Pop Quizzes
And
Stolen Kisses

Book Three of The Marchfield Series

A Hilarious Lesson in Second Chances

M. Jayne LaDow

To my students, the first of whom are now in their early fifties... I hope you still believe in the magic of reading and the power of love.

Go VBMS Seahawks!

Chapter 1

Rachel

What would you do if your friends wanted details about a past relationship?
a) Dodge the topic—some things are better left in the past.
b) Give them a vague, mysterious response and let them fill in the blanks.
c) Spill just enough to keep them entertained but leave out the good parts.
d) Grab a drink, sit them down, and reenact it dramatically.

At exactly 11:00 a.m., I stepped out of my carriage house apartment, locking the door with practiced precision. Not a minute early, not a second late. Punctuality was control, and control kept me from being the flaky mess.

The humid late August air hung oppressively, but I shrugged it off. Air conditioning was a girl's best friend during summer in Virginia. I turned toward my cute Smart car, but I didn't even make it three steps before—

"Rachel, honey!"

Barb's voice drifted from the porch of the big house where she rocked. Wrapped in a light kimono, her silver-streaked curls tucked under a scarf, she was the picture of motherly warmth.

I paused, the keys digging into my palm. "Morning, Barb."

She tilted her head, eyes twinkling. "You're off somewhere in a hurry."

"I'm meeting Audrey and Val," I explained, glancing at my car like I could will myself into it.

"Good, good! Girls' time is important." She gave me a knowing nod, then gestured to the book in her lap. "Speaking of important, I finished the last one you gave me." She held up *Lessons in Chemistry*. "Loved it. That Elizabeth Zott, she's got moxie."

A smile tugged at my lips. "She really does."

Barb patted the arm of her chair. "Got any other recommendations? I'm heading to Kiss and Tale later to stock up."

"When are you going? If it's after two thirty, I can go with you."

Her face lit up. "Awesome. What would I do without you keeping my reading list full?"

"Be tragically bored?"

Barb laughed, warm and familiar. "Probably." Then she waved me off. "Go on, now, before you're late."

Returning the wave, I slipped into my car. One minute behind schedule. But for Barb, it's worth it.

Stepping into Egglectic, Marchfield's go-to breakfast and brunch spot, I was immediately greeted by the rich scent of coffee and maple syrup.

"Oh my God, hi Rachel!" Val dashed across the room and swept me into a hug. Her arms tugged me close, and the scent of her perfume swamped my senses with a dizzying mix of coconut and citrus.

"It's great to see you, Val," I managed to say into her wavy dark hair. Thunking her on the back once, I shrugged out of her hug and retreated, skirting around Val to Audrey.

She'd risen much more slowly, her pregnant belly like a hard basketball between as we hugged. Her subtle smell of baby powder and fresh soap soothed me as much as her hug.

"Hi, Audrey," I said, as we sat down at the table.

The charming breakfast-and-lunch café buzzed with life. Forks clinked against plates, bursts of laughter floated from nearby tables, and the scent of freshly brewed coffee mingled with the sweet aroma of pancakes. Blocking out the symphony of distractions, I inhaled deeply and fixed my gaze on the sprawling mural behind Val. Its whimsical scene of rainbow-colored chickens strutting through a vibrant farmyard seemed alive with dazzling hues.

It had been months since I'd last seen either woman. When the teaching year ended in June, I returned home for the summer to help my mom. She'd traded the clamor of welding in the Salisbury shipyard for a new passion, sculpting intricate metal statues of fairies and goblins. Her work had become so popular, she recently opened her own gallery, a space brimming with enchanting creations.

I smiled at my friends.

My friends.

I glanced at Val and Audrey with a familiar pang of gratitude. I'd never had many friends, not the kind who stuck around once they got to know the real me.

Last year, these two had taken me under their wings, inviting me into their tight-knit circle. At first, I kept waiting for them to figure out I was too weird and back away slowly. But they didn't. They just kept showing up until one day I realized they weren't waiting for me to change. They'd accepted me as I was.

"How are you guys?" I asked, looking from Audrey's sun kissed face dotted with freckles to Val's olive one.

"Okay." Audrey rubbed her hand over her belly. "The baby's not due until November, but I'm already so uncomfortable, I'm not sure I'll make it."

Concern tightened in my chest, coiling like a knot I couldn't untangle. She joked about dying, but my mind raced with the possibilities: hemorrhage, eclampsia, infection—each one a shadow looming too close for comfort.

"Stop being dramatic, Aud." Val rolled her eyes. "You're fine."

Audrey frowned. "Just wait until you get pregnant. I'll spare you no pity."

I cleared my throat. "But the doctor says you're well?"

"Fit as a fiddle even though I can't see my feet anymore and my ankles swell at night." Despite her complaints, her smile lit up the room. "I'm fantastic."

I frowned but accepted the answer.

Turning to Val, I said, "How are you?"

"Great. I moved in with Evan when my lease ran out in July, so we spent the first three weeks of August naked in bed."

Audrey cackled. "Honestly, this pregnancy has made me so horny. I'm the one keeping Oz trapped at home in bed."

I shot her a look, half-expecting a smirk, but, nope, just that unmistakable, well-satisfied glow. Maybe I should be grateful things with Keith fizzled out when school ended. No way he and I could've kept up with that kind of energy.

The shiny, plastic-coated menu was a welcome distraction. The small, tightly packed text spilled across both sides, listing every imaginable variation of pancakes, French toast, and eggs cooked to perfection. My neck stiffened as tension coiled at its base as I drowned in the options.

Squinting at the egg-shaped chandelier hovering over our table, I frowned. Its blinding glow turned our cozy corner into something out of an interrogation room. Shielding my eyes, I dropped my gaze to the menu, only for the light to refract off the glossy surface, piercing my corneas like a laser.

Fumbling in my purse, I found my glasses case and slid my practical, brown plastic sunglasses on. Momentarily relieved, I sighed. At least now I could see without feeling like I was under a spotlight.

Val propped her hands under her chin. "What about you, Rach? Meet any men? Do anything naughty?"

"There was a—a guy who worked at my mom's gallery," I stammered. Rich was fifteen years older than me and flirted with anything in a skirt.

"Oooh, go on," Audrey prompted when I stopped there.

I wasn't sure how to tell them the story. Rich had followed me into the storeroom with a grin, teasing me about my skirt being shorter than usual. Clueless, I'd blinked and glanced down at my swing dress which I'd chosen for its pockets rather than any attempt at seduction. But before I could respond, he reached out and traced a finger down my jawline. Panic had surged through me, and I jumped away...straight into my mom's collection of Fae warrior statues. The metallic figures, absurdly endowed with enormous penises, toppled like a bad chain reaction. By the time Mom had found me, crouched in the wreckage with my hands over my ears, Rich had sprinted for the door, muttering something about needing fresh air.

"Did you flirt?" Val wiggled her eyebrows as if saying there was more to the story.

I shrugged. "That's not how my relationships usually go."

Despite carrying a little extra weight, men were drawn to my blonde hair and fair skin. But the spark fizzled once they realized I was different. All the men I knew wanted more neurotypical, less complicated women.

But not Keith. He embraced my quirks, reveled in my eccentricities, and never made me feel like too much. He had this way of looking at me, of focusing so completely that it felt like I was the only person in his world. With him, I wasn't an anomaly—I was something to be cherished.

Until the day I realized I wasn't special to him at all. I was just one of many, many women. And then he broke my heart, shattering it with the kind of casual ease that made it painfully clear that I'd been wrong.

"What can I get you, ladies?" Diane, Eggletic's owner, took that moment to approach the table.

She nodded to me to start. "I'll have the omelet."

Diane's warm smile never wavered as she nodded and asked, "Two egg whites with cheddar cheese, two slices of bacon, and wheat toast on the side?"

The first time I'd ordered here, Diane had noticed my struggle, slid into the seat beside me, and gently walked me through all the options, her patience endless. Now, she remembered my order by heart, as if it were her personal mission to make me feel seen and cared for.

I returned her kindness with a grateful smile and nodded. "Thanks, Diane."

After the others ordered, I changed the subject. "Have either of you seen your schedules yet?"

Val chose not to push. "I'm teaching four blocks of civics, but the curriculum's changed for the third time in two years."

"I hate that." Audrey nodded. "Teaching to the state tests sounds easy, but they make it so hard."

"Not to mention taking away all creativity," Val added.

"I'm teaching all advanced sixth-grade classes this year," Audrey said. "The administration wanted to keep it simple for the long-term substitute while I'm out on maternity leave."

I took a sip of my water. "That explains why I have all the sixth-grade core classes, Sped, ELL, and most of the 504s."

"Oh," Audrey reached out to pat my shoulder. "I didn't think about that! You're going to have your hands full."

"It'll be fine. I'll have help."

Audrey continued to look worried. "Do you know who your inclusion teacher will be?"

"I haven't heard."

Val's forehead wrinkled in thought. "Tina Keller's great."

Tina—a tall Black woman with an infectious laugh and boundless energy—was the perfect co-teacher. We had similar teaching styles, and her dedication to her work was unmatched.

"It could also be Riley Buchard," Audrey offered.

An older, seasoned special education teacher, Riley's no-nonsense demeanor often clashed with the students. Her sharp tone and unyielding rules made it hard to imagine her genuinely enjoying the work. I couldn't help but wonder why she stayed in the classroom when her attitude suggested she didn't like the kids at all.

Before I could respond, Val said, "Or it could be Keith."

No.

No.

No, no, no, no.

Keith and I had co-taught one English class together last year. He was a natural with the kids, helping them push past their limits and reach their potential. I'd loved working with him. His energy, passion, and way of connecting with every student had been part of the reason I liked him so much.

But I couldn't teach four blocks with him. All day, every day. No, it was impossible. Not after everything that had happened last year. Not after how it ended.

Flustered, my skin felt hot and tight, a strange prickling sensation running across my arms. Was I breaking out in hives? I'd take grouchy Riley or anyone else. Keith was too loud, too distracting, too... in my face.

Too sexy.

The uninvited image of him sleeping in my bed flashed into my mind. Sunlight streamed through the window, casting a soft glow over his wavy brown hair and beard, turning them into strands of gold. His thick eyelashes brushed against his angular face, his skin a perfect, sun-kissed golden hue.

Heat rushed to my face, and I could feel the flush creeping up my neck. With my pale skin, I wore my embarrassment like a flag—proud, bright, and unmistakable. At least my sunglasses hid some of it, a small mercy in the moment.

"Keith would be fun to teach with," Audrey said, her eyes catching the flush on my face but wisely not commenting on it.

Both of these women had crossed that invisible line between co-worker and more by falling in love with teachers in the same school. After a few growing pains and awkward moments, it had worked out for them.

But Keith and I? We'd imploded after only a few weeks.

And my friends knew nothing. It had all happened so fast. Keith went from friend to lover to betrayer in the blink of an eye. One minute, I was floating on air, the next, I was running home to lick my wounds, unsure how I'd gone from one extreme to the other so quickly.

"But Keith teaches the self-contained students," Val pointed out. "Mr. Kline wouldn't reassign him."

"You're probably right," Audrey nodded, changing the subject. "Did you hear Keith bought a house this summer?"

Keith bought a house? My stomach twisted. He loved his apartment—the first place he'd ever lived alone. A bachelor pad through and through, with mismatched furniture, a worn leather couch that probably had a permanent dent where he collapsed after long days, and a coffee table perpetually cluttered with empty beer bottles and takeout boxes. It'd suited him.

I could picture him there, lounging in the dim glow of his TV, surrounded by the women he once swore didn't matter to him anymore. I'd always preferred going to my apartment, where things felt less temporary, less tawdry.

"It's just down the street from us," Val added, her tone casual. "Evan helped him with some of the repairs this summer."

I glanced up to find both women watching me, waiting for my reaction. I forced a nod. "That's interesting." Hopefully, that was enough.

It wasn't. Both women exchanged a glance.

A familiar sense of otherness settled over me. I didn't fit in. I saw the world differently—like I was navigating a maze where everyone else had the map.

As a teacher, I understood my students' struggles with the material, but their challenges with friendship, flirting, and casual conversation? Those were as much a mystery to me as my own. I was good at my job, but feeling like part of the community felt out of reach.

Autism Spectrum Disorder. My diagnosis was both an answer and a puzzle. The developmental condition affected how I perceived the world and interacted with others. It turned social cues into a language I couldn't learn to speak.

"I'm sorry." The words slipped out automatically. Apologizing usually softened people's reactions to my ASD, made things easier.

"Rachel..." Val's voice was gentle as she covered my hand with hers. "You don't have to be sorry. Just say what you mean."

I swallowed hard. "I guess... I just think it's interesting that Keith would give up his sex pad for a fixer-upper."

Heat crept up my face, my chest tightening as I leaned back in my chair. Talking was hard sometimes.

"It took me by surprise too," Val said. "But he's thirty-nine. Maybe he's ready to settle down."

I snorted, regretting it immediately as Audrey and Val's narrowed eyes studied my face.

"Wait a minute..." Val glanced between me and Audrey.

My eyes rounded in horror. The room shrank and the air grew thick with the weight of my own discomfort.

"Did you and Keith..." Audrey started.

"Play hide the sausage last year?" Val finished.

I shook my head vigorously, as if trying to physically shake off the thought.

Audrey clapped. "You did. You did the deed of darkness with Keith."

My cheeks were hot, but I snorted. "Nope. No."

"Hmm," Val muttered.

"Nothing happened."

Only two hookups, a catastrophic argument, and a broken heart.

"Okayyy." Audrey giggled.

They were never going to let it go. And worse, they'd go home and talk to Oz and Evan. Small towns and small schools sucked sometimes.

"Okay fine." I threw up my hands in exasperation. "Keith and I paired up a few times last year."

"Paired up?" Audrey asked as Val whisper-shouted, "You took the hot dog truck to taco town with Keith!"

"Shhh," I said, my gaze flitting from one corner to the next.

Ignoring me, Val clapped. "I knew it."

Audrey narrowed her eyes. "You mean I knew it. I told you last year—"

"But you didn't know for sure," Val argued.

Audrey turned to me, her smile sweetening. "Give us the deets, Rach."

I inhaled, trying to settle my nerves. I hated being the center of attention. On top of that, I'd never had deets to dish before.

I released the air from my lungs and inhaled again. Where should I start? The Winter Carnival, when Keith first noticed me? The little jokes he whispered in my ear, meant to relax me during awkward social situations? Or the first time he held my hand under the table in this very restaurant last winter?

I took a deep breath and then another. My mind drifted in and out with the air, each inhale bringing me clarity. It was a technique I'd learned in therapy, and I was grateful for it now more than ever.

Diane dropped off our orders, and I continued to breathe, letting the world swirl around me while I stayed rooted in the moment.

Val and Audrey began to eat, wordlessly giving me the space I needed to gather myself. The smell of my omelet wafted up, its savory warmth tugging at my stomach, which growled loudly even as butterflies fluttered nervously in my chest.

"The first time was last spring at Polar Vortex during the open house party. Keith and I slipped out of the main room and did it in the janitor's closet and went back to my apartment after."

Val's mouth fell open, her eyes wide with surprise, and Audrey coughed turning bright red, her face scrunching in that panicked way people do when they gag on a piece of food. Instinctively, I thumped her back, as Val pushed a glass of water closer.

The two of them stared at me, their expressions a mix of confusion and curiosity. Normally, I'd feel a flush of embarrassment creeping up my neck. I'd get anxious, my heart racing in my chest, my mind spinning with ways to excuse myself. I might have run out of the restaurant, or I would've clammed up, shutting down and retreating into the safety of silence.

But today, for some reason, I did something outside my wheelhouse:

I laughed.

Chapter 2

Keith

What would you do if you were locked in a supply closet with your work nemesis?
a) Plot their demise while maintaining silence.
b) Make snarky comments to pass the time.
c) Accidentally reveal something personal and regret it.
d) Get into an argument that turns into something else.

"I'm sorry, Keith, but I'm not changing your schedule." Mansfield Kline, Marchfield Middle's principal, put his foot down after my third request. "I hope you understand that if I changed your schedule for personal reasons, then every teacher would be in my office with demands."

I gritted my teeth. I'd gotten up at the butt crack of dawn to drive to school a week before teachers reported, thinking I could sort out my schedule before things got chaotic. But Mansfield— what kind of name was that, anyway?—wouldn't even hear me out.

Around the office, pictures of smiling middle school students looked down on me, frozen in moments of cheer that felt so out of reach in that tense room. Kline leaned back in his chair comfortably.

Meanwhile, I was stuck in an uncomfortable hot seat, feeling every inch of the tight, unforgiving plastic under me. The disparity was ridiculous, and the knot in my stomach only tightened as I fought to keep my frustration from boiling over.

A large sign hung behind his desk:

Ledares can let yuo flai
and yet not lety oub e a faileur.

Studying the letters as they swam in and out of order, I took the time to decode the sign before speaking.

Leaders can let you fail
and yet not let you be a failure.

Fucking ironic.

"I'm not asking for personal reasons. I'm asking because I've developed a bond with my self-contained students. We're making progress, especially Javion, and I don't want all his hard work to stall with a new teacher."

Kline shook his head. "Ms. Buchard knows these students as well as you, Keith. They will be fine. We need you out in the inclusion classrooms where you can work your magic on more students."

He was giving my class to Riley? The old-school hard ass who couldn't care less about relating to kids? She'd probably bark at them all day, treating them like a bunch of discipline problems to be fixed with a glare and a lecture.

She had no idea how to engage or motivate them. Javion, especially. He'd shut down the minute Riley looked at him the wrong way. I worked so hard to build a trusting relationship with him; all that progress would come to a screeching halt. It would stagnate, fade into nothing, just like so many other kids who'd slipped through the cracks under the wrong teacher.

"I disagree. Ms. Buchard hasn't spent time building relationships with these kids. She knows their names only to yell at them. She doesn't know how to motivate them or meet them at their level."

Kline took a deep breath and folded his hands in front of him on the desk. "Keith, I hear your frustration, but I'm not changing the schedule."

I took a deep breath, trying to let go of my tension, though it felt like trying to hold back a flood with a paper towel. Was it hubris to think these kids needed me more than some teacher just biding her time until retirement?

Counting to ten, I rubbed my eyes as if I could somehow scrub away the frustration. Finally, I spoke, my voice tight but controlled. "At least tell me who I'm teaching with, then.

"Of course." He tapped some keys and used his mouse to locate the file on his computer. "Ah yes, we had to move some classes around in the sixth grade, to accommodate Ms. Freemont's maternity leave, so you're with Rachel Bright, sixth-grade English."

My head swam. The universe was dealing me a hand that I was destined to lose.

"English? My degree is in math. English is a problem for me."

"Your degree is in math and special education. Mr. Hernandez and Mr. Young co-teach math six, so we need you in English."

I shook my head, unable to verbalize what a cluster-fuck this was going to be. It had to be a joke. *A dyslexic math teacher walks into an English class...*

"You co-taught with Ms. Bright last year for one class, and the test scores were through the roof."

An image of Rachel's flushed cheeks, her head thrown back against the pillows as the sun filtered in behind the curtains, crept into my mind. The memory of her tight pussy clenching my cock followed. Fucking good fit.

Until I blew it. Took the best thing that had ever happened to me and torched it.

Shoving the guilt and regret aside, I cleared my throat. "I'm dyslexic, Mr. Kline. I'm sure you can see why teaching English full time would be impossible."

"Is that in your file?" Mansfield Kline swiveled his chair to a wide filing cabinet behind his desk and began rifling through the files. "I don't remember reading that."

"I assure you, it is," I said, leaning back in the uncomfortable plastic chair. "I provided the school with a letter from my doctor and my test results when I was hired."

Not that it was any of their damned business.

The principal turned back with my file. Why was it so fat? Sure, I'd been teaching for ten years, but that thing looked like it was about to burst at the seams.

He spread it out on the desk, flipping through page after page with no sense of urgency, just the quiet sound of paper rustling. My heart skipped a beat as I saw the copies of my evaluations and observations. Then there were my contracts, all neatly stapled together.

A few pages in, I saw them. Letters of discipline. Ouch. I swallowed hard, trying not to feel the heat of embarrassment creeping up my neck.

At the very bottom of the stack was the medical information.

About half of dyslexics hate school. It's a constant battle just to keep up, and many can't wait to leave the hallowed ground of education behind for a job where reading struggles won't be a daily reminder of their challenges. The odds had been stacked against me, too.

But I was lucky. I crossed paths with two incredible teachers, Mr. Martin and Ms. Greenwell, who saw potential in me even when I couldn't see it in myself. They worked with me through high school, making sure I had the support I needed to keep up with my classmates and develop the skills to succeed. Because of them, I didn't just survive school—I made it through college and found my way back to the classroom, not as a struggling student, but as a Special Ed teacher determined to be that same kind of lifeline for someone else.

But co-teaching English? That was a migraine waiting to happen.

"I don't know how I missed this, Keith." Mr. Kline seemed genuinely apologetic.

I nodded. "I'm sure you see the best solution for everyone is putting me back with the self-contained students."

Kline's eyes drifted away from mine. "Unfortunately, class schedules were mailed this morning, so I'm in a bit of a bind."

"Just swap me and Riley. I know she'll be okay with it." Better than okay. As a co-teacher, Riley wouldn't have to write lesson plans or make materials. That would suit her lazy ass just fine.

"Well, you see, I can't. Ms. Bouchard was assigned to the self-contained classes by the superintendent." He shrugged as if to say it was out of his hands. "I'm not privy as to why. Above my pay grade."

I would have challenged that as a lie, but his face was pinched, like he'd swallowed something bitter.

"Would you consider co-teaching with Ms. Bright until I can find another position for you?"

I crossed my arms over my chest and waited. I'd learned a long time ago that teachers always got the shaft when it came to scheduling. You could raise a fuss, demand answers, and maybe get lucky. Most years, though, you just had to accept what you were given and make the best of it.

Kline continued, "You could also take your pick from any open position in the city, but we'd hate to lose you here."

I didn't want to leave Marchfield. It wasn't just a job—it was home. I had friends here. I had students who depended on me.

And Rachel... Rachel was here.

But she'd made it clear she wanted nothing to do with me, so teaching with her would be a minefield of awkward silences and forced politeness.

But I could charm her. Women were easy that way... Who was I kidding? I was screwed.

****

At home, I grabbed a paintbrush and headed into the kitchen.

After twelve years of scrimping and saving, I finally had enough to put a down payment on a wreck of a house. The small Victorian was close to a hundred and fifty years old and had seen better days, but I'd make her shine. I'd gotten a new roof on her and patched up the porch.

Inside, I'd taken down some of the walls, turning tiny, cramped rooms into larger spaces. The walls were patched and ready for paint.

I switched on my portable speaker, letting the brush strokes keep time with the energetic beats of The Red Hot Chili Peppers and Pearl Jam. The light gray-blue I'd chosen for the walls was soothing, and it made the white of the cabinets pop, giving the space a clean, fresh feel.

I'd just started on the second wall when the back door banged open.

"You're actually painting?" Sunny's voice carried through the house as she dropped the laundry basket on the kitchen table. "I figured you'd live in a construction zone forever."

I turned, arching a brow. "I'm making progress."

"Sure, sure." She smirked, eyeing the unfinished trim. "At this rate, you'll be done by retirement."

I flicked a tiny bit of paint in her direction. "You want to help or just provide commentary?"

She dodged with ease, grabbing a soda from my fridge like she lived here—which, in fairness, she practically did. After Mom died, I'd raised her, and now, at twenty-four, she was working on her master's in social work at Old Dominion.

It should've meant I got to be her brother again, not the guy who worried if she ate well or slept enough between balancing her classes and an internship.

But old habits died hard.

She plopped onto one of my mismatched kitchen chairs and cracked open the can. "I just came home to do laundry, but I also wanted to check on my favorite brother."

I rolled my eyes. "I'm your only brother."

"Which makes the title that much easier to award." She took a sip, then gave me a knowing look. "So, when are you gonna tell me why you're really in here painting like it's therapy?"

I kept my strokes even. "Maybe because it needs to be done."

"Uh-huh." She wasn't buying it. "Not because you're trying to keep busy and not think about Rachel?"

My jaw clenched. "You don't know what you're talking about."

Inside, I bristled, my mind racing with thoughts I wasn't ready to confront.

She hummed in a way that said she absolutely did. "You messed up. She left town and ghosted you. And now, instead of dealing with it, you're over here trying to paint away your feelings."

I sighed, wondering again why I'd confided in her this summer. "I know I messed up, okay? But she's back. We're co-teaching."

"Oof." Sunny winced. "So, you have to see her every day?"

"Yep."

"And you still have feelings for her?"

I hesitated. Then, quietly, "Yep."

Sunny studied me for a long moment before nodding. "Then fix it."

I scoffed. "It's not that simple. She thinks I'm always bouncing from one woman to the next."

"Apologize. Mean it. Show her you've changed." She paused, giving me a knowing glance. "I've seen it, you know. You're not the same player you were before."

I rubbed a hand over my face. "What if she doesn't want to hear it?"

Sunny shrugged. "At least you'll know you tried. Then you can decide whether to let her go or fight for her." Grabbing her basket again, she walked away.

Sunny always knew exactly what I needed to hear, though there was little comfort in it tonight.

Her advice made sense, but I wasn't prepared to let Rachel go, even if, deep down, I knew it might be inevitable.

Chapter 3

Rachel

What would you do if your grumpy coworker was suddenly nice to you?
a) Assume they want something.
b) Try to figure out if they've been replaced.
c) Flirt just to see if they'll blush.
d) Ask them what took them so long.

Teachers always complain about professional development, but I actually enjoy it. There's something comforting about problem solving with like-minded adults. I fit in, and no one thought I was weird.

Entering the school library, I scanned the tables until my eyes landed on my friends sitting near the back. I hesitated, feeling uneasy at the thought of sitting there. I preferred the front, where the light was brighter and the space felt more open, but I forced myself to walk back anyway.

Val and Evan were an odd match on the surface—Val, all fire and chaos, her brain moving faster than her mouth, and Evan, steady and deliberate, his presence like an anchor in the storm. But somehow, it worked. She leaned into him, her fingers drumming a beat on his forearm as she spoke, her energy vibrating through the space between them. Evan, for his part, listened with that quiet intensity of his, the kind that made you feel heard even when you weren't the one talking. He didn't try to slow her down or tame her—he just let her be. It was the kind of balance that made you believe in fate.

Across from them, Oz and Audrey shared a different kind of connection—one built on history and an unshakable foundation of trust. Oz was larger than life, but Audrey softened him. His hand moved absently against her back, rubbing slow circles. Audrey, for her part, had that sleepy kind of contentment that came from being with someone who knew you inside and out. They were a unit—newlyweds and soon-to-be parents.

And then there was me. The fifth wheel.

Arranging my highlighters, pens, and pencils in a neat line, the smooth barrels clicked softly against the table. My fingers lingered over my favorite pen—a sleek, fine-tipped gel pen that practically glided across the page like magic. It was a small joy, but an important one. A good pen could make all the difference, turning even the most mundane notes into something beautiful.

With a deep breath, I flipped open a crisp, new notebook, the untouched pages full of promise. I'd cleaned out the office store of all their latest supplies, reveling in the sheer delight of fresh stationery. There was something so deeply satisfying about the smooth glide of a brand-new highlighter, the sharp click of a mechanical pencil, the cool weight of a perfectly balanced pen in my hand. This was my ritual, my armor against the chaos of a new school year.

The scent of fresh paper and ink filled the air as I meticulously arranged everything just so, grounding myself in the quiet comfort of my carefully curated tools. No matter how out of place I felt in this moment, at least here, in the lines of my notebook and the ink of my beloved pens, I was in control.

"Didn't any of you bring a notebook or a pen?"

"I have paper and a pen," Val said, fishing a folded sheet of printer paper out of her pants pocket along with a purple marker.

I recoiled, barely suppressing a gasp. Paper? Folded and crumpled beyond salvation? And a marker? My carefully curated collection of smooth gel pens and pristine notebooks trembled in the face of such recklessness. The horror clawed up my spine as I stared at the poor, mistreated sheet in her hands. It was a crime against stationery.

Forcing my face to remain blank, I asked, "Would you like to borrow a real pen?"

"No, this is fine." Val smiled, drawing a cartoon version of Evan in the corner of the page in purple.

Teachers still trickled in the door with only two minutes left before the mandatory two-hour class about collecting and using data to teach effectively began. I glanced around the other tables in the library for Keith.

Not that I was looking for him.

I just didn't want him to be late and embarrass himself in front of the entire staff.

I spotted him at a table to my right with Mel, Bobby, and a few new teachers. He was smiling, his full lips framed by a dark mustache and beard, trimmed short to highlight the angular lines of his face. He wore a flannel shirt with the sleeves rolled up, exposing long tan arms dusted with dark hair. He slouched in his chair, long legs stretched out, every muscle of his lean, muscular frame completely relaxed.

His gray eyes shifted, meeting mine. Our gazes clashed, but I couldn't read the expression on his face. Then he dipped his chin in a small nod, and a jolt of heat curled into a tight ball at the base of my stomach.

I yanked my eyes away and turned to face the front of the room, trying to ignore the flare of warmth spreading through me.

Mr. Kline began to speak. "Good morning. I'd like to begin by setting our instructional focus for this year on using data to assess student mastery. Let's begin by discussing the types of data teachers gather in the classroom and make a list with your tablemates."

The noise level in the room increased as everyone began talking.

"Have you guys chosen a name for the baby yet?" Evan asked.

Baby names? Mr. Kline had a timer set for this activity, so we needed to stay on topic. I shifted uncomfortably in my seat.

What if he called on us to present our ideas, and we didn't have any?

Audrey wrinkled her nose. "I read that vintage names are in now, so we're considering Eustice or Harold."

I tried to interject, my hand tugging at a strand of my short hair nervously as I spoke. "I think we should—"

Val gasped and steamrolled over me. "Audrey, you aren't!"

"Do you know how hard it is to be a teacher and name a baby? So many names have bad memories. Like Aiden."

"Shhh," Oz shuddered. "We agreed we'd never talk about him again. Now all I can think about is the cupcake fight Aiden started after the National Junior Honor Society inductions."

Evan nodded. "That red frosting was impossible to get out of those robes. They had to be dry cleaned twice."

"See? We can't use Aiden or Garret. Isabel and Toni are out, too. The list is a mile long."

I bounced my leg restlessly under the table, the tap of my foot against the floor a repetitive rhythm I could almost lose myself in.

"I see your point," I began, hoping to take control of this trainwreck. "Now about the question—"

"But you can't name the baby Eustice or Harold." Val insisted. "They're grandparent names."

"Why not Rhysand or Nesta?" Evan asked, naming two of characters from *A Court of Thorns and Roses* series. Val had bought Evan all the novels for his birthday, and he'd just finished them.

"Gah!" Audrey slapped her hand over her mouth, then squealed, "Cassian! I could name my son Cassian!"

"We're not naming our son after some winged Fae book boyfriend of yours." Oz crossed his muscular arms over his chest.

"Let's discuss it later." Audrey stroked his arm but winked at Val and me.

Seizing the opportunity to try again, I said, "I really think we should spend a minute discussing the data we collect in the classroom—"

But Mr. Kline was already moving to the front of the room. "Time's up. Let's go around the room and have each table share their lists."

My mouth dropped open. This was my worst-case scenario. The principal would call on me, and I wouldn't have an answer. Everyone would laugh. I'd have to quit and move out of town.

My heart rate increased, and my breath sounded shallow. I could feel the panic race across my senses, so I closed my eyes and focused on my breathing.

In for the count of three.
Out for six.
In for three
Out for six.

"You okay?" Val whispered.

I felt her hand on my shoulder, but I couldn't open my eyes. "Shh," I whispered. "You're going to get us in trouble."

She tapped me on the shoulder until I met her eyes. Uncapping her marker, she wrote on her wrinkled sheet of printer paper:

Are you okay?

I nodded, but she nudged the pen toward me. I reached for a pen, my fingers tapping rhythmically against my leg—light, quick beats, like a soft drumroll. I focused on the self-soothing rhythm. It grounded me enough so I could write.

I'm fine.

She grabbed the paper, shaking her head while she scribbled.

If you breathe any faster, you'll hyperventilate. What can I do?

My pulse raced, each beat drumming against my skull, and a sharp pressure tightened in my chest. Anxiety coiled in my stomach, twisting and churning, making it hard to breathe, but I needed to handle this on my own.

I just need a minute.

But I didn't get one. With the instincts of a shark, Mr. Kline smelled my blood in the water. He wandered through the tables, stopping behind Val and me.

Looking down at the notes we'd written, he scowled, tapping the table with his finger. "How about over here? Who wants to share?"

My eyes flew from person to person. What were we going to do?

Audrey stood, her round stomach brushing against the table. "Teachers use all types of data from attendance to grades. We discussed formative and summative data, pulse checks, and poll questions."

She lowered herself into the seat, her back straight. Oz rubbed her lower back while I prayed the principal would move on to another table.

"I'm interested in the term pulse checks," Mr. Kline asked. "What is that exactly?"

Our table fell silent. No one wanted to answer the question.

"Can you field this one, Rachel?"

"It's, um..." My voice croaked like a frog. The tapping of my fingers turned into quick slaps across my thighs. "It's, um, like a pop quiz with no wrong answers. Just a few questions to get students thinking and sharing their feelings."

A pretty brunette sitting between Keith and Bobby raised her hand. "We learned in our education classes that pop quizzes were no longer considered good teaching practices. It heightens anxiety in some students."

My worst fear had happened. Not only had I answered incorrectly, but my stimming behaviors had burst out into the open for everyone to see.

I slid down in my chair, my head tipping forward until my chin rested on my chest. My arms instinctively wrapped tightly around my body, trying to pull myself together. My heart thudded loudly in my chest, every beat echoing in my ears. The walls of the room seemed to close in, and I could feel my breath catching in my throat.

Mr. Kline grinned down at his shoes for a moment before responding. "The term pop quiz is a bit antiquated, but I'm sure Ms. Bright meant a questionnaire or a short survey. And don't worry, Ms. Stuart, we'll develop the look-fors together at the end of the session."

One teacher I didn't know nodded before asking, "What are the instructional look-fors you'll use to evaluate us on this topic?"

"At my old school, we used a Pineapple Board to schedule observations," another person added. "Will it be the same here?"

Mr. Kline returned to the front of the room to answer the question and resume the class.

My face burned, heat rushing to my cheeks. My hands felt clammy. I fought the urge to bolt, to hide somewhere, anywhere. I hated how vulnerable I felt. How could I have been so stupid? I wasn't prepared for this. I wasn't ready to be exposed, not like this.

Adrenaline hit me like a train, amping my anxiety even higher. I was making a huge deal over nothing. I knew this, but my body didn't. Chemicals in my brain elicited a fight or flight response, and I felt helpless to stop it.

Shutting down on the outside ensured I wouldn't cry or say anything else embarrassing, but inside, my body churned with a sense of being out of control. I gripped the edge of my chair, feeling the wood beneath my palms as if it were the only thing keeping me grounded. My chest tightened, and every breath felt shallow, like there wasn't enough air in the room. Why couldn't I just be normal?

I glanced up, hoping no one noticed the panic on my face. And Keith's gray eyes met mine. For a moment, everything else in the room faded away. I felt a brief flicker of comfort, then the overwhelming sense of exposure hit me again.

His gaze lingered for just a second longer before he turned away, but I was left with that spark of recognition, the reminder of how much I'd let myself get tangled up in the mess of my own emotions.

Out of the corner of my eye, I saw Keith whisper something to the pretty woman at his table. She giggled, flipping her long, straight hair over her shoulder and angling her body toward him. She might as well have been in his lap.

I wished the floor would open up and swallow me.

What was I doing? He didn't care about me. Not like that. His attention was clearly on someone else. Self-doubt flooded in like a wave, pulling me under.

Of course, he was into someone like her.

I had no right to feel hurt, no right to even be here in this room, surrounded by people who had their shit together while I felt like I was on the verge of falling apart. I was beyond tapping my fingers. I squeezed my hands into fists, digging my nails into my palms, trying to anchor myself.

I could feel tears pricking the back of my eyes, but I refused to let them loose. Not here. Not now.

My heart raced, painfully bumping along, making it hard to catch my breath. My mind roared with a barrage of insults and questions:

I'm an idiot!
Why can't I calm down?
Everyone is looking at me. They think I'm a weirdo.
I need to get out of here!

"Rachel?" Val's voice was softer now, careful. Controlled.

"Sweetie, are you alright?" Audrey's words stretched, distant and warped, like they were coming from the other end of a tunnel. The room was too bright, the hum of the overhead lights too sharp, every noise slicing through me like static. My pulse thundered in my ears.

Something warm and solid nudged against my hand. Audrey. She didn't grab, didn't force, just set a pen there. My favorite one. I curled my fingers around it, focusing on the smooth barrel, the way it fit perfectly in my grip.

"You're okay," Val murmured, her voice even and steady, like a lighthouse cutting through the fog. "We're right here."

Audrey shifted, blocking some of the noise, her presence a buffer against the press of the world. I traced the ridges on the rubber grip, the words filtering in. My breath hitched, then evened. The edges of the tunnel widened.

"There you are," Audrey said softly. "Any better?"

I heard other voices, but they were muffled and indistinct. Mr. Kline responded, asking questions, and eliciting responses, but they spoke in another language.

My body was rigid. Muscles clenched tightly, I knew they would ache when I finally relaxed. More than anything, I wanted to run. Just get up and leave. But the thought of everyone watching seemed too much to bear.

I'd have to stick it out somehow.

"Hey, Princess." Keith's soft voice was a soothing balm on my senses. "You okay?"

Rough fingers rubbing along my clenched knuckles. "Breathe, Rach. In through your nose and out through your pretty lips."

He breathed in and out in rhythm until my harsh breaths joined his. The world grew still around us. It was just Keith and me in a bubble of safety. My muscles unknotted, letting go one at a time as the panic retreated. I cracked an eye open.

Keith crouched beside my chair, concern etched in the creases on his forehead. His eyes were kind and sympathetic. "Why don't we step outside for a minute and get some air?"

My eyes darted around the room. Everyone around us was working, writing on large sheets of poster paper with markers. Mr. Kline wandered along the far side of the room, speaking with individuals. No one stared at me. There were no pitying looks. Or laughs.

I met Keith's eyes and nodded.

***

The air was hot and humid when Keith and I stepped outside. A typical late August day in Virginia, the sky was hazy even as the sun beat down relentlessly.

He led me around to the side of the school where picnic tables were set out under an awning. Nearby the rain gardens teemed with sound and movement. Cicadas screamed high in the trees while butterflies danced from flower to flower. A bullfrog rumbled long and low in the tall grasses nearby as I sat on a bench in the shade.

Keith sat next to me, but he gave me space as the outdoors settled me. I breathed in the scent of warm earth, fresh grass, and his citrusy cedar cologne.

A few moments passed, and my mind opened to the world around me. Being outside reminded me that my problems were specks in the universe, and I felt connected to the bigger picture.

I turned to Keith. He was watching the monarch butterflies feed on the late-blooming flowers.

I knew I should tell him to leave me alone. To go back inside to the pretty new teacher and ask her if she was interested in a zero-strings hook-up. Or better yet, lie to her about wanting more, then pull away when she begins to believe it. But my messy, emotional baggage came with a shitload of anxiety, so I retreated to the safe world of facts.

"Those monarchs will fly between two and three thousand miles to get to Mexico before winter."

Keith responded without looking at me. "Yeah?"

"They can travel more than a hundred miles a day and fly over a thousand feet in the air."

He tipped his chin toward me. "Impressive."

"Monarchs live up to nine months; compared to other butterflies, that's an eternity." I point to a yellow and black striped butterfly sharing the milkweed with the monarch. "That tiger swallowtail over there only lives about ten days." I focused on the words as if they could anchor me in the moment.

"You know a lot about butterflies."

"I read a lot of books." Heat rushed to my cheeks. Ever since I could read, I would dive deep into topics, learning as much as I could about a subject. Butterflies and moths, dinosaurs,

Shakespearean sonnets, World Cup soccer, sexual positions... the list was long and varied.

He smiled, winking when I dared to look at him. "I remember."

Of course, he would. He'd seen the bookcases and boxes full of books in my apartment, everything organized alphabetically by author or subject.

"What are you reading now?"

I tucked my chin into my chest. "Smut." His question relaxed me. I could talk about romance novels all day. "Dark romance. Fantasy. Fae smut."

"Sunshine's reading *Fourth Wing* by Rebecca something. Is that the kind of book you're talking about?"

I blinked at the mention of her name. I knew about Sunshine. Keith's younger sister who he'd raised after their mom passed. I'd heard stories, caught snippets of their conversations last year, but I'd never met her. Still, the way he said her name, so casually woven into our conversation, made it clear how much she meant to him.

"Yarros," I said, tapping my fingers against my palm.

"Huh?" Keith replied, frowned.

"The author is Rebecca Yarros."

"Oh, gotcha." He scratched the back of his neck before clearing his throat. "Rachel, I'm sorry about how things ended last spring. I hope we can move on as friends. I—"

His phone buzzed with a notification, and I jumped. Pulling my arms tighter around myself, my fingers fidgeted with the hem of my sleeve.

Sighing, he swiped his finger across the screen.

"I have to take this."

Of course, he needed to answer his phone.

The knot twisted again in my stomach as he walked back toward the school's door before answering to call, the familiar sting of abandonment creeping in.

A year ago, I'd heard all the stories. Keith dated all the new teachers, always chasing the next thrill, never sticking around when things started to get serious. Everyone warned me, but I'd fallen for him anyway. And when he promised me things were different, I believed him.

Swallowing the bitterness rising in my throat, I scolded myself for not learning a damn thing.

Chapter 4

Keith

What would you do when you realize you want a second chance at love?
a) Follow her around like a puppy.
b) Make snarky comments to get a reaction out of her.
c) Be honest with her and regret it later.
d) Ignore it because you know she's over you.

After all the meetings and preparations wrapped up, I stayed late in the classroom I shared with Rachel. She'd chosen to spend the day working in the library, and I thought I could get all my work done without distractions. But I'd barely put a dent in my to-do list because no matter how hard I tried to focus, my mind kept drifting back to Rachel.

Watching her shut down during the faculty meeting had been gut-wrenching. It'd felt like the air left the room when she withdrew. Her whole body pulled inward as if she were trying to disappear.

At first, I'd been unsure if I should try to help. Afraid I'd just make things worse. But the longer I watched Rachel fold in on herself, the more convinced I became that I needed to intervene.

Her breathing was shallow, her hands gripping the edges of the table like she was bracing for impact. When Val and Audrey noticeably started to panic, I did what felt right and gave her something to focus on. A steady voice. A distraction.

I'd leaned in, kept my tone even, and talked her through it, grounding her in the moment. Bit by bit, I saw her come back to herself. Her grip loosened. Her breathing slowed. The tension in her shoulders eased just enough. For a brief moment, I thought I'd done something right.

Then my damn phone rang.

The second I pulled it out of my pocket and saw Mya's mom's name on the screen, I knew I had to answer because rescheduling her annual IEP meeting couldn't wait. But in the split second before I picked up, I caught the flicker of hurt in Rachel's eyes. Then her walls slammed down. By the time I hung up, she was gone, leaving behind nothing but an empty space and a sick feeling in my gut.

I rubbed my temples, trying to shake off the helplessness that sat on my chest like a boulder. School started Monday, and there'd be no avoiding her then. We'd be co-teaching, in meetings, side by side in the classroom all day long. If I didn't figure out how to fix this, we were in for months of tension while she shut me out and I pretended it didn't gut me.

What if I'd already ruined things? What if she never let me back in? I had to fix this before it was too late.

I needed advice. Fast.

As if summoned by my thoughts, Bobby and Mel walked into the classroom, their laughter cutting through my thoughts like sunlight through storm clouds. Bobby's dark brown hair was cut in short angles, and her sharp eyes missed nothing. Mel was warmth and light, her curvy body always in motion. Her long, light brown hair bounced with every step.

"Hey, you good?" Bobby asked as she sat down across from me, a knowing look in her eyes.

"Yeah, just... dealing with some things." I glanced up, a hesitant smile flickering on my face. "Actually, I could use your advice."

Mel raised an eyebrow, her sparkling eyes full of curiosity. "What's up?"

I sighed, shifting in my seat. "I've screwed up with Rachel."

Bobby leaned forward, a little surprised. "What do you mean?"

I rubbed the back of my neck, feeling the weight of the situation. "It's complicated."

Bobby raised an eyebrow. "Complicated how?"

Mel tilted her head, her sharp eyes narrowing like she was already halfway to figuring it out.

I let out a slow breath. "Rachel and I... we had a thing last year. It was brief, and it didn't end well."

That was an understatement.

Bobby leaned against one of the desks, arms crossed. "Define thing."

I ran a hand through my hair. "It started casual." I hesitated, my jaw tightening. "But she's special, you know?" I shook my head. "I caught feelings."

Mel and Bobby exchanged a look.

"Don't look at me that way." I huffed out a humorless laugh.

"Why didn't it work out?" Mel asked quietly.

"I was an asshole and screwed it up." I tapped my fingers against the desk, a restless energy building in my chest. "Now, we have to co-teach all year, and I don't know how the hell I'm supposed to fix things."

Bobby whistled low. "Damn."

Mel sighed. "Rachel's different. She processes things in her own way. If you get in her space, she's gonna shut you out."

Bobby leaned back in her chair, crossing her arms. "So, what's your plan? Gonna grovel? Maybe serenade her in the teachers' lounge?"

I shot her a flat look. "Yeah, that'll go over great. Maybe I'll throw in an interpretive dance while I'm at it."

Mel rolled her eyes. "Look, if you push, she's just going to dig in deeper. Give her space, but don't disappear. Show up, be steady, let her come to you."

"The long game," I muttered, dragging a hand down my face.

"She's worth it," Mel said.

I didn't even have to think. "Yeah. She is."

Bobby smirked. "Then quit whining and start playing smart."

I grumbled something under my breath, but the conversation stuck with me long after they left.

By the time I got home, exhaustion crept in. The first week back always hit hard, and between the meetings, lesson planning, and watching my step around Rachel, my brain was fried.

Collapsing onto the couch, I barely got my shoes off before my phone buzzed, but a glance at the screen had me smiling.

"Hey, Sunshine," I answered, my voice warming at the sound of my little sister's name.

"Keith!" Sunny's voice was bright but held an edge of stress. "You home?"

"Just walked in," I said, stretching out. "How's college treating you?"

She let out a dramatic groan. "Ugh. I have so much reading, and my child psychology class is kicking my ass. I swear my professor enjoys watching us suffer."

I chuckled. "You'll survive. Just don't leave everything for the night before."

"I make no promises." Her voice turned teasing, but then she hesitated. "Actually... there's something I wanted to tell you."

I stretched my legs out, already wary. "That sounds ominous."

She groaned. "It's not a big deal, but... I'm seeing someone."

I sat up a little straighter. "Oh yeah?" I kept my tone light, but my protective instincts flared up fast. "What's his name?"

"Seb Parker."

The name wasn't familiar, but something in Sunny's voice made my stomach tighten.

I ran a hand over my face. "Tell me about him."

She hesitated, and that hesitation told me plenty. "He's great. Smart, funny, really sweet."

Sweet. *Right.*

"And you've been seeing him for...?"

"Since school started," she admitted. "I really like him, Keith. He's different."

Different. That word sent a prickle of unease down my spine.

"Different how?"

She let out a small laugh, but I caught the nervous edge to it. "I don't know. He gets me."

I leaned back, gripping the back of my neck. "Where'd you meet him?"

"At a party."

Of course.

"Keith," she warned, hearing my silence stretch.

"I didn't say anything."

"You didn't have to."

I exhaled through my nose. "Look, I know you can take care of yourself. But don't expect me to trust some random guy from a party."

I'd heard that before from women who wanted to believe the best, even when the warning signs were there. I might not know Seb Parker, but I knew his type.

And I hated that it felt like looking in a damn mirror.

I exhaled slowly. "Just... be careful, alright?"

She sighed. "I knew you were gonna say that."

"Because I know guys like him." I hesitated. "And you know why."

She didn't respond right away, but I heard the shift in her breathing. Yeah, she knew.

"He's not you, Keith," she finally said, soft but firm. "I know what I'm doing."

I wished I had her confidence.

"Fine, fine." I leaned my head back against the couch. "Anything else stressing you out besides psychology and Seb?"

She sighed. "Just... I don't know. The master's program is a lot. I miss you."

My chest tightened. "I miss you too, kid. You're doing great. Just keep working through it."

"Yeah, yeah." Her silence grew for a few seconds before she asked, "What about you? How's school? How's Rachel?"

I exhaled slowly, rubbing my temples. "Complicated."

"She still hates you?"

"Feels that way."

"Are you being an idiot?"

I let out a dry laugh. "Probably."

Sunny sighed. "Keith, just... don't make it worse. And don't be stubborn."

"I'll do my best."

"Good." She yawned. "Alright, I should probably get some dinner and then sleep. Love you."

"Love you too, Sunshine. Call anytime."

As the call ended, I stared at the ceiling, the weight of the day settling over me again. I needed to fix things with Rachel. And if my little sister, who had zero patience for my stubbornness, was telling me to get it together, maybe I needed to figure out how.

Chapter 5

Rachel

What would you do if your ex showed up at your usual coffee shop?
a) Walk out without making eye contact.
b) Act unbothered.
c) Exchange polite small talk, but keep them at a distance.
d) Make sure they regret letting you go.

I unlocked my classroom door, closing it softly behind me. Leaving the lights off, I navigated through the desks by the soft morning light to the book nook at the back of my classroom.

Sinking down into a beanbag chair, I hid behind the bookshelves to gather myself. The calm before the storm. I rested my head back against the shelf of colorful young adult book covers and closed my eyes.

The first week of school had crept by. Every day seemed more insurmountable than the last, each moment dragging on like the hands of the clock were moving slower just to test my patience.

The constant hum of classroom, the murmur of students, the pressure of preparing lesson plans, and the weight of expectations—all of it felt suffocating. I couldn't shake the feeling of drowning in a sea of tasks, the waves of work crashing over me, one after another. Every time I thought I could take a breath, something new would come up.

And then there was Keith.

We were assigned together every moment of the day, and honestly, it felt like a cruel joke. I had no escape. We planned together and walked the students down the hall together—every damn moment together. My me time was gone. We couldn't even go to the bathroom without crossing paths. The constant need to speak with him exhausted me. He was everywhere. Even during lunch, I had to listen to him ramble on about the kids or the lesson plan or whatever irrelevant nonsense was on his mind.

I could feel myself winding tighter and tighter with every passing second. Why did I have to be stuck with him?

His casual comments, the way he leaned in too close when we were planning, the way his voice always seemed to get under my skin... ugh! I hated all of it. It was too familiar. He invaded my space, in my head, and I couldn't get away. Was he deliberately putting himself in my path?

And then there were the phone calls. The way he'd step out of class for a few minutes, always with some excuse, always acting like it was no big deal. I tried not to notice. Or care.

But I did. Because it was just another reminder of what I should have seen all along.

Every time he cracked that stupid smile or flashed those stupid dimples, I wanted to scream. But I couldn't. I had to work with him, pretending he didn't drive me absolutely insane.

He'd already moved on. And damn it, it hurt more than I admitted.

A soft knock sounded on my door, interrupting my thoughts. I braced myself as I peeked out of my hiding spot.

Val and Audrey pressed their noses to the small glass window in the door. Chuckling, I raced over to let them in.

"We weren't sure you were here yet," Val said as she pushed past me. She wore forest green pants and a floral top. Her designer heels added three inches to her height.

"I'm reorganizing the book nook," I lied, the words slipping out before I even had time to think about them. I didn't want to tell my friends the real reason they'd found me hiding. They would think it was strange, maybe even overdramatic. Of course, they'd probably chalk it up to me being too sensitive, or worse, pity me. I couldn't stand the thought of that.

Audrey followed Val in carrying a drink holder with three steaming cups. Her tan and brown dress emphasized the red of her hair and made her green eyes sparkle. She handed me a cup and closed the door behind her. "Admit it. You were hiding."

"Okay, yes." Sometimes it shocked me how well these two women could read me. "I needed a few minutes before the Friday insanity began."

Val walked back to the nook and flopped onto a bean bag. Kicking off her shoes, she said, "If I had one of these in my classroom, I'd never come out."

Audrey rubbed her hand across her belly. "There's no way I'd ever get out of it."

I hurried to my desk and pushed the comfortable adult chair over to her and joined Val on the floor in the other beanbag chair. "What's in the bag?"

"I figured we all could use a pick me up." Val opened the bag and passed out chocolate croissants.

Audrey passed me a drink. Taking a sip of the mocha latte, I sighed happily. "You guys are the best."

"You're welcome." Audrey smiled. "Take a bite and then give us the details. How is teaching with Keith?"

I bit into the pastry, savoring the sweet, flaky treat as I considered what to say. "He's a great teacher. He knows enough Spanish to communicate with our ELLs, and enough psychology to get kids to do their work."

"Very politically correct." Val brushed crumbs off her shirt. "Now tell us the truth."

I pointed to his desk, stacked high with piles of paper, water bottles, and coffee cups. Did the man even know how to throw anything away? "His part of the room is a mess. It makes me anxious just looking at it."

Audrey snickered. "At least he's not leaving dirty socks in the living room. I swear, Oz never puts them in the hamper."

"Evan never puts the toothpaste in the vanity," Val complained. "And he leaves his dishes in the sink. Why is it so hard to put them into the dishwasher?"

"A few of many unanswered questions," Audrey sighed. "Is that it?"

My frustration and anger slipped out. "I don't know. Last year, Keith and I had a rhythm. We moved together like we were on the same wavelength. He could practically finish my sentences during class, anticipating my every word. Now, it's like he's constantly under my feet. We keep tripping over each other, stepping on each other's toes. It's like he's everywhere, always in my space, always throwing me off balance. I can't breathe, can't think straight, without him in the way. And I'm sick of it."

Val reached over from her spot on the floor and rubbed my shoulder. "That sounds pretty bad."

"Planning is miserable. I can't concentrate with him in the room, so I'm already behind. I send him out to make copies, but he comes back too soon. I walked in on him yesterday after the kids left, and he was changing his shirt!"

Audrey bit her lip, but I could tell she wanted to laugh. "Is it horrible?"

"Yes," I answered automatically then changed my mind. "No. I don't know. The kids love him, and they'll do anything for him. Honestly, I'm jealous because it takes me weeks to build relationships."

I'd spent my life wishing I could be someone different, easy-going, the life of the party. A loud extrovert with a quip always at the ready. The kind of person who could walk into any room and make instant connections.

But that wasn't me. I was shy and awkward. The one who stood off to the side, overthinking every word, every gesture. I often found myself deep inside my own head, replaying conversations, second-guessing everything. It made relationships hard. I couldn't just jump into something like everyone else seemed to do. I had to analyze every little detail, and even then, I didn't know if I was doing it right.

I sighed, frustration settling deep in my chest. "Sometimes I think I imagined it. But then I'd catch him staring."

His eyes would linger just a bit too long, his gaze soft in a way that made my heart race. He'd stare, his eyes dark and searching, like something still lingered between us. Something more than just professional. But then, like mist in the morning sun, it slipped away.

"Oooh." Val wiggled around in her chair to see me better. "The good kind of stare? Like you are so hot, I can't keep my eyes off you?"

I scoffed, the bitterness rising in my throat. "It doesn't matter. He's moved on, and I should too."

The words felt wrapped in poison, but I choked them out. Keith acted like I belonged to a forgotten chapter in his life.

The whole thing felt like a cruel, painful joke. I had to move on. I couldn't keep clinging to the ghosts of what might have been. But the anger still churned inside me, a constant reminder that he had betrayed me without a second thought, leaving me tangled up in all the things he'd said, all the things he hadn't.

I hated him. I hated the way he could flip the switch so easily.

But most of all, I hated how much I still cared.

The sound of a key unlocking the door interrupted us. The door swung open, and the lights came on.

"Hi, Keith," Audrey called, waving from her chair.

He tossed his keys onto his desk. "What are y'all doing in here?"

"Breakfast meeting," Val grumbled, rolling out of the beanbag onto her knees before standing up, her irritation clear in every movement.

Keith noticed the crumpled pink bag in her hand. "Anything left for me?"

Val's eyes narrowed. "Nope."

Keith glanced from Val to Audrey and then to me, his expression unreadable. "Should I leave?"

"No," Audrey barked, frowning at Keith. She stood with a hand pressing against her lower back. "I need to check with Mr. Kline to see if he's found a long-term sub for me yet."

"Oh," Val interjected, "I've been meaning to ask you. What do you think about Yona? She's finished most of her education classes and will be ready to teach full time next semester."

Yona wasn't just any substitute. She was Evan's friend who'd come to town for a fresh start with her two daughters after the tragic death of her husband.

"That's a great idea," Audrey brightened. "I'll call her now and ask her to contact the school."

"I need to post my lesson on the portal," Val sighed, rubbing her head as if it hurt. "Is it four o'clock yet?"

I stood too, wishing I could leave with them, the pull of escape so strong. Val and Audrey made me feel safe. They had no expectations, so I felt no awkwardness around them.

Staying behind, stuck in this classroom with the lingering tension, made my skin itch. I wanted to be far from Keith's presence.

But instead of following them out, I went to my desk and booted up my laptop. The familiar hum of the machine helped me focus on something simple that didn't involve complicated emotions or unresolved issues.

Keith turned on his own computer, the click of the power button unnervingly loud in the quiet room. The screen glowed to life, casting a pale light across his face, but he didn't immediately start typing. Instead, he sat there, staring at the screen like he wasn't sure what to do next, his fingers hovering over the keyboard.

Locking my eyes on my monitor, I refused to look up. The rhythmic clacking of my keys filled the silence, a deliberate attempt to drown out the tension building between us. But my traitorous eyes caught him shifting in his chair, his jaw tightening as though he held back words. Or maybe that was my imagination, playing tricks on me. Either way, I wasn't about to make this moment easier for him.

"Want me to do the warm-up today?" he asked softly, his voice almost tentative.

My fingers froze over the keyboard as the words landed, stinging in a way I hadn't expected. Did he think I couldn't do it? Doubt slithered under my skin, sharp and unwelcome. I clenched my jaw, refusing to look at him or give him the satisfaction of seeing how much it affected me. "Sure."

He glanced at the day's agenda written on the board. "And the brain break?"

"Okay." I opened my email and scanned the messages, wishing he'd stop talking to me.

Keith walked around his desk, coming toward mine. "And I'll take a small group into the hall to review after your lesson on commas."

I deleted two spam messages from universities pushing me to learn more about a PhD in education, my lip curling at the thought. Did they really think I had time for that?

"That's fine." I forced the words out, my fingers tightening around my coffee cup. But the only thing I swallowed was the irritation bubbling up, bitter and persistent.

He stopped beside my desk, leaning his hip against the edge like he belonged there. "Are you ever going to talk to me again?"

The truth was I didn't know. My emotions felt like they'd been tossed into a blender. They were raw, messy, and impossible to sort out. So, I did what I always did when everything felt too big. I shut it down. Compartmentalized. Focused on what I could control.

Eyes on my screen, I opened an email from the assistant principal and jotted a note in my planner about Monday's adjusted schedule for testing. A quick reply to the testing coordinator followed, confirming I'd be in early to help set up. Each small task was a lifeline, pulling me further away from the chaos swirling in my chest.

Across from me, he sat in a student chair, his fingers drumming lightly against the adjoining desk. His knee bounced—a telltale sign of his impatience—but he stayed quiet, watching me, waiting.

When I finally met his eyes, my voice sounded detached. "I am talking to you."

He sighed, throwing his hands up. "We used to be friends."

The muscles on my face were frozen as I said, "Do we have to talk about this now? I really need to finish responding to these emails."

His voice rose in frustration. "You can't keep shutting me out, Rachel. We have to work together."

"We're doing fine," I lied.

"Really?" he spat out. "Because we can't even co-teach anymore. I know English isn't my strong suit, but you never made me feel like a hindrance last year."

I could barely meet his eyes. "Stop yelling at me."

He stalked away but didn't make it far before he turned back, his clenched fists betrayed the effort it took to rein himself in. "If you'd just talk to me, we could figure this out."

Figure it out. Like it was that simple.

He made it sound easy, but I wasn't wired for easy. Even the simplest interactions felt like walking a tightrope. On a good day, I balanced. On days like this, when stress and emotions tangled into a suffocating knot, one misstep meant freefalling.

I loved my job because it gave me purpose. It challenged me to confront my struggles head-on while helping kids like me find their footing in a world that didn't always make sense. But relationships? None of that made sense.

Last year had stripped away every romantic delusion I'd allowed myself to indulge in. No rose-colored glasses, no sugar-coated fantasies—just the sharp clarity that it would never be.

But I couldn't say any of that to Keith, so I said, "We already figured it out."

"When? I gave you space like you asked, and you left for two months without a word."

My mind went blank. I didn't know what to say.

I sidestepped around him, keeping my voice even. "I can't do this right now. The kids will be here in a few minutes. You should answer your phone."

Brushing past him, I slipped out the door, my heart pounding harder with every step down the hall. The faculty restroom was mercifully empty, and I locked myself in a stall, leaning against the cold metal door.

The seconds ticked by as I tried to calm the storm in my chest, but the knot in my stomach only tightened. I stared at the floor, focusing on the tiny flecks in the tile to keep from replaying his words.

When the bell finally rang, signaling the start of class, I took a deep breath, straightened my posture, and stepped out of the stall. The mirror reflected a composed face, but underneath, I felt anything but.

Chapter 6

Keith

What would you do if you had to work with a cute but irritating co-worker?

a) Exchange playful banter and pretend they don't get under your skin.
b) Try to stay professional... but secretly enjoy the tension.
c) Challenge them to a competition just to wipe that smug grin off their face.
d) Give in and find out if the chemistry is as electric as it feels.

By mid-October, I felt ready to tear my beard out. How had I ever thought I could win Rachel over with a little charm? We spent five days a week, eight hours a day together, yet she still treated me like an uninvited guest in her classroom.

Rachel had two sides. The first, her professional facade—polite, composed, and annoyingly conciliatory. She wore it like armor in meetings, in front of students, even around our friends. Maddeningly effective, it made her seem untouchable, impervious to anything I said or did.

But then came the other side—the fiery, frustrated Rachel that only emerged when we were alone. This side lacked politeness; she turned sharp, sarcastic, and maddeningly real. And damn it if I didn't find myself drawn to that version of her. More than a challenge, she became a puzzle I couldn't stop trying to solve.

I wasn't proud of it, but I stirred the pot on purpose sometimes, just to crack through her icy exterior and see the fire beneath. Which explained why, at the end of another long day, I stood in her way after school, gearing up for yet another round of verbal sparring.

She tried to ignore me, her hands overflowing with papers, her bag slipping off her shoulder. But I refused to let her escape that easily.

"Today was a struggle from beginning to end," I said, crossing my arms and planting myself firmly in her path.

The way her eyes flashed with irritation sent a thrill through me, even as I braced for her inevitable retort. Reckless and probably stupid, but I couldn't help it. Rachel in a temper captivated me more than any version of her polite silence ever could.

"Tomorrow, we should switch it up," I continued. "Try to add more pizzazz to the lesson."

"More pizzazz?" she echoed, her tone hardening.

"The kids couldn't connect with the lesson today. It was boring," I offered unhelpfully as I watched her fists clench.

"You distracted them by telling dad jokes."

"It woke them up." I crossed my arms, feeling oddly insulted. "Besides, dad jokes are a tried-and-true method of engagement. Who doesn't appreciate a well-timed pun?"

"Me," she hissed, her teeth clenched.

"Strategic humor is one of the fundamentals of education. You should try it." I leaned back, arms crossing over my chest, a smirk tugging at the corner of my mouth. Riling her up was too easy, but damn if it wasn't my favorite part of the day.

Her sharp exhale signaled I'd hit my mark, and in a few quick strides, she closed the distance, planting herself on the other side of the desk. "I'd just gotten them settled down."

I met her glare head-on, squaring my shoulders and biting back a grin. "Additionally, Marco and Zuri were confused about the assignment."

Her face could've melted steel. "Because they were listening to you while I gave directions. In. Two. Languages."

Okay, fair point. Time to pivot. "Speaking of the assignment," I said, leaning casually against the desk, "we should probably talk about how we're going to handle the group projects next week. The seating arrangement alone is a ticking time bomb."

Her face reddened with anger, her eyes hot. As much as I hated poking at her, I reveled in the honesty of her emotion. She hated me. Wanted to flay me alive.

"The seating arrangement is f-fine!" she spluttered, her words tumbling out in a mix of frustration and disbelief.

I stood, giving her a smirk. "And your Spanish needs work. I'd be happy to tutor you."

Her eyes narrowed, lips pressing into a thin line. "Right, because clearly, I'm the one who doesn't understand things."

I paused, watching the storm brew in her eyes. Anger rolled off her in waves, but underneath it, I caught a flicker of hurt, maybe even betrayal. My own frustration ebbed, replaced by the familiar pull to fix things, to make it better somehow.

I ran a hand through my hair, exhaling slowly. "Look, I didn't mean to—"

"Be a jackass? I don't think you can help yourself."

She was glorious in her fury. Her fire called to me on a primal level. My cock responded to her while my mind buzzed with images of taking her on the desk—her full breasts, plump with nipples taut and ready for my mouth in my hands. Her pussy wet and aching for my fingers and mouth.

I swallowed hard. "Tell me how to fix this, Rachel. I'll do anything."

She threw her hands up with an exasperated groan, her frustration radiating off her.

"You're crazy." Her voice cut sharp through the tension between us, but emotion only deepened the flush in her cheeks. She looked wild, untouchable, and somehow that only made me want to reach for her more.

"I know," I admitted, my voice quieter, almost resigned. I wasn't sure if I was confessing to her or to myself, but the weight of it sat heavy in my chest. I was crazy for pushing her. Crazy for wanting her. Just... crazy.

"I don't have time for this. Get out your phone and call a woman who cares." She lashed out, sharp and bitter, like she'd been holding it in for months.

The accusation hung in the air, cutting to the root of our problem.

"I deleted it all off my phone."

Her head jerked up, her blue eyes locking onto mine with an intensity that made my chest tighten. Finally, we were getting somewhere. For the first time in weeks, she wasn't looking through me.

"What?"

"I canceled my membership and deleted my profile." My voice was steady, but inside I held my breath, waiting for her to say something that would crack the wall between us.

There were questions in her eyes, and I mentally dared her to ask them. I'd tell her the truth if she asked.

She shook her head, planting her fists on her hips. "Don't bullshit me. You've been sneaking out to take calls during class. Scheduling dates the old-fashioned way now?"

"Do you want to look?" I dug my phone out of my back pocket, unlocked it, and held it out to her.

I wasn't hiding anything. If she needed proof, she could have it. But the fact that she didn't believe me stung. Frustration knotted in my gut. And disappointment. Because I'd done this to her, to us.

Her fists uncurled by her sides and I held my breath, hoping she would take it. "Put it away. Deleting an app doesn't fix this. It doesn't fix us."

I tossed the phone down between us on the desk as we faced off. "Maybe it's a start."

"We're here now, trapped in a classroom together for the rest of the year."

I accepted her view, and maybe she was right. But I couldn't stop hoping this could be our second chance.

"You can believe me, Rach."

She laughed, a bitter, ugly sound that scraped across my nerves. "I will never trust you again, Keith."

Her lower lip wobbled as she fought off tears, and I hated myself more with every second that passed. Turning away, she stalked back to her desk and shoved papers, notebooks, and planners into her bag, her movements jerky and uncoordinated.

I moved around to the other side of the desk but stopped short, suddenly terrified that pushing even a little more might shatter her completely. "You can't hate me for things that happened before we met," I said, my voice quieter than I intended.

She froze, her back to me, then straightened, stiffening her spine, bracing for a blow. "No," she said, spinning around to glare at me, "but I can hate myself for being gullible. And I do. I was available, and you saw it as an opportunity to have some fun."

"That's not fair," I said, my frustration creeping into my tone. "You're putting words in my mouth. Why not just ask me the truth?"

Her laugh came again, sharper this time. "Do you think I want to know? Do you think I want to sit here and listen to you tell me how it meant nothing? That you were still swiping through women's profiles the whole time we were together?"

"It wasn't like that!" I insisted, my fists curling at my sides.

"Oh, really?" She stepped closer, pointing at my phone, her eyes blazing. "Are you saying I didn't see it? That the proof was right in front of me the whole damn time?"

I shook my head, trying to keep my voice steady. "It didn't mean anything."

Her face darkened, and I could see the hatred shining in her eyes. I'd pushed too hard, and now her anxiety ran rampant, fueling her anger.

"I can't do this," she said, her voice cracking as she slung her bag over her shoulder. Grabbing her lunch box, she shot me one last glare. "I have to go."

"Rachel, wait—"

But she had already stepped out the door, her footsteps echoing down the hallway.

I leaned against the edge of my desk, rubbing a hand over my face. "Fucking hell."

***

Late that night, I stretched out on my bed, trying to unwind. The king-sized mattress took up most of the room, leaving just enough space for a small nightstand crammed between the bed frame and the wall. Normally, this bed was my sanctuary. The perfect blend of softness, wrapped in crisp sheets and a thick black-and-gray comforter. After a rough day, it offered the one place where I could sprawl out and shut my mind off. Not tonight.

I closed my eyes, forcing myself to breathe deeply, counting each inhale and exhale like it might hypnotize me into sleep. It didn't.

With a groan, I rolled over and reached into the nightstand drawer, rummaging blindly until my fingers brushed against the bottle of melatonin buried in the clutter. I fished it out, unscrewed the cap, and popped a couple of gummies into my mouth.

Returning the bottle, my hand brushed something else. I pulled out a handful of the small packages and stared at them.

Condoms.

Extra-large. Ribbed for her pleasure. Lubricated. Neon colors.

A buffet of bad decisions, a variety pack for every potential escapade. I turned one over in my fingers, the corner of my mouth twitching in a wry, humorless smile. How ironic that they mocked me now, dusty and untouched.

I didn't regret my life choices. While my friends were out living it up in college, I attended parent-teacher conferences and chaperoned field trips. I'd been the responsible one, the one who always had to be the role model for Sunshine.

Then Sunshine graduated from high school and left for Old Dominion University. Suddenly, I had free time. A lot of it. And energy. So, I cut loose.

I deserved it. I was single, no longer tied down, and free to do whatever the hell I wanted.

Did I take it too far?

Maybe.

Definitely.

Pretty soon, the rumors started flying around Marchfield, and I discovered I had a reputation as a player. I couldn't help but laugh. After all, wasn't I just doing what any other guy would do in my shoes?

My phone beeped, pulling me out of my thoughts. I rolled over, reaching out to grab it off the charger.

Before I could unlock the screen, it buzzed again.

Rachel would probably say this was proof—evidence that I couldn't be trusted, that I hadn't really changed. It didn't matter who was calling. I was guilty and no matter what I did, she still expected me to mess up.

I exhaled sharply, gripping the phone tighter. "Unbelievable," I muttered, swiping at the screen with more force than necessary.

Sunshine.

I swiped to answer, forcing the tension from my voice. "Hey, little sis," I said. No matter what was going on with Rachel, my sister didn't deserve to catch the heat from it. "What's up?"

"Hey, Keith." Her voice sounded light, yet something felt off.

I frowned. "You good?"

She hesitated. "Yeah. I just... I might come home this weekend."

I sat up straighter. It had only been two weekends since Homecoming, and she'd seemed fine when we went to the football game together. So why the sudden urge to come home?

"Everything okay?" I asked, trying to keep my voice casual.

"I just need to get off campus," she said, a little too fast.

That hit harder than I expected. My gut twisted. Sunshine was independent—she didn't ask for much. If she reached out, something was wrong.

Exhaling slowly, I asked, "Is it Seb?"

I'd met him at Homecoming a few weeks ago. He'd smiled and laughed, but it felt off. Like he was acting. Or trying to prove something. Whatever it was, it rubbed me the wrong way.

I hadn't said anything at the time. Sunshine liked him, and she was an adult. But now, with her suddenly wanting to come home? Yeah. My instincts told me I should have trusted my gut.

"Yeah," she said softly. "It's Seb."

I leaned back, trying to keep my voice casual, but the frustration in my chest started to burn. "What's going on, Sunny? You can talk to me."

There was a long pause on the other end of the line, and I could almost hear her wrestling with her thoughts.

"I don't know," she finally said, her voice tight. "I thought things were going okay, but now he's acting weird. Like, distant. And then there's this whole thing with his friends..."

My stomach tightened, and I exhaled slowly, trying to keep my frustration in check.

Hearing Sunshine doubt made me think of Rachel. Had I pushed her to doubt herself, just like Seb was doing? The thought gnawed at me.

"Has he treated you badly?" I asked, my voice rougher than I meant it to be.

"Yes." Sunny hesitated. "No. I don't know. I'm confused."

I rubbed my hand over my face, trying to reign in the instinct to hunt down Seb and give him a piece of my mind. But the truth was, I hadn't been any better. The way I'd treated Rachel, had made her feel the same way—confused, uncertain, unsure of what was real.

"Listen," I said, my voice softer now, "don't settle for someone who makes you confused. You deserve better." The words felt hollow, like I was convincing myself as much as her.

Should I back off, let Rachel move on? Maybe I wasn't the guy she needed right now, or ever. She deserved someone who didn't make her question her own instincts. Someone who didn't add to the noise in her head. But as much as I told myself I needed to walk away, I just couldn't.

"Hey," Sunny interrupted my thoughts. "I just need a few days to think, that's all."

I swallowed, pushing aside the storm of thoughts about Rachel for the moment to focus on Sunny.

"Okay," I said. "I'll be here. Just let me know when you're on the way."

"Great! I'll see you Friday." Her voice softened. "Love you."

"Love you too, Sunny."

The call ended, but the tightness in my chest didn't ease. I set my phone back on the charger and tried to relax, but my mind wouldn't stop turning.

Tossing the blanket off, I sat up. The room felt too small, the air thick with thoughts of everything I couldn't control.

I rubbed my eyes, trying to shake off the exhaustion that had been building all day, but my brain refused to quiet. Rachel's face kept resurfacing, her angry words from earlier echoing in my ears. I wanted to go back to when things had felt simpler between us, but I didn't know how. Hell, I didn't even know where to start.

And then my mind drifted back to my conversation with Sunny. Who was I to give advice? I told her she deserved better, yet I kept making the same mistakes with Rachel. It made me feel slimy. I'd confused Rachel, made her question herself when all she ever wanted was honesty.

My stomach twisted, the weight of the guilt pressing down on me as I recalled Rachel's furious expression. The distance she'd put between us, the things I'd said, they weren't fixable with a simple apology. But what else could I do? I couldn't take back the mistakes I'd made, and I couldn't promise her that I wouldn't mess up again. I wanted her in my life, but I wasn't worthy.

***

Last May, before everything fell apart, we'd been celebrating Audrey and Oz's wedding, the air buzzing with energy. Rachel and I had hooked up a few weeks before, but one taste of her had only whet my appetite. Twirling her around the dance floor, both of us laughing, I couldn't take my eyes off her. She was radiant, her cheeks flushed from champagne. Then she leaned in, lips brushing my ear as she whispered, "Do you want to go somewhere more private?"

Before we could slip away, she pressed a quick kiss to my cheek and murmured, "Meet me by the door, I just need to run to the restroom."

I went back to the table to grab my jacket, pulling my phone out, half-distracted as I scrolled through notifications. Out of habit—because that's all it was at this point—I tapped open the dating app known more for hookups than its relationships. I wasn't even really paying attention, just flicking through profiles the way someone mindlessly scrolls social media. It didn't mean anything. At least, that's what I told myself.

When I spied Rachel heading toward the door, I slipped the phone into my pocket. Coming up behind her, I grabbed her hand, and we slipped out of the reception and into my car, the cool night air sharp against the heat of my skin.

"Where do you want to go?" I asked, driving away from the farm and heading toward town.

She trailed a finger from my knee across my thigh, her touch leaving a trail of fire in its wake. "My apartment is closest," she said, her voice low and inviting.

Rachel couldn't keep her hands off me in the car, stroking her fingers down my neck and around the edge of my collared shirt. Her touch burned through my clothes, driving me crazy.

When she trailed her hand down to my crotch, I folded her hand into mine. "If you do that, I'll drive us off the road."

She laughed. "Then you better drive faster."

I turned into the driveway, heading back toward Rachel's carriage house apartment. Braking hard, I kissed Rachel, dragging her close. She practically dragged me inside, and I wasn't complaining.

She made quick work of my clothes. Stripping off my suit, almost choking me before loosening my tie. We teased and joked. I didn't remember the last time I'd laughed during sex.

I'd barely peeled her out of her bridesmaid's dress before she pulled me down on the carpet and straddled my hips.

"The bed's right over there." My hands were busy unhooking her bra. Distracted by the beauty of the round globes and pink nipples, I forgot all about moving.

Rachel slipped out of her panties. Her naked body straddled mine.

"Slow down," I murmured, but she had other plans.

Her wet center was hot as she held herself over my cock, and there was no place I'd rather be. I held my breath, waiting.

"Do you have a condom?" She blushed, her entire body turning pink.

I dragged my pants over and handed her a packet.

Her warm hand surrounded me, pumping up and down a few times before tearing open the condom and rolling it slowly down my sensitive skin.

My hips jerked.

And then I slid inside her.

I groaned, and she giggled breathlessly, then shifted her hips.

"You feel so fucking good," I said, but it came out in Bart Simpson's voice. She laughed hard, tears of joy filling her eyes as she drove both of us higher.

It only took a few more frantic movements, and we were both coming, the joy of it sweeping us up and over the edge until we were left panting on the floor.

A long time afterward, I grabbed my phone, wanting to snap a picture of her face. Rachel was totally relaxed and happier than I'd ever seen her. I made some crack about wanting to photograph her naked, and we tussled for the phone.

She poked me in the armpit, and I dropped my phone with a yelp, her laughter echoing in the tiny apartment. But I remember then that her laughter stopped.

Because that's when she saw it.

The screen of my phone still lit with notifications. A woman's face—ready for me to swipe left or right.

Rachel's expression shifted so quickly it felt like a slap. The joy in her eyes evaporated, replaced by something raw and heavy. Distrust. Sorrow. Disappointment.

She stared at me, and I couldn't find a single word to explain.

My tongue felt heavy, my chest hollow. Then she moved, wrapping herself in a blanket like it was armor.

She reached for my phone without saying a word, her fingers cold as she swiped through it quickly, and my chest tightening with every movement. I could feel her eyes on me, each glance a silent accusation that cut deeper. She found the dating apps first, the familiar icons staring back at her, but she didn't stop there. She scrolled through the names of the women I'd hooked up with in my contacts, then flicked through my photos and all the selfies with women. Each swipe felt like another nail in the coffin, and I knew then that I had destroyed any chance of explaining, of making her believe it wasn't what it seemed.

When she threw my phone at me, the crack of it landing on the hardwood floor felt like a gavel coming down, sentencing me.

"You need to go." Her voice stayed steady, but a tremble lingered beneath the surface, a crack threatening to widen.

I scooped up the phone, as if that would somehow erase what she'd seen.

"That's what you were doing earlier." Her laugh rang bitter, sharp. "Scrolling through women's pictures. At the wedding." She pointed at the door, her hand shaking. "Please go."

I froze, my feet glued to the floor. Every instinct screamed at me to stay, to throw myself at her feet and beg her to hear me out. But her face. God, her face—so closed off and resolute.

So, I left.

I walked out the door with dread solidifying into a cold heavy weight in my gut.

But that was then.

Since then, every time I walked away from Rachel, the weight in my chest got heavier, settling deep like a stone. Every step from her felt like tearing out pieces of my heart, leaving behind something raw and exposed. I told myself it would fade, but the truth was, it hadn't.

Rachel was different. She was the only woman I'd ever wanted to cuddle all night long, the only one whose presence felt like home. With her, I wanted to sink in rather than escape. She made me think about a future in a way I'd never imagined. Not because I didn't want it, but because wanting meant risking, and risking meant the chance of losing her for good. And maybe, just maybe, that had already happened.

But now, she wanted me gone.

And I feared she'd never change her mind.

Chapter 7

Rachel

What would you do if your boss asked you to go on a work trip with your nemesis?
a) Politely decline, citing other commitments.
b) Accept and wonder if it's an opportunity for something more.
c) Agree, but make sure you book your own room.
d) Use the trip as an excuse to network and make new connections.

I stepped into the classroom, already feeling the weight of the day on my shoulders. The door creaked as I pushed it open, and there he was.

Keith sat at his desk, looking way too damn fresh for someone who'd been up before the sun. He was relaxed, like he had everything under control, and that pissed me off. He sat there like he owned the place and didn't have a care in the world.

His dark brown hair was tousled just right, his beard perfectly trimmed, and his clothes fit him in all the right places. The sunglasses perched on his head only added to his laid-back charm.

And it irritated the hell out of me.

It wasn't like him to be early. I always got here first, so I could be calm and composed before he strolled in. But today, he was already at the desk, shuffling through papers and muttering under his breath, completely unaware of me standing there, shooting daggers with my eyes. I hated it. I hated how effortless he made everything seem when my world felt like it was crumbling around me.

"Of course, you're already here," I muttered, my voice laced with frustration. "Can't let me have one thing today, huh?"

Keith glanced up, his eyes narrowing on my face. "What happened to your eye, Princess?"

Of course he had to ask, but I wasn't a child. What happened to me on my own time wasn't any of his business, and I could do without his judgment.

Reaching up to touch the sore spot near my eye, I winced as my fingers brushed over the tender bruise. "Bolt happened," I muttered, trying to brush it off with a shrug. "I was sleeping on the couch, and I tripped over the little idiot when I woke up. Instead of crushing him, I overcompensated and ended up falling into the damn floor lamp."

Keith's confused expression added to my irritation. I could feel my annoyance rising, but I kept my tone level as I quickly added, "I'm fine, it's just a stupid accident."

I turned on my heel, heading toward my desk and dropping into my chair with a little more force than necessary.

"Bolt is your tortoise, right?"

His tone edged with condescension and disbelief, like he found the whole thing amusing. I wasn't in the mood to deal with it.

"Yes," I snapped. "He's a marginated tortoise. Native to Greece and Italy, and his shell's unique—kind of like a wedge. Not that it matters to you." The words tumbled out faster than I could control, and I cursed myself for letting him get under my skin.

Keith raised an eyebrow, a grin tugging at the corners of his mouth. "Well, at least you didn't get into a bar brawl." Without missing a beat, he slid his aviators down from the top of his head and handed them to me.

"Put 'em on or people will think we've been fighting."

I opened my mouth to protest, but the playful glint in his eyes made me pause. I wanted to stay angry, but there was something about Keith that made it hard.

Maybe it was the way he didn't take himself too seriously, or that the whole situation had become ridiculous. Either way, I couldn't help but let go of some of the frustration I'd been holding onto.

I rolled my eyes. "No one will think that," I muttered, but the edge in my voice had softened. "Everyone knows what a klutz I am. Assault by lamp is much more believable."

Keith's grin widened, his voice light and teasing. "Wear the glasses anyway. It'll stop the kids from gawking at you during class."

A laugh slipped out before I could stop it, the sound soft but genuine. I shook my head, slipping the sunglasses on with a sigh. "If you insist."

I felt silly, but at least they had the desired effect. The kids quickly shifted their attention back to their work, and I found myself relaxing.

The rest of the day went surprisingly smoothly. The tension that had been between Keith and me seemed to evaporate with the exchange. We settled into a comfortable rhythm, and for a brief moment, I forgot all the things that had been weighing on me.

When Sawyer pushed his chair back and lifted two legs off the ground, Keith was right there, his hand on the chair before it could rock too far. When I fumbled with the score of the review game, Keith effortlessly took over, making sure the score tallied correctly. And when I'd explained the difference between an adjective and an adverb for the fourth time, Keith swooped in and clarified it three more times, breaking it down in a way that even the most confused students seemed to understand.

But just as I started to think the day was a success, the classroom phone rang, and I went to answer it while Keith continued to supervise the students, guiding them as they cleaned up.

"Hi, Rachel. This is Rhonda from the office. Mr. Kline would like you to stop by his office after dismissal."

My stomach clenched automatically. Getting called to the office was rarely good news.

"Sure. Okay."

Rhonda continued, "Is Keith there, too?"

"Yes. Would you like to speak with him?"

"That's not necessary. Just bring him with you."

The questions swirled in my mind. Each possibility more unsettling than the last. What could this be about? Did someone hear Keith and me fighting? Or maybe Mr. Kline found out about last year's non-relationship sex?

My anxiety spiked as I hung up, the familiar rush of panic flooding my chest as my heart pounded loudly in my ears.

The loudspeaker crackled to life, droning on about the football game starting at five tomorrow. Blah, blah, blah. The bell rang, signaling the end of class. The students hurried out, chattering and laughing, leaving the room empty except for Keith and me.

He sat down at his desk with a groan, leaning back in his chair like he'd just run a marathon.

"Don't get too comfortable," I said, trying to sound casual. "We need to go see Mr. Kline after the buses roll."

Keith's eyebrows shot up, a mix of curiosity and concern flashing across his face. "Did they say why?"

I shook my head.

We followed the mass of students toward the exit, the halls buzzing with the familiar chaos of dismissal. Lockers slammed, shoes squeaked against the floor, and the air filled with the overlapping sounds of chatter and laughter. A girl with a cello case dashed past, her strides quick and determined, the case bumping against her legs like a steady drumbeat.

The chaos was palpable. Students weaved in and out of the crowds, some with backpacks slung carelessly over one shoulder, others pushing past one another to get to the door faster. Teachers were scattered at various points, herding kids out the door or answering last-minute questions.

In the middle of all this, Keith and I moved in slow motion, trying to navigate through the crowd toward Mr. Kline's office.

We entered the office, where Rhonda, a plump brunette with a no-nonsense expression, sat like a gatekeeper in front of the inner sanctum of the admin offices. Her desk was stacked with papers, half-empty coffee mugs, and a family of stress balls that looked like they'd seen better days.

"Mr. Kline's expecting you," she said as if this was just another one of the many daily routines she oversaw. She barely looked up from her computer screen as she gestured toward the closed door behind her.

I glanced at Keith, who raised an eyebrow, his expression unreadable. He knocked on the office door.

"Hi, thanks for coming down," Mr. Kline said, his tone polite but with a hint of warmth that helped ease some of my nervousness. His smile, faint but reassuring, made me wonder if this wouldn't turn into the disaster I'd envisioned.

Mr. Kline gestured to the small group of chairs clustered in front of his desk. Keith and I sat.

"Before I start, may I ask why you're wearing sunglasses, Ms. Bright?" he asked, his eyebrow quirked in curiosity.

I blinked, momentarily confused, before remembering I still had Keith's aviators perched on my face like some kind of clueless disguise. "Oh, right." I flushed slightly. "I got in a scuffle with a tortoise and a floor lamp..."

I lifted the glasses off, and both men winced at the sight of my bruised eye.

"I'm very sorry to hear that," Mr. Kline said, his voice shifting into genuine concern. "Be sure to ice it tonight."

"Okay," I agreed, feeling a little sheepish. I was willing to pretend everything else was normal for a moment. I folded the glasses in my hands and passed them to Keith.

"I asked you to come down because I have some great news," Mr. Kline said, his voice steady, almost cheerful. "This year's Middle School Conference theme is co-teaching. Every school gets to send two teachers who work together to the conference, all expenses paid, and I've picked you."

I tried to focus on what he was saying, but the words felt like they were bouncing off me. Co-teaching? Middle School Conference? Why would he pick us? Had I volunteered for this last year and just forgotten about it? My brain raced, trying to piece together any memory of even discussing it. Anxiety rose in my chest, spreading through me like a sudden storm. Was this a test?

"It's in Charlottesville this year. December first through the third."

Charlottesville. December. Should I know what that meant? My head swirled with a thousand thoughts at once, and I couldn't get a grip on any of them.

I glanced at Keith, hoping for some kind of sign that this was normal. But his brow was furrowed, his lips turned down slightly. He looked just as thrown as I felt. The silence between us stretched a little too long as my discomfort built.

"I chose you two because I see great potential in you both as leaders in the school," Mr. Kline continued.

Keith and I exchanged a look, but I couldn't process his expression. All I could focus on was how much I didn't want to go.

It was a crazy idea. Keith and I couldn't go to a conference together. Charlottesville was hours away from Marchfield. I could barely make it through a school day in the same room with Keith, let alone spend an entire weekend. I couldn't even imagine it. I opened my mouth to protest, but the words stuck in my throat.

And then the worst possible thing happened. Keith nodded. "Thank you for the opportunity. I'd love to go to the conference."

My mouth fell open.

I stared at him as he sat with that goofy grin on his face. He wasn't suffocating under the thought of a weekend full of forced bonding and awkward conversations.

How could I say what I thought without sounding completely irrational?

"I, uh…" I cleared my throat. "Umm."

Mr. Kline nodded. "Education conferences are a lot of fun."

It wouldn't be fun. Traveling was a nightmare. I always left something vital at home and being surrounded by strangers made me nervous.

And then there were the meals. Eating in strange restaurants was always a gamble, and hotel rooms? I could never get comfortable, and no matter how many pillows I piled up, I couldn't sleep.

And Keith. The thought of spending an entire weekend with him, forced into proximity, no easy escape. Just the thought of it made my palms sweat.

But what choice did I have? I could lie, of course. Say I had plans. Like, I don't know, brain surgery. Or a therapy retreat. Something that sounded both urgent and impossible to reschedule. But I knew that would only lead to more questions, and I was a horrible liar.

And I didn't want to disappoint Mr. Kline. He'd hired me and put his faith in me. I took a deep breath. I had to do this. For my students. For the school.

I could probably avoid Keith the whole weekend. He'd be off partying with the other teachers while I holed up in my room.

"Okay," I said, my voice almost squeaking.

Keith's grin widened, but I couldn't bring myself to meet his eyes.

Instead, I clutched the edges of my chair. All I had to do was survive. I could fake it until I made it until I could escape back to my safe little bubble in Marchfield.

"I'll go."

Chapter 8

Rachel

What would you tell your bestie about the irritating person you work with?
a) I catch myself staring way too often... and I think they've noticed.
b) If they ever leaned in too close, I don't think I'd be able to resist.
c) I've imagined way too many scenarios involving the supply closet.
d) I don't just want them—I want them on my desk.

Steam curled from my coffee cup as I wrapped my hands around it, soaking in the warmth. Thursday mornings were always better with Barb, even if I had to wake up an hour early to make time for her.

Barb sat across from me in a wicker chair, her favorite blanket draped over her legs as she gazed out over the fog-covered yard. I sat across a small table from her, leaning back into the comfortable chair.

"So," she said, tearing open a sugar packet and dumping it into her cup. "How's it going with Keith? Are you still plotting his demise?"

I rolled my eyes. "It's been fine."

"Fine?" She arched a knowing brow. "I thought you hated him. What were your words? Ah yes, Keith was an annoying worm you wanted to grind under your boot."

I sighed, taking a sip of my coffee before admitting, "It's been... easier. We don't step on each other's toes as much, and he actually listens when I make a suggestion."

Barb smirked. "And?"

"And what?"

She leaned in, eyes twinkling with mischief. "And you don't hate him anymore."

"I never hated him." I felt the heat rise in my cheeks. That had never been the problem. I'd been exasperated by Keith, frustrated beyond belief, constantly annoyed at how he absentmindedly checked his phone, thumbing over the screen like he was waiting for someone. But hate? No.

"Mm-hmm." She took a sip of her drink, still watching me like a hawk.

I ignored her and took a book from my bag. Barb's gaze dropped to the cover. "For me?"

I glanced at the cover. A brooding duke loomed in the background, his dark hair windswept. The heroine stood in the foreground, bodice barely hanging on, her curls wild as if she'd just escaped some scandalous encounter. Her hand clutched a jeweled hairpin, poised like a dagger, while the duke's smoldering gaze practically dared her to use it. "It's a good story, but it could never happen in real life."

Barb raised an eyebrow. "What evidence do you have to base that on?"

I snorted, taking a sip of my coffee. "Love just doesn't work like that."

She tapped the book against the table. "Then why do you read romances?"

I shrugged. "Escapism. They're fun to read, but real relationships are messy and disappointing. People lie. They leave. They break promises."

"You're very cynical about love."

I narrowed my eyes, my heart beating a little too fast. Was it cynicism, though? Or was it just the truth? I had seen enough to know that love wasn't like the stories in romance novels, where everything fell into place with a happily-ever-after.

"Because I know better." I tapped my screen to turn the page. "Love makes people irrational. It makes them ignore red flags and do stupid things. I've never seen anyone like me in a romance, so it's hard to believe it's something that could work for me."

Barb sighed, setting the book down. "I used to think that too."

I glanced up, skeptical. "Really?"

She nodded. "Before I met Mike, I swore I'd never fall in love, but when he walked into my life with that ridiculous smile and his terrible jokes, everything shifted." She shook her head, a fond smile tugging at her lips. "Loving him didn't mean either of us had to change. We just grew together."

"Real life fairy tales are rare."

Barb leaned forward, her expression soft but firm. "Love isn't a fairy tale, Rachel. It's work, but it's worth it." She tapped the book again, her gaze steady. "You don't have to believe me now. Just follow your heart when the time comes."

*****

The conversation with Barb lingered in my mind as I gathered my things and headed to school. I tried to push the nagging thoughts about love aside and focus on the day ahead. The drive was quiet, the hum of my Smart car's engine a dull backdrop to my swirling thoughts.

By the time I pulled into the parking lot, the morning fog had lifted, but I still felt off-balance. Walking inside, I tried to shake off the odd feeling. The hallways were quiet, most of the teachers still gathering materials or chatting in the breakroom.

Entering my classroom, I saw Keith was already there behind his desk.

He glanced up as I entered, his lips quirking into that familiar half-smile. "You're here early," I said, trying to sound casual, even though I could feel the pulse of my heart surge.

Too much caffeine. That was the only explanation.

The jump in my heartrate had nothing to do with Keith's half-smile that made him the most handsome man on earth.

Nope, that was biology. An involuntary reaction, like sneezing or shivering when it's cold. Not attraction. Definitely not the beginning of anything ridiculous, like feelings. My heart racing? That was just a fluke. Nothing more.

Keith stretched his arms above his head. "Thought I'd get a jump start on the lesson plan. Any interest in integrating some creative writing today?"

I nodded, moving toward my desk to drop my bag. "That works. We could focus on character development, maybe have the students write a short scene using only compound and complex sentences."

Keith leaned back in his chair, tapping a pen on the desk. "Good idea. They could develop characters for a story they write later on."

"Exactly," I said, my nerves easing just a little as the conversation turned to work. "They'll have fun with that. It's always good to shake things up."

The unmistakable sound of footsteps outside our door caught both of our attention, but what got us moving was Oz's frustrated tone:

"I really think we should call the doctor."

"I need to see if my seating charts are current and make copies." Audrey's voice trembled breathlessly.

Keith and I raced into the hallway as Audrey crumpled against Oz, her face pale with a mix of panic and pain. She moaned, her breath coming in quick, shallow bursts as she gripped her massive belly.

"I'm not ready to have this baby!" she cried.

"We've got to call the doctor, Audrey." Oz's face was a picture of helplessness as he tried to steady her, his eyes wide and frantic.

Before I could move forward, Keith's deep voice cut through the tension. "Hey, Audrey, just breathe. You've got this. Let's take it one step at a time."

Audrey's eyes flickered to him, looking as if she wanted to argue but clearly not having the energy. Instead, she let out a shaky breath, her hands gripping her belly tighter.

"Keith's right," I said, trying to steady myself as I approached them. "We don't need to panic. Why don't we sit down for a minute?"

Oz stepped back, still looking unsure as Keith guided Audrey into our classroom, his movements smooth and confident.

I stepped aside, clearing the way as they shuffled past me, Audrey leaning into Keith with every step, trying to steady herself.

One of the benefits of having ASD is that in moments of crisis, my brain tends to lock in on the details of the situation. Audrey was in pain, she needed help, and I had to keep my cool.

I moved toward Keith's desk and cleared off the clutter, preparing a place for Audrey to sit. My hands moved automatically. I didn't panic. "How far apart are the contractions? Did your water break?"

"Are you a doctor?" Audrey snapped. Her voice was laced with irritation as another wave of discomfort passed through her.

"No, but I've read ten labor and delivery books since the beginning of November," I replied without missing a beat, trying to keep things light even though the situation was anything but.

Audrey's response was a weak, breathless laugh. "Of course you have."

My phone beeped in my pocket. Glancing at the screen, I realized Keith had sent a group text to Val, Bobby, and me.

7:43 AM
Keith: SOS. Audrey is having contractions.

"This is just a false alarm," Audrey insisted, her hand against the small of her back, rubbing the muscles. "Everyone is getting worked up over nothing."

Keith stepped in beside her, his voice calm but firm. "And if it's not? Let's just be smart about this, okay? No harm in making sure." He put his arm around Audrey's shoulder, his tone softening. "We'll handle whatever comes next. Right now, let's get you sitting down and breathing through it."

Another beep let me know someone had responded to Keith's text.

7:43 AM
Val: Holy shit. I'm on my way.

"Does your back hurt?" I asked, watching Audrey closely.

"Oh God, yes. I couldn't sleep at all last night," she admitted, her voice strained as she shifted uncomfortably.

I nodded. All the books said that back pain was a classic sign of labor, but I knew it could be a while before things progressed. Her water hadn't broken yet, so she might still have hours to go.

"I've got pillows," I offered, thinking it might help her get more comfortable.

"No, I can't sit. I need to stand up," Audrey replied, her voice laced with urgency. She reached for my hand, and I helped her to her feet, supporting her.

She began to waddle in front of the smart screen, one hand gripping her back and the other cradling her belly. Every time she moved, a grimace would cross her face, but she kept going, her determination to manage the pain visible.

Keith stepped in beside her, his hands outstretched but not quite touching, like he was ready to catch her if she toppled over.

"Pacing is good," he said evenly. "Just don't overdo it. You don't have to be a hero, Audrey."

Audrey shot him a glare. "Says the guy who's never been pregnant."

Keith smirked but didn't argue. Instead, he exchanged a glance with me. "I'll shut up then and time the contractions."

Just then, Bobby burst through the door and rushed over to Audrey. "Hey, beautiful. Are you having a baby today?" Her voice was full of concern and affection, but Audrey wasn't in the mood for jokes.

Groaning loudly as another contraction hit, her face twisted in discomfort. Audrey grabbed Bobby's hand so tightly that Bobby grunted in surprise.

"I can't. It can't be today," Audrey cried, her voice breaking. "The baby isn't even due yet. I have two more weeks."

Her distress was palpable, and I could see the panic rising in her eyes. She wasn't ready—physically, mentally, emotionally. But labor wasn't asking for permission. It was happening whether Audrey was ready or not.

"Statistically, only four percent of babies arrive on their due date," I said, rolling the chair closer, hoping Bobby could get her to sit.

"Shut up, Rachel." Audrey flailed her fist in my direction.

Bobby laughed, catching Audrey's fist. "As Salt-N-Pepa say, it's time to push it."

I smothered my laugh as Audrey groaned. "Do not get that song in my head. It's too soon!"

Keith, who had been standing back to give Audrey space, stepped in with a steady, practical tone that made people listen. "Okay, deep breaths. We're not delivering a baby in a middle school classroom." He slid a supportive hand under Audrey's elbow. "Your contractions are five minutes apart. You've got this, but let's get you off your feet."

Audrey sank into my rolling desk chair and let out a shuddering breath. "I'm never forgiving any you for this."

Before Audrey could argue, Oz rushed back into the classroom, phone in hand. "Dr. Martinelli says she'll meet us at the hospital."

"I can't go. I don't have my baby music or my overnight bag." She crossed her arms tightly over her chest, her gaze flicking nervously around the room as if the missing items would appear.

Like a miracle, Val ran into the room, puffing hard. She carried a small brown duffle bag. "I've got your stuff, and the playlist is on your phone."

"Come on, Red, tuck up your feet," Oz prompted his wife. "I'll roll you back to the car."

"What about my seating charts? My sub plans? I still need to make copies."

I moved closer. "I'll take care of everything. Don't worry about school. I've got you covered."

Audrey's lip trembled. "Thank you, Rachel."

For the first time all morning, awkwardness struck. I never knew how to react when someone thanked me. It felt too personal. "You're, ah, welcome."

Audrey nodded weakly, her face drawn with exhaustion, and then looked around, her eyes landing on Val. "Val? You're coming, right?"

Val didn't hesitate. She picked up the duffel bag from the corner, slinging it over her shoulder, and grabbed Audrey's hand. "I've already told the office that you, Oz, and I are out today."

"My emergency plans are on my desk," Oz muttered to Bobby, who gave him a thumbs up.

Bobby nodded. "Gotcha, Sarge. Good luck."

"Emergency plans?" Audrey shrieked as Oz carefully rolled her toward the door in Keith's chair. "Why didn't you tell me to make emergency plans?"

Oz leaned down, brushing a kiss on top of her head as he guided the chair with practiced ease. "I only mentioned it two dozen times."

"You did not," Audrey roared, her voice filled with indignation as he rolled her down the hallway. "And stop humming that song, Bobby, I can hear you."

"*I'm Coming Out* by Diana Ross just feels appropriate."

"Ugh!" Audrey's wail of dismay disappeared down the hallway.

Keith let out a low chuckle. "I mean, she's not wrong."

"Ignore them, Red," Oz muttered, adjusting his grip on Audrey as they moved toward the exit.

Val paused for a second, glancing back at us. "I'll keep you updated," she assured Bobby, Keith, and me, her voice steady, though I could see the concern in her eyes.

"You better," I responded.

Keith crossed his arms. "And tell Oz to breathe before he passes out."

With that, Val followed them out the door, the sound of Audrey's protest still echoing in the hallway.

*****

The day dragged on, each minute stretching longer than the last. Keith and I split our classes, and he took half of them to the think tank down the hallway for some project work.

I usually enjoyed having more one-on-one time with the students, giving them more individualized attention. But something about today felt different. Maybe it was the silence in the room without Keith's usual banter or his steady presence beside me. I missed the way he would jump in to help with a question or add his own spin to the lesson.

When Sawyer Sinclair told me that a synonym was the stuff he puts on his toast, I wanted to roll my eyes, but Keith wasn't there to back me up. And when Kelly Linzel came back from the bathroom crying, I found myself wishing Keith was there to talk to her, too.

By the time the students left for the day and Keith returned, I was itching to talk to him.

Keith put his computer on his desk and looked over at me, his face weary from the long day. "How's Audrey doing?"

"She's still in labor."

"She got the meds, right? The epi-whatever?"

"The epidural? Yeah," I replied, glancing over at Keith as he grabbed his jacket off the back of the chair.

He nodded, running a hand through his hair, the familiar gesture making him look slightly messy and utterly gorgeous. "I thought I'd drop by the hospital for a minute, but I promised to feed their cat, Stevie." He paused, glancing over at me with a raised eyebrow. "Do you want to ride over with me?"

I shuffled a little, feeling that old unease stir in my stomach. Hospitals made me nervous. The lights were too bright, the sounds too sharp. The smell of antiseptic and illness clung to everything, and the doctors spoke in hushed, urgent tones. I might be good in a crisis, but in the hospital, I was a mess.

I paused, my fingers instinctively tightening around the edge of my sleeve. I'd always kept this part of my life to myself. It wasn't something I shared with just anyone. But things with Keith had been going well lately, like he genuinely cared.

I thought about it for a second, feeling that familiar knot in my stomach. "I used to go there a lot as a kid... long stays, tests, things that never really made sense to me." I glanced away, almost as if I could push the memory out of my head. "It's just easier to avoid them."

Keith didn't say anything right away. He didn't push or look at me like I'd just said something strange. It was like he was simply letting me say it, letting me be honest. And for some reason, that made me feel a little lighter.

"I didn't talk until I was almost four and spent a lot of time in medical clinics before and after I was diagnosed with ASD. My father is a scholar, and wanted to understand how my brain worked, so he might find a cure. My mother put her foot down when I turned twelve, and the testing stopped."

The hazel of his eyes darkened, becoming stormy. He had long, thick eyelashes. His voice was gruff when he responded. "There's nothing wrong with you. You just process the world differently."

"Yeah, well, the world doesn't always understand that," I muttered, my eyes darting back to the screen.

Keith stepped a little closer. "Maybe not, but that doesn't mean you're any less." His nostrils flared and his forehead furrowed.

"Are you angry?"

"Yes."

"Oh." My head dropped and I took a step back, but he caught my hand, twining his fingers through mine.

"Not with you, Rach, with the circumstances. I can't imagine putting a child through all that. You're perfect the way you are."

I was far from perfect, but it was kind of him to say. "I'm just me." I shrugged. "Why don't you like hospitals?"

Keith's voice dropped, and he stared down at our intertwined hands. "I was twenty when Mom was diagnosed with leukemia, but I had to step up. I didn't think twice about leaving college behind. Sunshine needed me, and so did my mom. We watched Mom go from this strong, independent woman to someone I had to help with the simplest tasks. And the days in those hospital rooms... they never really leave you."

My heart hurt for him. He'd been younger than I was now when he'd sacrificed everything for his mom and sister. No wonder he didn't like hospitals.

I studied the tops of his black sneakers, unable to look at him. "I'm sorry for your loss," I said.

It felt inadequate, but I didn't have more words.

"It was a long time ago. Are you ever going to look at me again?"

Looking into Keith's eyes made me uncomfortable. I could see unspoken questions and emotions I couldn't deal with. It was too personal. Too intimate.

"Eye contact is hard for me."

"I understand." He squeezed my hand. "Your blue eyes are so pretty. I hope I get to see them again."

I glanced over at my desk piled high with papers. "I better finish up this work, or I'll never get out of here."

Moving away from him, I tried to focus my thoughts away from the weight of our conversation. Audrey's lesson plans were just the thing to provide a distraction. Since we were both teaching a writing unit next week, our objectives were aligned. I opened a computer folder, scanning for the advanced lesson we'd used last year, but forcing myself to get to work wasn't easy with my mind still lingering on what Keith had shared.

Keith sat in front of his laptop, too. His face was turned toward the smart screen, but I couldn't help noticing the way his jaw clenched tight. I wondered if he was still thinking about his family.

He spoke quietly, using text-to-speech to complete Oz's lesson plan. His deep voice soothed the sharp edges of my embarrassment, and with his dark head bent over the keyboard, I took the chance to observe him unnoticed.

His face was angular, with high cheekbones that gave him a striking look. The well-kept beard accentuated the strong lines and edges of his jaw, adding to his rugged appeal. His neck was long, and his broad shoulders filled out the shirt, the fabric stretching slightly over the muscles in his arms. I couldn't help but notice the way his posture seemed to command attention.

It was annoying how magnetic he was. Even now, even after everything, a part of me responded to him. The heat in my chest, the twist low in my stomach, the way my gaze lingered a second too long, and a traitorous part of me didn't want to stop.

He glanced up and our eyes met.

"I can feel you looking at me." His firm lips parted into a teasing smile.

My eyes darted away, but my lips curved up in response.

Re-focusing on the task at hand, I used my access to Audrey's classes and set up the assignments for her students, then sent the lesson plan document to the printer.

I retrieved the printed plan from the workroom. Now, I had to go back and get my things before I could go home.

Keith was on the phone when I walked back in. He hung up, his face full of excitement. "Audrey had the baby."

I dropped the paper I was holding. "That's great!"

"They want us to stop by and meet him."

I hesitated, the words caught in my throat. It wasn't just the hospital that made me uneasy. Big groups of people, with their chatter and noise, always set me on edge. And babies... babies cried. The sound always seemed to pierce through me, filling the air with a tension I could never shake off.

"I'm sure they are all tired. Maybe I'll go tomorrow."

"Audrey specifically told me to tell you to come."

I couldn't say no to Audrey. She and Val were the best friends I'd ever had, and they'd been there for me more times than I could count. Maybe I could just stop in for a minute, check on her, and then slip away. I'd handle the anxiety, somehow.

"Okay." I picked up the paper I'd dropped and then gathered my things.

Keith turned off his computer and followed me out to the parking lot.

"Oh no, I forgot that I rode my bike today," I said, staring at the bright red ten-speed with a basket on the front while wondering if I could use this as an excuse to go home.

Keith gestured to his Toyota truck. "I'll drive."

Tipping my head back, I stared up at the few stars that had risen in the sky. The night was clear, crisp. I took a few deep breaths, willing my nerves to settle, and walked over to the passenger side of his truck, trying not to think about the strange mix of comfort and unease Keith's presence brought.

***

At the hospital, we followed the sounds of celebration into Audrey's room. Her face was pale, and she looked ready to sleep for a week, and yet she also glowed from the inside. There was a softness to her now, like the world had paused just for her to bask in the joy of the moment.

A tiny bundle nestled in her arms, and when she saw Keith and me, she beckoned us over, a tired but wide smile stretching across her face. My heart squeezed in my chest as I looked at the little one, so small, so perfect. Audrey's eyes sparkled with pride as she carefully adjusted the baby's blanket, revealing a tiny face with a mop of dark hair. "This is Liam Douglass Taylor, all eight pounds, two ounces, and nineteen point four inches of him. Liam, this is Keith and Rachel, Mommy and Daddy's friends."

His tiny, squished red face, completely mesmerized me. His eyes were closed, but his mouth moved in a steady rhythm, his little pink tongue popping out. Liam looked impossibly delicate despite how his fingers curled into miniature fists. I'd never been this close to a newborn before, and the wonder of it hit me all at once.

I moved closer. "Hey, buddy, glad you're finally here."

"It took him long enough," Val groused from the sofa nearby. "Eight hours plus some."

"That's pretty fast for a first baby," Bobby chimed in from where she sat next to Val.

Oz came in with a can of soda and a Snickers bar. "So, what do you think of Liam?"

"His face is kind of smooshed," I said.

Oz laughed. "Yeah, they all look like that at first. It's just the way they're crammed in there. He'll be all round and cute in no time."

Keith grinned, leaning in for a closer look. "But it's kind of cute. Gives him some character."

Audrey smiled tiredly, holding Liam closer. "I think he's perfect," she said, her voice soft but filled with love. "Smooshed face and all, he's mine. Do you want to hold him, Rach?"

I shook my head. "I don't think that's a great idea. I've never held a baby."

But she held Liam out with expectation in her eyes. My heart skipped a beat as I processed the situation, but I didn't want to disappoint her.

I reached for him slowly, my hands feeling unsteady as I accepted the small bundle. Pulling him close, I held him against my chest as Audrey had.

"Support his head." Keith tucked Liam's head into the crook of my arm.

I looked down at the baby. He had a tuft of blond hair on top of his pale head, so soft it almost seemed like a feather. The smell of baby powder mixed with pure innocence filled my senses. His tiny mouth trembled, his lips curling in a slight frown before he let out a soft grunt, then settled. His warmth seeped into my chest, and I held him tighter, instinctively.

A feeling swept over me, sudden and overwhelming. Deep in my belly, I felt an ache, like a tugging at something I didn't even know was there. For a moment, I thought it was just anxiety, my brain spinning at the unfamiliar sensation of holding someone so small. But it wasn't panic. It was a yearning, a longing that I couldn't quite place. It wasn't a thought, more like an instinct that made me want to protect him, to give him everything I never had to offer. The feeling was unfamiliar but also comforting, like something I'd been missing without even realizing.

"I can see it on your face," Audrey spoke quietly. "You want a baby."

I gaped at her in horror. The very idea of having a baby sent a wave of panic crashing through me. I could barely manage myself some days, let alone care for a tiny human, but then my eyes met Keith's.

His warm hazel eyes seemed to speak volumes, and for a moment, I thought maybe I could trust him.

Before I could look away, Keith's phone buzzed in his pocket. Pulling it out, he hesitated, glancing between me and the screen before answering.

"Yeah?" His voice dropped into that casual, almost indifferent tone he used when he didn't want to be overheard. A pause. Then a sigh. "No, I told you—I'll handle it later."

The moment shattered, and reality came rushing back in. Of course. Keith was always juggling something or someone. It wasn't like I didn't know that. He was unreliable, impulsive, and he never fully committed to anything long-term.

Anxiety settled in my chest, making it hard to breathe. I was over-stimulated, and I didn't even know how to begin dealing with it.

Passing Liam back to Audrey, my hands trembled as I let go. Every part of me screamed to bolt, to run until the sterile scent and relentless beeping were distant memories.

I was already in the lobby, halfway to the doors, before it hit me. Keith had driven me here.

My chest tightened, breath catching as the realization crashed down. I had no way to leave. Trapped. The urge to run warred with the fact that I had nowhere to go, and suddenly the walls felt closer, the air too thin.

Chapter 9

Keith

**What would you talk about on a road trip with a person who
drives you crazy in the best way?**
a) Embarrassing childhood stories to see who has the most
ridiculous one.
b) Deep "what if" scenarios that get more absurd as the miles
pass.
c) Flirty debates over the best road trip snacks and music
playlists.
d) Confessions—silly, serious, and maybe even a little steamy.

A few weeks later, I stood in Rachel's driveway, the
unusually frigid December air settling deep in my bones. And it
wasn't just the weather—the air felt heavy with everything
unspoken between us.

Rachel had kept her distance since running out of the
hospital. She stayed late at school most nights, met with Yona
during our planning time, her silence sharper than words. I tried
to give her space, checking in just enough to remind her I hadn't
gone anywhere. But despite my efforts, I couldn't shake the
feeling that something was off.

Thanksgiving break had come and gone in a whirlwind. Rachel took off early to visit her parents in Salisbury, and Sunshine and I went with Oz and Audrey up to Delaware to celebrate with his mom and sister. It had been nice, almost like a brief escape. Sunny and Stella had hit it off, making plans to get together over Christmas break. It was a relief knowing Sunny had someone else to lean on, since she'd been quieter than usual. She'd ended things with Seb, but she'd been hurt. Seeing her sad made me want to track him down and make him regret ever messing with her, but I knew she'd never forgive me for it.

Even in the midst of the holidays, Rachel lingered in my mind. No matter how many distractions, she was always there, just beneath the surface.

And now, here I was, on a cold December morning, about to drive three hours to a conference with her. I didn't know what I was walking into, but I wouldn't ride in her excuse for a car.

"I'm not going to fit in there."

Rachel put her gloved hands on her hips, her pink puffy jacket puffing out like a tiny, defiant cloud. The pink slouchy hat covering her short blond hair bobbed as she tilted her head in defiance. "She's bigger than you think."

"It's a Smart car. It's designed to be small," I said, eyeing the tiny vehicle like it might try to swallow me whole.

"She gets better gas mileage than your gas-guzzling truck," she argued, gesturing toward my maroon Toyota Rav 4 like it was single-handedly responsible for global warming.

"Sure, but at least my truck doesn't look like it should come with a wind-up key on the back," I shot back. "Seriously, Rachel, I've seen golf carts with more legroom. I'm pretty sure if I sneeze in there, I'll knock out the windshield."

She crossed her arms and smirked, clearly unimpressed. "That's just because you're used to sitting on a throne in your truck."

"It's not a throne," I grumbled. "It's comfort and style. Something your shoebox on wheels can't offer."

"Just get in the car, Payt," she said, her grin widening. "You might even like it. It's cozy."

"Cozy? That's code for cramped." I sighed, shaking my head. "Please, Rachel. I promise you can make all the rest of the decisions this weekend."

Her forehead wrinkled in thought. I'd learned to love those little lines. I hoped their appearance meant she was at least considering my point of view.

"You should take him up on it, Rachel," a voice chimed in from behind us, smooth as butter and twice as cheeky.

Rachel and I turned to see an older woman standing on the path from the main house, her red bathrobe cinched over flannel pajamas and Uggs snug on her feet. She held a fat romance novel in one hand and a box of cookies in the other, looking like she'd just stepped out of a Hallmark Christmas movie.

"Keith, this is my landlady and friend, Barbara Bartlett," Rachel said, smiling but already looking like she might want to bolt.

"A pleasure to meet you, Ms. Bartlett," I said, giving her a nod.

Barbara's eyes twinkled as she looked me up and down, clearly enjoying herself. "He's so polite, Rachel. And those muscles! I bet he could pick up a woman and—"

"Barb!" Rachel's voice shot up an octave as she darted toward her friend. "Keith and I need to get going. Can I help you with anything?"

Barbara grinned like the cat that got the cream and handed Rachel the cookies. "I have a long list of things Keith could do for me, but I just wanted to return this book and give you some treats for the road."

"Thanks, Barb. I'll see you Sunday." Rachel's words came out in a rush, her cheeks visibly pink under her slouchy hat.

Barbara winked at me as Rachel hustled her back toward the house. "You're welcome. And, Keith," Barbara said, her voice dripping with mischief as she leaned in just enough to make Rachel visibly squirm, "treat my Rachel like a lady... but not too much like a lady, if you know what I mean."

Rachel groaned, burying her face in her hands. "Barb!"

She wagged a finger at me with a wink. "She's a treasure, Keith. Handle with care, but feel free to unwrap her if the moment's right."

"Okay, that's it!" Rachel nearly yanked the box of cookies from Barbara's hands. "We have to go. Thanks for the snacks, Barb!"

Barbara laughed as we made a hasty retreat. "Drive safe, you two! And remember, Rachel, life's never too short for great coffee or naughty men!"

Rachel practically dragged her landlady down the path before turning back and giving me an apologetic wave. "Let's go before she thinks of another embarrassing thing to say."

I pulled her suitcase out of her tiny car and stowed it behind the front seat of my truck. Rachel slid into the passenger seat, looking both flustered and amused. "I'm sorry about that. I've created a monster by loaning her my spicy romances."

I chuckled as I started the engine. "No worries. If anything, I'm flattered. I had no idea I was protagonist material."

"Don't let it go to your head," she said, but her lips twitched like she was fighting a smile.

As I backed out of the driveway, she glanced at me, her tone shifting to something more serious. "I want to drive halfway."

"Deal." I held out my hand to seal it.

Rachel hesitated, her gaze lingering on my outstretched palm. Then she slipped her hand into mine, her fingers soft but firm. Two pumps, quick and efficient, and then she pulled away.

But in that fleeting moment, something sparked between us, and I could've sworn I heard a crack in the wall she'd built around herself. I couldn't help but hope that something had shifted between us.

***

Unfortunately, by the time we merged onto the highway, the silence between us felt heavier than the luggage in the back seat. The silence grew so thick it could have been its own passenger. As she gnawed on her lower lip, her hands twisted together in her lap.

I rolled my shoulders and shifted in the driver's seat, trying to release the tension that crept in. I reached for the radio.

"Want to listen to music?" I asked, keeping my tone light.

She shook her head. "Not really."

I let out a breath and reached to turn it back off. Just then, the announcer's voice cut in over the soft static:

"It's not time to get the snow shovels out, but there's a thirty percent chance of wintry weather this weekend. While this is unusual for December, it's not unheard of for us to get ice or snow in Virginia..."

Rachel tensed, her eyes flicking to the windshield like the forecast was about to materialize on the glass.

"Relax," I said, trying to sound casual. "Thirty percent is nothing to worry about."

She shot me a look, arching one eyebrow. "That's probably what Noah said before it started raining."

"I'm just saying, it's not exactly a blizzard warning. And it certainly won't snow for forty days and nights."

"Famous last words," she muttered, crossing her arms and leaning back against the seat.

A grin tugged at the corner of my mouth. If nothing else, at least the silence was broken.

Rachel's fingers were white on the armrest. I wondered if she'd pull away if I touched her hand. "Are you okay?"

"You're driving fast."

I glanced at the speedometer. Sixty-five miles per hour. "I'm driving the speed limit."

"Limit means the absolute highest speed a driver should go."

I eased off the gas and set the cruise control for sixty. "Better?"

I caught her nod from the corner of my eye. "How about a trivia challenge?"

"I'm the Scholastic Bowl coach and a member of Quiz Pro Quo. We meet at Barrel for Trivia nights. I don't think it would be fair for me to challenge you."

I shot her a quick glance, surprised. How had I not known that?

Rachel straightened in her seat, her chin lifting slightly. The pink of her puffy jacket made her fair skin look even brighter, and her short blonde hair peeked out from beneath her slouchy hat, the ends curling slightly at her neck. She exuded a quiet confidence, like she didn't need to brag—her smirk said it all. "There are three of us. Some of the other teams have more players, but we hold our own."

I let that sink in for a moment. "Quiz Pro Quo? Please tell me you came up with the name."

Her lips twitched. "I can neither confirm nor deny."

"Well, Miss Scholastic Bowl, put your money where your mouth is."

She hesitated before she said, "Betting against me would be illogical."

"Okay, Spock. I'll bet you..." I let the words hang as I leaned toward her slightly. "Loser has to give the winner a back massage."

She paused, chewing on her lip for a moment. Was she nervous or stalling?

"Deal. Give me a question."

I smiled, trying to act casual, even though my brain was suddenly working overtime to come up with a trivia question that wasn't too easy or too hard. Something that wouldn't make her regret saying yes.

"What's the capital of Wyoming?"

She turned to me with a look of mock offense. "Cheyenne. Please tell me that's not your idea of a challenge."

I smirked. "Just warming up. Keep going, genius. My shoulders are killing me. What was the name of the Roman god of doorways and transitions?"

Her mouth opened, then closed, and she squinted at me. "Janus. I only knew that because I took a college mythology class. Surprisingly clever for you, though."

"Surprisingly clever?" I pressed a hand to my chest in mock hurt. "I'll have you know, Rachel, I'm a wealth of useless knowledge. What's the strangest fact you had to know to win a match?"

She thought for a second and then said, "What animal sweats milk?"

I smiled. "Easy. Platypus."

Her brow wrinkled. "What is the formal name for the hashtag?"

I waggled my eyebrows at her. "An octothorpe. What's a group of bunnies called?"

She smiled. "A fluffle."

Half an hour passed with us trading questions back and forth before she cued the *Trivial Warfare Trivia* podcast up on her phone and linked to my sound system.

An hour later when I pulled into the rest area near Richmond, she seemed more relaxed. "You're really knowledgeable."

I shot her a smug grin. "That's a very flattering way to admit you never expected me to know anything."

"No," she said quickly. "No. You're brilliant. I just didn't realize how much random knowledge you've got stored up."

"Careful," I said with a grin. "Flattery like that might make me unbearable."

She rolled her eyes, but I caught the hint of a smile before she turned to look out the window.

"And you won our bet," I pointed out, letting my voice dip just enough to make her blink. "Which means I owe you... a backrub at the time of your choosing."

Her lips twitched. "I'll have to check my calendar."

I grinned. "Take your time. I'd hate for you to waste such a golden opportunity."

She giggled, and the sound seemed to lift the weight in the car, making everything feel a little lighter. The urge to throw my arms up and dance in celebration almost overwhelmed me, but I bit it back, not wanting to embarrass her.

Or myself.

A few minutes later, Rachel settled behind the wheel, her focus shifting as she made the necessary adjustments to the mirrors, seat, and steering wheel. At some point, she'd peeled off her hat and coat, and now the soft fabric of her shirt stretched just enough to make a row of tiny buttons down strain across her chest. And, somehow, that ruined my ability to think straight.

Finally, she backed out of the parking space, her hands steady on the wheel, and merged back onto the highway like she'd driven a truck a thousand times.

"Want a snack?" I asked, opening the box of cookies Barbara had given us. "I have cookies. They're pink and shaped like..." I looked up at Rachel, a grin tugging at my lips. "Penises."

Rachel's eyes widened for a second, then she burst out laughing, her hand flying to her mouth to stifle the sound. "Oh my God, Keith!" she gasped between fits of giggles. "You can't be serious."

I shrugged, offering her the box with a mock-innocent smile. "I didn't pack them. But I'm happy to share."

"I can't eat those."

I popped a cookie in my mouth, chewing slowly. "Says who?"

"That's disgusting."

I took another cookie. "If you were watching the road, you wouldn't be able to see me."

She shivered unpleasantly. "I can hear all the crumbs in your mouth."

"Okay," I said, putting the cookies away. "Your loss."

"There are grapes in my bag. Can you hand them to me?"

"Grapes, huh?" I said, pulling the small plastic box from her oversized purse. "Nature's candy."

"That's raisins, not grapes," she shot back. "The California Raisin Company used that slogan in the 1980s to make dried fruit seem cool."

"Fascinating," I said dryly. "Now, open up." I popped a few grapes off the stem and held them out to her.

"Just hand me a bunch, please."

I pinched a grape between my thumb and forefinger. "Don't bite me," I teased, holding the fruit in front of her.

"I won't make any promises," she said, rolling her eyes.

When she opened her mouth, I gently placed the grape between her lips. She accepted it with a smile and a soft sigh, clearly savoring the sweetness. Her eyes flicked up to mine as she chewed. And the air charged with something unspoken. My cock twitched, lengthening as I watched her bite into the fruit.

"This is silly," she said, her face flushed pink.

I raised an eyebrow. "Is it? Or do you like being waited on?"

She shot me a look, clearly fighting the urge to roll her eyes. "You didn't wash your hands and that can lead to the spread of germs, foodborne illnesses, and respiratory infections."

I grinned, unbothered. "Well, I guess I'll just have to live dangerously then." I waggled the grape in front of her.

She hesitated, then, with a resigned sigh, opened her mouth. "Fine."

She took another grape, her fingers brushing mine as she did, and I couldn't help but notice the way her touch lingered just a second longer than necessary.

This time her tongue brushed my fingers, and my heart almost exploded. I had to look away before I made a fool of myself. Thrusting the bunch of grapes at her, I covered my lap with my hands, hoping she hadn't seen my reaction.

Outside, the highway twisted its way into the Blue Ridge Mountains, winding through thick patches of pine and oak trees.

The air grew cooler, crisp with the scent of earth and wood, and the sun began to filter through the branches in golden slivers. Snow clung to the mountain peaks in the distance, giving the landscape a dreamy, almost ethereal quality.

"Have you ever been to Charlottesville before?" Rachel asked as she adjusted the mirror, eyes still on the road.

"Sunshine and I went to UVA before she applied at colleges. It's a nice town."

"She didn't like it?"

I shook my head, a small frown tugging at the corner of my mouth. Sunny was still sad, and no matter how much she insisted she was fine, it stirred a knot in my stomach. I needed to call her as soon as we got to the conference, just to check in.

"Not really. She loved the campus, but the vibe of the town that didn't sit right with her. She said the mountains creeped her out."

Rachel nodded as if that made perfect sense.

"She's been having a rough time at ODU lately," I added, not sure why I'd shared this with Rachel.

"College can be hard."

"She broke up with her boyfriend. He was... into a lot of girls." I ran a hand through my hair, letting out a frustrated sigh. "I think he really liked Sunny but couldn't be the guy she needed."

Rachel's expression softened. "I'm sorry to hear that."

A twinge of guilt ricochetted through my heart. I hadn't been ready for Rachel when we'd met. Not the guy she deserved. If I'd been more honest with myself, I could've done better; instead, I'd hurt her. And I'd regretted it every minute since then.

"Me too," I muttered. "Sunny's one of the strongest people I know, but I can tell she's been struggling."

Rachel nodded, her eyes glued to the road. "Breakups can be devastating, even if they are for the best."

My heart tightened as Rachel's words sank in. I knew exactly what she meant. Our breakup had torn her apart, but she thought she'd made the right choice.

I'd never experienced that gut-wrenching emptiness except when it came to Rachel. And it was all my fault. We'd broken apart, and now she couldn't trust me enough to give us a second chance.

Ahead of us, the road curved and the summit of the mountain appeared. The view opened up in breathtaking clarity. Ridge after ridge of undulating peaks stretched endlessly to the horizon, their deep blue and green hues fading into the distance. Dark shadows of clouds swept across the forests of pine and spruce, moving fast. A thin veil of gray began to settle in the distance, blurring the edges of the farthest ridges.

Despite the regret that gnawed at me, I didn't want to stay in that space. Not with Rachel beside me, not with that spark of something still flickering between us. I needed to lighten the mood, to push past the serious talk. I glanced at her, her focus on the road, and the mischievous side of me reared its head.

I shook off my heavy mood and asked playfully, "Are you speeding, Rachel?"

"What? No. The speed limit is fifty-five."

"And how fast are you driving?"

"Fifty-four."

"You're full of hot air, Ms. Bright. Giving me a hard time this morning!"

She laughed. A little tinkle of mirth that stroked down my body. Her laughter hit me like a freaking aphrodisiac.

"I like it when you laugh," I said, my voice husky.

She gave me a quick glance. "Your laugh is pleasant too."

I chuckled. "Is it?"

The pink deepened, and she squirmed a little in her seat, gripping the steering wheel as if it tethered her to reality. "Don't make me run off the road."

"From laughing?" I teased, unscrewing the cap off my water bottle and tipping it up for a drink.

She sighed, almost too softly to hear. "I wish you weren't so handsome."

The words were so quiet they barely registered, but when they did, I choked on the water, nearly spitting it out. Coughing, I managed to sputter, "You think I'm handsome?"

"Did I say that out loud?" Her hand slapped over her mouth in a flash, her eyes wide in horror. The truck swerved slightly, and I had to steady the wheel to keep us on course.

Wiping water off my chin with my sleeve, I grinned so wide it almost hurt. "You can't take it back now."

She sent a quick glare my way, but the pink in her cheeks betrayed her. "Don't let it go to your head."

"Too late," I said, smirking. "I mean, you've already admitted you think I'm handsome. Next thing I know, you'll be writing smutty novels about me."

Rachel rolled her eyes but couldn't quite hide the smile tugging at the corner of her mouth. "Oh, please. No one wants to read that."

We took the exit toward Charlottesville, and as she navigated through the maze of traffic lights and roundabouts, I kept the teasing alive.

"You know, if you want to jot down a limerick about me later, I wouldn't mind."

"There once was a man named Keith," she said, her voice dripping with sarcasm, "who never stopped grinding his teeth. He teased and he joked, but I wasn't provoked—"

"Come on, finish it," I egged her on when she paused.

"Because his wit was as dull as his sheath."

I clutched my chest like I'd been shot. "Ouch, Ms. Bright. You wound me."

Driving along Business Route 29, Rachel steered us toward the Omni Hotel and Conference Center and pulled into a parking spot in the crowded lot. As the car came to a stop, the playful tension of our earlier conversation faded and seriousness crept back in.

She killed the engine and turned to face me, her expression suddenly serious. "Listen, before we go in there, we need to set some ground rules. I'm here to learn how to be a better co-teacher, not to flirt or mess around."

I raised an eyebrow, feigning offense. "Ground rules? Come on, Rachel. What do you think I'm going to do? Sweep you off your feet in front of the entire conference?"

Her lips twitched. "I wouldn't put it past you. You do have a knack for being extra."

"I'll have you know, I'm always just the right amount of extra," I shot back, leaning in slightly.

Her voice rose. "I'm not having sex with you this weekend."

I sobered at the pain threading through her words, though I'd been expecting her to say it. Of course, she didn't want to sleep with me. I'd hurt her last year, and she still wasn't over it. "Okay, rule one: no sex."

Her shoulders relaxed, and she offered a small, grateful smile. "Thank you."

But sometimes, the devil in me just had to provoke. "Unless, of course, you ask me to make love to you."

She stiffened, folding her hands primly in her lap. "That won't happen."

God help me, but when did I start finding the prim and proper routine sexy? She was buttoned-up perfection, and yet I wanted to undo her, one deliberate moment at a time. My gaze lingered on her flushed cheeks and the way her lips pressed into a thin line, as if holding back some cutting remark. I was tempted to lean over and kiss her, if only to hear her squeak in outrage.

"Let me live in hope," I said, my grin slow and lazy. "What's rule two?"

Her eyes narrowed, a storm brewing in those hazel depths. "No flirting. Nothing that could be construed as you hitting on me."

I laughed, low and easy, leaning back in my seat. "That's going to be tough. I'm naturally charming."

She leaned toward me, wagging her finger in my face like a schoolmarm scolding an unruly child. "I mean it, Keith. None of your smooth lines or... or that smile."

Her eyes were so blue. Looking into their depths was like staring at the mesmerizing beauty of the ocean. Her scent washed over me, sunshine and fresh flowers. My whole body coiled, ready to spring.

God help me. I wanted to unravel her. Not just peel back the layers of her carefully constructed walls but discover every hidden corner of her. The way she tipped her chin up in defiance but kept her hands folded in her lap like she didn't trust them to stay still. The way she drew her boundaries with sharp edges, only to soften when she thought no one paid attention.

Tasting her mattered more than breathing. The ache in my chest went beyond longing—it burned, raw and unrelenting. Every muscle pulled tight, my body tense from holding myself back. I caught her finger gently, her skin soft against mine. "Want to wager on if I can behave myself?"

She raised an eyebrow, a playful smirk tugging at her lips. "What will I win? Because I know you can't do it."

I leaned in slightly, my voice dropping to a teasing whisper. "I'll let you choose… I'll buy your lunch for a week at school or coffee from your favorite shop."

Her eyes sparkled with challenge. "You're on. But I'm warning you, I'll break you."

I took her hand to shake it, pressing my palm to her soft skin; the warmth of her touch sent a jolt of electricity up my arm. Her fingers curled against mine, and I had to swallow the unexpected heat that rushed through me.

Her breath hitched, a little gasp that slipped past those perfect lips. Her teeth caught her bottom lip, worrying it. Blue eyes flickered downward, catching on my mouth. My pulse kicked like a piston, and my world narrowed to the small space between us.

Her lips parted, and for a moment, I thought she might spit fire. Instead, she huffed out a breath, snatched her hand away, but her tongue darted out, pink and soft, to swipe across her plump lower lip. An unconscious, small, habitual movement, but it sent a jolt through me so fierce it almost hurt. She wasn't even trying, and I was ready to come undone.

I wanted to pull her close, tilt her chin, and taste her right then and there. But I didn't. I couldn't. Not when she'd made her lines so clear. So, I rooted myself to the spot, my knuckles whitening on the armrest, willing my body to relax.

I'd settle for the knowledge that she didn't walk away untouched. That, maybe, I wasn't the only one fighting this pull between us.

"Just behave yourself," she muttered, her tone laced with exasperation.

I chuckled, settling back into my own seat. Oh, I'd behave, all right. But only enough to keep her guessing.

Chapter 10

Keith

What would you do if you ran into your crush at a conference?
a) Play it cool and casually start a conversation.
b) Blurt out something awkward and immediately regret it.
c) Use the opportunity to flirt and see if there's a spark.
d) Pretend you didn't see them... but secretly hope they notice you.

An hour later, we found ourselves in a cavernous conference room packed with teachers from across the state. The chatter of a hundred conversations echoed off the high ceilings, blending with the shuffle of papers, the rustle of tote bags, and the occasional clatter of travel mugs against tabletops. The air smelled faintly of burnt coffee and the sharp, metallic tang of stress.

"Education is a rainbow in a stormy world of chaos," Dr. Gina Mickle, the perky keynote speaker gushed. She'd already compared teaching to whitewater rafting, dancing, and, I kid you not, the art of bonsai. She was going to burst into *The Rainbow Connection* or *Kumbaya* any second.

I slid my phone from my pocket to text Sunny.

3:23 PM
Me: You woudn't believe the uniocorns and utopia nonsene at this convenstion.

Beside me, Rachel ate it up, laughing at the jokes and nodding with every metaphor. Her eyes were bright, locked on the speaker like they were the only two people in the room. Every so often, she'd scribble something in her notebook, her pen moving with purpose, as though she'd been waiting her whole life to hear this wisdom.

She leaned forward in her seat, her chin resting on her hand, the faintest smile tugging at her lips. Rachel looked like she'd landed in TED Talk heaven, and needed to soak it all in. I should've let her have her moment, but her intensity was so cute.

"It says in the pamphlet she hasn't been in the classroom for more than five years," I whispered to Rachel.

She shot me a sidelong glare. "Shh."

I leaned in closer. "Bet you five bucks she only taught advanced kids."

"Keith!" Her voice dropped to a low hiss. "Shh."

On stage, Dr. Mickle continued, "When I look at a student, I see more than their grades or records. I see a butterfly in its cocoon, waiting for just the right moment to break free and show the world its colors."

Squinting at the screen, I slowly scrolled through the message. My thumb moved over the words with a deliberate slowness, pausing every few seconds to decode the words until I made it to the end with a smile.

3:37 PM
Sunshine: Send me pics of the unicorns.

I felt Rachel watching me and saw her frown grow as her eyes flicked between the phone and my face. Like she wanted me to explain myself.

To distract myself, I shifted in my seat and scanned the crowd. Women of all shapes and sizes filled the seats around me, their expressions ranging from politely bored to downright enamored with Dr. Mickle's pep. Some looked like they'd been cast right out of *Teachers Weekly*—polished, perky, and ready to save the world. The rest were more down-to-earth, with coffee-stained shirts and jeans with a *I Haven't Slept Since 2022* glaze over their eyes.

And then it hit me. Rachel was the only one in the room I wanted to talk to, and the weight of that realization left me reeling. When had she become the only one I couldn't stop thinking about?

Sensing my eyes on her, she shot me an irritated look, but the faint blush on her cheeks betrayed her.

I smirked, leaning closer. "What workshops are you going to?" I asked, waving the brochure under her nose.

"You pick first," she whispered. "Then I'll choose different ones."

"So you're avoiding me all day?"

"Yes," she said, smiling sweetly.

I made a show of pouting. "You're no fun."

The speaker continued to wax poetic while I skimmed through the workshops again. I'd already used text-to-speech to read them at home, so I knew which ones looked tolerable. *Teach Together, Thrive Together: Building a Dynamic Duo in the Classroom* caught my eye, along with the brilliantly punny *Full SPED Ahead: Navigating the Road to Inclusive Education.*

The crowd rose to their feet as Dr. Mickle concluded, "Thank you, everyone! And stay sparkly!"

Rachel stood, joining the crowd in a standing ovation, her face alight with enthusiasm. She nudged my shoe with hers, a silent command, and I rose to my feet, clapping half-heartedly because most of my attention was fixed on the way Rachel's beautiful eyes sparkled.

As the applause faded, Rachel turned to me with her pen ready. "Did you pick your workshops?"

I showed her my choices, and she crossed them off her list. "I guess we should meet later to exchange notes and set up our plan for tomorrow?"

"Why don't we grab dinner? And go to the mixer after?"

"Oh," she said, pausing. "I thought I'd just grab something from the vending machine and stay in tonight."

"Let me get this straight. You'd rather sit alone in your hotel room with stale chips and room-temperature soda than join me for a proper meal?"

She glanced away, her voice softening. "I assumed you'd be busy."

"Doing what?" I asked, knowing exactly what she would say, and that I'd hate it.

She waved her hand vaguely. Her gaze flickered back to me, reluctant but honest. "You know, flirting and adding notches to the bedpost."

Her gaze flickered back to me, reluctant but honest.

I raised an eyebrow, feeling a mix of amusement and something deeper I couldn't quite name. My pulse quickened, but I kept my voice steady. "I'd rather flirt with you."

The words hung between us, and I realized how much I meant them. I wondered how long I could pretend the playful banter didn't mean anything.

"That," she said, wagging her finger under my nose, "would break the rules."

"At least let me buy you dinner. Healthier than vending machine starch and salt."

She bit her lip, hesitating. I held my breath.

"Fine. What time?"

"Six-thirty. I'll knock on your door."

She hesitated for a moment longer, then sighed, clearly giving in. "Fine. But don't expect me to be easy to impress."

I grinned, the thrill of getting her to agree settling into my chest. "I wouldn't dream of it," I teased.

She rolled her eyes but couldn't suppress a smile. "You're insufferable."

***

The hotel restaurant bustled with teachers when we arrived, so we opted for seats at the wide mahogany bar. The polished wood gleamed under the warm, amber lighting, its rich surface reflecting the flicker of nearby flatscreen TVs.

The bar area hummed with chatter, glasses clinking, and the soft swish of bartenders pouring drinks. A mix of sports played on the screens: football and hockey games blaring with cheers and whistles, while the muted news broadcasts scrolled headlines across the bottom, a sharp contrast to the rowdy atmosphere.

There weren't any open tables, so we took seats at the bar. Rachel climbed onto the stool, her long turquoise-colored skirt catching on the edge as she adjusted herself, clearly trying to avoid making a scene. She adjusted it with a quick tug, but the soft fabric still clung to her legs, accentuating her graceful curves. Her pale skin contrasted against the vivid color of the fabric, and her hair caught the low light in the room, turning into shimmering gold.

Sitting next to her, I said, "I didn't know we were dressing for dinner."

"I wanted a shower and new clothes after my last workshop. A lady behind me coughed and sniffled, and I could feel germs on me."

"A teacher's immune system is tough. I'm sure you'll be fine."

"Tell that to that lady behind me who sounded like death warmed over."

I chuckled, changing the subject. "What did you learn today?"

Whipping her notebook out of her bag, she said, "I took six pages of notes, but basically we are already co-teaching our asses off."

"Agreed. We could teach one of these classes."

"No thanks. Give me children and teens all day." She shivered, a wry smile crossing her face. "Adults in large groups scare the stuffing out of me."

On the TV behind the bar, the weatherman silently pointed to a front approaching from the west. The radar showed pink and white precipitation moving in tomorrow. The European model predicted only a light dusting, while the NAM forecasted much heavier accumulations. It was anyone's guess whether we'd get a few flakes or a full-blown snowstorm.

"We should keep our eye on the weather," Rachel suggested.

I shrugged. "I have all-weather tires and four-wheel drive. I'm sure we'll be fine."

With that settled, we ordered patatas bravas, garlic shrimp, calamari, and Spanish meatballs off the tapas menu, along with two beers.

As we waited for our food, I couldn't help but notice how easygoing Rachel seemed. I'd dated plenty of fussy women on restrictive diets who demanded meals that were mostly water and tasteless, but Rachel? She was up for anything.

"I'm so hungry," she said, rubbing her stomach. "I missed lunch."

"Me too. The last thing I ate was Barbara's penis cookies."

"She's an excellent baker, but sometimes you have to watch out."

"You mean she puts weed in them?"

Her chuckle sounded like wind chimes on a breezy day. Her eyes sparkled, the corners crinkling as she grinned. The sleek strands of her hair shimmered, and her lips held an irresistible curve.

"One time I ate one of her brownies. An hour later, I gave every student an A on their essay."

"I bet they loved that," I laughed.

"I was also so..." She broke off, turning pink.

"So what?"

Shaking her head, she muttered. "Nothing. Never mind."

I pressed my mouth to the edge of her ear. "Were you horny?"

She nodded slowly, her expression thoughtful yet composed. Her steady blue eyes contained a faint flicker of something deeper hidden within them, perhaps vulnerability or curiosity.

Was she thinking about breaking her rules?

"You should have called me," I whispered, desperate to kiss her neck. To inhale her scent.

She paused, her eyes flicking around the room as if weighing her options. Then, a small spark of defiance flashed in her eyes. "BOB took care of me."

Jealousy ripped through me. "Who the hell is Bob?"

She giggled. "He always pleases me, never breaks my heart, and recharges quickly."

Catching on, the sharp edge of envy diminished. "Sounds like a great guy. Why aren't you with him?"

"I can't take him out in public." She laughed, and I joined in as our food arrived, the clatter of plates and silverware mixing with the sound of our shared amusement. The smell of sizzling garlic shrimp, spicy potatoes, and the rich, savory meatballs filled the air, making my stomach growl in agreement with my earlier hunger.

Rachel's eyes widened as she took in the spread. "This looks amazing." Her voice held a note of relaxation, and as we dug in, the tension from earlier faded.

Some women photographed every plate, posting it to Instagram and then checked their phone all night to see how many likes they'd received, but I much preferred Rachel's reaction as she dove in, chewing slowly, her eyes going glassy with pleasure.

"I love watching you eat."

She swallowed, putting her fork down. "What!?"

"It makes me happy that you're enjoying it."

"Oh," she said and popped the rest of the potato into her mouth.

Laughing, I opened my phone and snapped her picture. Her lips pressed together in a soft smile, her eyes half-closed as she savored a bite, and the satisfied look on her face radiated a quiet contentment that reminded me of how she looked after an orgasm.

She snapped her fingers, demanding to see the photo. "Delete that picture. I'm a mess."

I grabbed back my phone and shoved it in my pocket. "I like you unwound, relaxed, and happy."

"You mean tired and unkempt."

"Sexy." I leaned over the table between us, watching her eyes darken with awareness.

She blinked hard, breaking the moment, then waved me off like a stray thought. "Stop."

"I'm serious." I leaned in slightly, my gaze never leaving hers.

"Don't be silly." She took a slow sip of her drink, eyeing me over the rim.

"You're beautiful, Rachel."

Her fingers tightened around her glass as she let out a breath. "We said... You promised," she stammered.

"I promised no sex or flirting. I only stated the truth. Have I broken my word?"

"No, but..." She sucked in her bottom lip, her teeth sinking into it just enough to make my brain short-circuit.

"But?" I prompted, voice lower now.

Her eyes flicked to mine, her resolve visibly wavering. "You're making it really hard not to want to break the rules."

The corner of my mouth curled. "That a complaint or a confession?"

"An observation." She lifted her chin, feigning indifference, but the heat in her gaze gave her away.

"Good to know. I'll add it to my notes."

"Your notes?" She arched a brow.

"Yeah, I'm compiling a list. *Ways Rachel has Forgiven Me.* So far, I've got: doesn't roll her eyes every time I speak, tolerates me in her personal space, and only threatens me occasionally."

Her lips twitched. "You forgot how I let you sit at my lunch table."

"Oh, that's a major milestone." I nodded seriously. "I marked that one with a gold star."

She shook her head, but the smile she fought against finally surfaced. It was small but real, and damn, it hit me harder than I expected. My chest tightened, and for a moment, I forgot how to breathe.

She sighed, swirling the ice in her glass. "I don't know why I let you get under my skin."

"Because you like me," I said simply.

She scoffed, but the sound lacked conviction. "You're awfully sure of yourself."

"Nah," I murmured, my gaze locked on hers. "I'm just paying attention."

Her fingers tapped against her glass, and I smiled.

"And what, exactly, have you noticed?" she asked, pretending she wasn't holding her breath.

I leaned in just a little. "That even when you say stop, you never really want me to."

She inhaled sharply. I watched as the words hit, as she felt them—just like I did. But instead of running, instead of shutting down, she let the moment stretch, let the air between us hum with something unnamed but impossible to ignore.

For once, she didn't look away.

And neither did I.

Then her lips curved ever so slightly. Not quite a smile—more like the expression of someone realizing they just won a game they weren't even sure they were playing.

"You do realize," she murmured, tilting her head, "that you just lost?"

I frowned. "Lost what?"

"Our bet." She propped her chin on her hand, eyes bright with satisfaction. "You flirted with me, so I win. And if I win..."

Groaning playfully, I said, "I bring you lunch every day for a week."

She leaned back, looking entirely too pleased with herself. "I like sushi on Wednesdays. Just so you know."

I dragged a hand over my face, but I wasn't even mad. If anything, I liked when she played back.

"You're dangerous," I muttered.

She picked up her glass and took a slow sip. "And you're paying for my lunch."

"Worth it." I leaned in closer, my focus locked on Rachel, but before I could say anything else, a woman bumped my hip as she leaned against the bar. I barely reacted, too caught up in the way Rachel's fingers tightened around her glass, her chest rising just a little faster than before.

Then the woman cleared her throat.

I leaned in closer, my focus locked on Rachel, but before I could say anything else, the woman bumped me again.

"Oh! Sorry about that," she said with a warm laugh, steadying herself with a hand on my arm. "Didn't mean to interrupt anything."

"No problem." I barely glanced at her, already shifting back toward Rachel.

The woman, completely oblivious, kept talking. "I swear, I only come to conventions for the catered breakfast and a night without my kids climbing into bed with me." She laughed and patted my arm. "You presenting tomorrow?"

I forced a polite smile, turning my head toward her. "Nah, just attending."

Rachel's grip on her glass tightened further. Her gaze flicked from the woman's hand on my forearm back to my face, something unreadable in her eyes.

Rachel tensed beside me, then slid off her stool. She grabbed her purse and stormed out of the restaurant.

My chest tightened as I watched Rachel disappear through the door without glancing back. The weight of her absence crushed me. She was pissed, no doubt about it.

Forcing a smile, I said to the bartender, "My friend needed some air. Can I get the check?" I couldn't keep my eyes from flickering to the exit, wishing I had stopped Rachel before she left.

The woman caught my shift in focus. "Oh, I hope she didn't think I wanted to steal you away. My husband would have a fit."

She flashed a wedding band before grabbing her drink from the bar and walked off.

I couldn't wait any longer. I stood, throwing bills on the bar in a hurry. I had to leave, had to fix this.

Rachel paced in front of the elevator when I caught up with her. The lobby sat mostly empty, the faint thrum of dance music filtering through the ballroom doors where the mixer buzzed with life.

"Why are you chasing after me?" she snapped, voice sharp.

"I can't help it."

She threw up her hands defensively. "Go back to the bar. That woman seemed interested in you." Rachel's emotions, usually so carefully tucked away, spilled out in a flash of anger in her blue eyes. It sent a jolt through me.

"But I'm not into her," I said, keeping my voice steady.

Her fists curled near her chest as though shielding herself. "Why not?"

I shrugged. "I like you."

The elevator chimed, and the doors slid open and four women stepped out. I knew them from an earlier workshop, and we'd had some laughs during the discussions.

"Hey, Keith!" a tall woman with long red hair called out, waving at me with a friendly smile. The others chimed in with casual greetings.

"We're heading to the mixer," Nadine explained. "Who's your friend?"

I smiled and nodded in their direction, but my attention was fixed on Rachel. "Hi, Nadine. This is Rachel. We were just heading up."

The woman with red hair shrugged, grinning. "I hope we see you at the mixer later, and in the sessions tomorrow."

Another woman nodded and said, "It's nice seeing familiar faces at these things."

I nodded distractedly as Rachel stepped into the elevator with an exasperated grunt, stabbing the close button. I caught the door with my shoulder just before it shut, and it jolted back open. "Good to see you all, too," I muttered, barely looking at the group. "Enjoy the rest of the night."

We rode up to the fourteenth floor in tense silence. When the elevator stopped, Rachel charged ahead, her footsteps brisk as she hurried to her room.

"Rach," I called after her, quickening my pace.

"Leave me alone," she shot back without slowing.

I caught up as she scanned her keycard. "Why are you running from me?"

The lock beeped, and she pivoted to face me in the doorway, one hand gripping the frame as if to anchor herself.

"Those women," she said, her voice thick with frustration, "they looked at you like they were starving."

"Did they? I was too busy chasing you to notice," I said, holding her gaze. "We met at the inclusive teaching workshop. They took pity on me—a dyslexic fish out of water."

Her hand trembled slightly on the doorframe. "I can't be like them. You should be with someone… normal." The room behind her stood dark, the only light spilling in from the window.

She squared her shoulders, her expression pained. "You're probably the most handsome man I've ever seen, and you've got this cocky confidence, like you know exactly who you are. But I'm not like that. I'm overweight, autistic, and nerdy. I struggle every day with anxiety. I'm not the woman for you, Keith."

I spread my hands wide, searching for the words that felt stuck in my throat, desperate for her to hear what I already knew. "None of that matters, Rachel. I'm not interested in anyone but you." I took a step closer.

Her lips parted. A flicker of something lit up her eyes before doubt settled in. "But…"

"I haven't slept with anyone since you," I interrupted. "And I don't want anyone else."

Her gaze flicked away, raw vulnerability in her expression. As if she wanted to believe me, but something inside her just couldn't. Then she stiffened. The walls went up. The distance stretched between us even though neither of us moved.

"I wish I could believe you," she murmured, her voice barely a whisper.

I took a step forward, wanting to reach out, to tell her what was in my heart, but then my phone rang. She turned away, disappearing into her room.

I stood there in the dim hallway, the sound of my phone ringing echoing in my ears, my heart racing in my chest as loneliness crept in.

Chapter 11

Rachel

What would you do if the man you'd been dreaming of appeared at your door?
a) Stare in stunned silence, questioning reality.
b) Invite him in and casually play it cool (while freaking out inside).
c) Flirt shamelessly and see where it leads.
d) Panic, slam the door, and then immediately regret it.

My alarm woke me the next morning, and my mind felt fuzzy and slow. I'd tossed and turned late into the night, unable to settle knowing that Keith was right next door. The argument from last night replayed in my mind, each word sharp and unforgiving.

When I finally fell asleep, he haunted my dreams.

Lying back against the pillows, I closed my eyes, the last dream vivid in my mind. His soft brown hair had a natural wave to it, tousling just enough at the sides and back to make him look effortlessly undone. It framed his face, adding to the rugged charm that seemed to make my pulse skip every time he looked my way. I couldn't help but imagine his neatly trimmed mustache and beard brushing against my skin, the soft tickle of it sending a shiver through me.

In the dream, his heavy body pressed into mine as he kissed, licked, and nibbled my sensitive skin. Moaning aloud, I savored the memory of him. His teeth and lips on my clit. The feel of his fingers pushing inside me.

My hand slid down, heightening my pleasure as the images flew faster through my mind. I could smell my arousal, my fingers slick as I rode the wave toward climax. My hips arched and my breath caught in my throat. My body tightened, curling in on itself. I was so close.

Bang. Bang. Bang.

I froze, my body aching for release. What kind of sadistic person would knock on my hotel door at seven in the morning?

"Rachel, are you in there?"

Keith's voice cut through the stillness of the morning, startling me. I froze. My fingers went numb against my clit, my heart pounding against my ribs.

I flew out of bed before I could think better of it. Wrenching the door open, I found him standing there, his hand raised in mid-knock.

I glared at him, painfully aware of how the thin fabric of my tank top did nothing to hide the way my body reacted. A flush crept up my neck as my gaze lingered on the flannel shirt that hugged his muscles, the subtle pull of it only adding to the heat between my legs. His eyes widened, traveling down to my low-riding pajama shorts and bare legs.

"What do you want, Keith?" My voice came out sharper than I intended, but I couldn't hide the crack of embarrassment beneath it. The sting of last night still clung to me, hot and confusing.

"Good morning, Princess," he said, his tone infuriatingly casual, like he hadn't disappointed me just hours ago. Like I hadn't walked away feeling like a fool.

I crossed my arms, more for self-defense than defiance. "Morning? It's barely that," I muttered, my body tensing.

Pretty, friendly, outgoing women approached him so easily. With their confident smiles and easy laughs, they looked at him with hungry eyes. I couldn't compete with that. I was foolish for even thinking I had a chance.

And yet, I knew deep down that Keith hadn't encouraged them. But that didn't stop the ugly, sinking feeling in my stomach. Because why wouldn't they flirt with him? He was a charming, easygoing guy. Why wouldn't he flirt back, when I pushed him away at every turn?

I clenched my jaw, shoving the thought away before it could take root again. It didn't matter. It shouldn't matter.

Keith leaned against the doorframe, his posture relaxed, but when I met his eyes, they simmered with heat.

A rush of reaction flooded through me, a stark reminder of how close I'd been to orgasm just minutes ago. The memory of that simmering tension made my breath catch in my throat.

"We need to talk," he said, his voice softer now, the easygoing act slipping a little as his gaze raked over me again.

God, why did he have to look at me like that? I shifted my weight, my body drawn to his. My nipples hardened in reaction, and I had to fight not to look away, not to lose myself in it, but I didn't want him to see how badly I wanted him.

"I don't think we do," I said, my voice cold, even though inside I was anything but. My heart pounded in my chest, and I couldn't catch my breath. Seconds away from throwing myself at him.

"Rachel—"

"No," I cut him off, shaking my head, trying to shut out the way his voice seemed to stroke across my skin. "I get it. I misread the situation. It won't happen again."

He exhaled, watching me, measuring every word, every shift in my posture, like he knew what I was thinking.

He blinked, shaking his head as if to clear the fog. "They've canceled the rest of the conference. It's going to snow."

The words barely registered. My thoughts were still caught in the web of his gaze, in the quiet intensity that wrapped around us. I tried to pull myself back, unable to separate myself from him.

I frowned, confused. "What?"

I pivoted away from him, needing space to breathe, to think. My feet carried me toward the window before my mind caught up. I yanked open the curtains.

Dark clouds gathered, rolling in over the mountains like a threat. The parking lot below was full of people hurrying to their cars, wearing coats and scarves wrapped tight around their necks. Their breath rose in frosty clouds. The scene outside should have been normal, but it only served to make me feel more off-balance, more out of sync.

"But there's only a fifty percent chance," I said, staring out the window. Change wasn't my strong suit. I preferred to have a plan and stick to it. This unexpected storm was difficult for me to process.

"The front is interacting with another low that's developing to the south of us," Keith explained from where he leaned against the bathroom threshold. "The new forecast is six or more inches."

Keith waited in silence as I processed. I wanted to explain, to make him understand what was happening inside me, but the words stuck in my throat. Instead, I just stood there, staring out into the gathering storm, my heart a storm of its own.

I took a steadying breath. I needed to focus on practical tasks. Showering could wait. I needed to get dressed, pack up, grab some breakfast, and check out.

I was done letting my thoughts spiral. I had work to do.

"Can you get me some coffee while I get my stuff together?"

"Sure, I'll get my duffel and meet you in the lobby."

"Give me fifteen minutes."

He lifted a brow, clearly skeptical that I could be ready so quickly, but he didn't argue. I was already moving before he slipped out the door.

Twelve minutes later, I was pressing the elevator button, my hair brushed back under a slouchy black hat that covered my bed head, and my face was shiny and clean. Makeup was a luxury I didn't bother with. I'd thrown on jeans and a fuzzy black sweater, my pink puffy coat draped over my arm.

When the elevator doors opened to the lobby, I spotted Keith sitting near the entrance. He had two steaming cups of coffee in front of him, along with a small paper plate of danishes.

"I've checked us both out," he said, taking the handle of my suitcase and lifting it easily. "Put your coat on. It's cold out there."

We hurried through the parking lot toward Keith's truck. The icy wind sliced through my coat and hat, cutting straight to my bones. The tall pines surrounding the lot swayed and creaked under the gusts, their needle-covered branches whispering ominously. Overhead, the clouds were heavy and gray with the promise of snow.

I scrambled into the cab, my hands already aching from the chill. He turned the key, and the engine roared to life. The heater blasted weakly, struggling to push back the cold that had settled into the cab.

As we pulled out onto the road, the silence between us was thick with unspoken worries. Keith's hands gripped the steering wheel, his knuckles pale against the leather, his jaw set in concentration.

Heading toward the highway, Keith retraced the winding, forest-lined route we'd taken the day before. The narrow road twisted and turned, climbing steadily toward the mountain pass. My eyes flicked nervously to the sky.

The first flake landed with a soft splat against the windshield, melting instantly. I held my breath, watching as another followed, then another, until the glass was peppered with tiny, fleeting snowflakes.

Keith glanced over at me, his expression unreadable. "We've got this," he said, but the tension in his voice betrayed him.

I nodded, trying to swallow the knot in my throat, but the snow continued to fall, its pace quickening with every mile.

"All snowflakes have six sides," I said, my voice steady as I clung to the calming effect of trivia facts. "The average snowfall in Chicago is thirty-eight inches."

"Good to know," Keith said.

The highway switch backed on its way up the mountain as more flakes came down. So far, the snow was melting on the driving lanes, but a sheen of ice collected on the grass.

We approached an overpass just as a silver hatchback in front of us hit an icy patch. The car fishtailed sharply, sliding several feet before the driver regained control. Keith immediately eased his foot off the gas, letting the truck coast over the bridge with careful precision.

"We should stop," I said, gripping the armrest. "This is a bad idea."

Keith shook his head, his voice steady but firm. "We just need to get over the mountain. Once we're on the other side, it'll be fine."

The road continued to climb, taking us higher into the thickening snow. Heavy clouds cast the world in twilight even though it was early morning. Keith switched on the windshield wipers as the flakes came faster, clinging to the glass and piling at the edges. The hum of the engine and the rhythmic swish of the wipers filled the silence as we crept forward, mile by cautious mile.

At the mountain's summit, the view was swallowed by a dense wall of clouds. Traffic ahead ground to a halt, red taillights glowing faintly through the falling snow. Around us, the landscape was quickly transforming, the snow gathering in drifts that blurred the boundaries between road and shoulder.

Keith turned off the car. Startled, my eyes swung to his. "We should've gotten gas before we hit the road," he muttered, his voice tense. "Now we're stuck here with a quarter tank, and we've been sitting in this snow for over an hour."

My hands were suddenly restless in my lap, so I clenched them together. "I mean—well, yeah, but—" I stumbled over my words, trying to calm myself. "Did you know that traffic in snow can reduce your fuel efficiency by up to thirty percent? And if we're idling, it's only making it worse. We really should've planned for this." I swallowed, realizing I was rambling. "Do you have gas cans in the back?"

Keith leaned back, a slight grin tugging at his lips as he glanced at me. "No cans, but I do have a shovel."

I stared out at the steadily piling snow, my voice soft but steady. "Snow isn't white, you know. It's translucent."

Keith looked over at me. "I'm sorry you're nervous."

I attempted a smile. "I'm not. Why would you think that?"

"I don't know, Rach. Maybe I just assumed you're nervous because I am."

"You never seem apprehensive."

He laughed. "I get nervous all the time."

"Anxiety disorder affects thirty-one percent of the population. Women are more likely to develop it than men."

Eyes on the road, he responded with a different fact. "One in five people have dyslexia. It's more common in males than females."

Of course, I knew Keith was dyslexic, but he'd developed strategies to navigate it—tools and methods that allowed him to overcome the challenges it presented. Anxiety, on the other hand, was a different beast entirely. It wasn't something you could outsmart. It required medication, therapy, and constant vigilance, and even then, it lurked in the background like a silent predator. "That's interesting, but not relevant."

He was silent for a moment before saying, "You should get out your phone and find the next exit."

"Okay," I said, unlocking my phone and typing into Google.

"Maybe look up a hotel nearby. Read the reviews to make sure it's decent. And restaurants, too, if you can."

"On it."

Through the storm of swirling snow, I could see flashing red lights ahead. Keith tapped his fingers against the steering wheel, the tension in his jaw mirrored in the rhythm of his movements.

"How long do you think it'll take you?" he asked.

I shrugged. "Maybe ten minutes? I can try to go faster if you want."

He nodded slowly. "It'd take me an hour. Maybe more. And after, I'd have a headache, and my eyes would feel like they'd been wrung out."

I glanced at him, startled by the weight in his tone. "Keith, I'm sorry. I didn't mean to—"

"I know, Princess," he said, cutting me off gently but firmly. "It's not your fault. It's just... something I live with every day.

Dyslexia doesn't go away. I've learned how to manage it, but it's always there, making simple things harder. Just like anxiety or autism, it shapes how I move through the world."

His words settled in the air between us, heavier than the snow piling up outside. I swallowed hard, my chest tightening with an ache for him I hadn't fully felt until now.

I'd never considered Keith's dyslexia on the same level as ASD and anxiety. It was almost like I'd crowned myself the queen of hardship, believing my struggle was somehow more valid or consuming than anyone else's. But that wasn't fair. Keith's challenges were just as real as mine. He carried them with a quiet resilience, so much so that I often forgot he faced them at all. That realization humbled me and gnawed at my conscience.

Another hour went by before a policeman appeared. The snow around him swirled in frantic gusts, the wind whipping it into stinging flurries that clung to his coat and hat.

Keith lowered the window so we could talk to him. The cold wind blowing flakes into the truck. "Officer, what's going on?"

"The road's closed ahead. We're turning everyone around. There's an exit about a half mile behind you."

Keith nodded and carefully swung the truck around, slowly heading in the opposite direction. Other cars followed us back toward Charlottesville.

It felt like an eternity before we finally reached the exit for Afton. Keith focused intently on driving, his hands steady on the wheel, while I sat in silence as we slid down the mountain.

Finally, lights cut through the storm ahead and The Pine Lodge materialized on the left side of the road. The sign glowed faintly against the swirling snow, and soon the gray, boxy building came into view.

The parking lot was nearly full, snow piling on the parked cars, but Keith maneuvered into a spot near the entrance. I zipped up my jacket and shoved my hat on my head. I grabbed my purse and stepped out into the freezing cold. The wind bit at my cheeks as I gingerly navigated the icy lot, my sneakers sliding with each step.

Keith was right behind me as we entered the lobby. Inside, warmth and light enveloped me. A group of people gathered near a large stone fireplace, steaming coffee cups in hand. The scent of fresh cookies wafted through the air, and a wide table in the center of the room was laden with a tray of baked goods. Around it, comfortable chairs and sofas invited weary travelers to sit and shake off the storm.

"Hello," a cheerful male voice called from behind us. "Welcome to the lodge. Do you have a reservation?"

"Um, no..."

The older man listened as we explained our situation. He had a kind face and laugh lines framed his eyes. His gentle smile carried a warmth that put me at ease. He gave off dad vibes, and I knew he'd help without a second thought.

"We were hoping to stay here tonight," I said with my fingers crossed in my pockets.

"Not a problem." The man beamed at Keith and me. "We have one room left."

Chapter 12

Keith

What would you do if you unexpectedly had to share a room with your crush for the night?
a) Offer to take the couch and try to play it cool.
b) Suggest building a pillow fort to keep things "friendly."
c) Pretend to be totally unfazed while internally freaking out.
d) Take the opportunity to finally make a move.

"No, no, no," Rachel whispered, shaking her head so hard that her loose pink cap fell off. When she bent down to retrieve it, I shifted closer to the reception desk.

Her discomfort radiated like an electric current, and I knew she didn't want to share a room with me. But the snowstorm outside was relentless, and we were stuck. We didn't have any other option.

"Hi. I'm Keith," I said, extending my hand.

His smile shifted from polite to a beaming megawatt joy. "Gene. I'm the owner of The Pine Tree Lodge."

"Likewise. We'll take the room, but I was wondering if you have anything else. You see—"

Across the desk, Gene had his hands clasped over his chest. "Aren't y'all the cutest?"

Rachel's eyes widened, her face turning bright red. "No, we're not cute together at all. I mean, we're not even together like that. Not *together* together. More like, stuck-in-the-snow-together. But not, you know, TOGETHER in any romantic way. No, nope." She tripped over her words, stepping closer and wedging herself between me and the desk.

I stifled a laugh. New drinking game word: *together*. Where were the shots?

"Give us a second, please. Don't give away that room." I gave Gene a smile while pulling Rachel away.

Gene winked at me. "Okey dokey."

I pulled Rachel a few steps away. "Hey, Rach? Can you let me talk to the guy to see if he can help us out?"

She wouldn't meet my eyes. "I can't share a room with you."

I raised an eyebrow. "I'll sleep in a chair or something. It'll be fine."

She shook her head, her voice barely above a whisper. "No, that's... that's not the problem."

"Then what is?" I leaned in slightly, trying to catch her gaze, but she was looking everywhere but at me.

She shifted uncomfortably, crossing her arms tighter. "It's just... they'll know."

"Who?" I whispered back, leaning closer. "Cause if it's aliens, I wouldn't mind letting them run naughty experiments on me."

Rachel smacked me on the shoulder, not hard, but it was enough to tell me I was making her uneasy. "Not aliens. People. The conference crowd. I recognize some of them."

I scanned the group near the fireplace. A few women were staring, and I could feel Rachel's discomfort. She was caught between wanting to do the practical thing and fearing how it might look.

"Would you rather sleep in the truck, Princess?" I asked, with a raised eyebrow. "Because I don't exactly see a ton of other options here."

Her eyes darted toward the crowd and then quickly away, her teeth nibbling on her bottom lip. "It's just... being close to you is..."

"What?" I asked, voice softer now, trying to get through the mess in her head.

She hesitated as if unable to say the words, her eyes searching mine for something—maybe reassurance, maybe the courage to speak a truth she wasn't ready to face.

I leaned in, my voice dropping. "Am I that irresistible?"

She snorted. "Absolutely not."

My voice dropped to a teasing whisper. "Not irresistible? Then what's the problem with sharing a room?"

She spun away, her footsteps quick and sharp as she paced across the lobby, muttering under her breath, "Unbelievable. Absolutely unbelievable."

With a deep breath, I walked over to Gene, who was still standing near the counter, looking like he was doing his best to avoid eye contact.

"Gene," I started, my voice casual but firm. "I know it's a tricky situation, but we're just looking for some way to make this work." I gave him a quick nod toward Rachel, who was staring at the fire. "I'm not asking for the world here, just some space to crash for the night. Is there any chance you've got a cot or something?"

Gene shook his head. "We only have two, and they're already spoken for. I realize this isn't ideal, but there are two chairs in the room. Maybe one of you could sleep there?"

Rachel approached. "Sleeping in a chair limits blood flow to the extremities and can lead to compressed nerves," she said, her voice higher than usual.

Gene's expression shifted, and I couldn't tell if he was worried about a lawsuit or just regretting his life choices. I took the room keys from his limp fingers. "Is there anywhere we can grab some food nearby?"

"I don't recommend going out." Gene looked out the window, the snow still falling in thick layers. "We have a small catering kitchen on premises. My wife is making cheese pizzas by request."

I glanced at Rachel, who seemed to contemplate the idea. At least we wouldn't have to starve.

"Cheese pizza sounds perfect," I said, feeling a little lighter.

"I'll let her know. Why don't you both get your things and get settled? We have cookies and hot drinks in the lobby if you'd like to join everyone."

Rachel and I made our way back toward the main door. She zipped up her coat and pulled her hat back over her hair.

"You can stay here," I said, fishing the keys to my truck out of my front pocket. "I need to make a quick call, and then I'll get the bags."

Rachel's eyes flicked to the phone in my hand, her posture suddenly tense. "A call?" she asked, her voice edged with something I couldn't quite place.

I nodded, already stepping toward the door. "Yeah, I promised Sunny I'd check in. She's been bugging me about the storm and all. I won't be long."

Rachel shifted uncomfortably, her arms wrapping tightly around herself. "Oh. Right." Her lips pressed into a thin line despite her casual words.

I frowned, sensing the shift in the air but not fully understanding it. "It's just a quick thing, Rachel."

"I'll help," Rachel replied, and with a quick, dramatic swish of her coat, she strode out into the cold.

It was only noon, but the sky was dark. The wind hit us like a runaway train, and snow blasted across the pavement like it had somewhere important to be. It was like the entire sky had decided to dump another ton of frozen precipitation on us. Snowflakes whipped around, sticking to my beard and eyelashes.

I pulled my coat tighter around me, bracing against the Arctic blast, and quickened my pace to catch up with Rachel. I'd call Sunny later when I wasn't so cold.

We grabbed our bags, which seemed more like stubborn mules than helpful luggage, and started back across the slick pavement, taking baby steps to avoid wiping out. I stepped up onto the sidewalk in front of the hotel, and BOOM.

I clutched the strap of my duffel tighter as my feet betrayed me, sliding out from under me with all the grace of a newborn deer. A half-frozen puddle broke my fall. The icy slap of water and muck soaked straight through my pants.

Rachel turned just in time to catch the disaster unfold, and I didn't miss the way her lips twitched, barely holding back a laugh.

I lay there for a second, sprawled like a crime scene outline. One leg stretched north, the other pointed west, my coat half-on, half-off, and my dignity nowhere in sight.

Rachel sighed, clearly torn between helping me and saving herself. "You okay?"

I waved a hand, attempting nonchalance, but as soon as I pushed up, my foot shot right back into the puddle. "Just... peachy."

My shoes let out an audible squelch as I shifted. Fantastic. I was now a human sponge, soaking up every bit of the frozen slush. My duffel, lying nearby, wasn't faring much better.

Rachel dropped her bag to reach for me. She braced herself, offering her hand. I took it, my fingers numb and stiff.

The moment I tried to get my legs under me, she slipped.

In slow motion, I saw the horror on her face as her arms flailed, her balance betrayed. Then her knee drove straight into my kidney, her full weight crashing down on me, submerging me deeper into the icy sludge.

"Can you get up?" I asked, my teeth chattering like castanets.

She attempted a push-up, barely lifted two inches, then slid right back down. "No!" she yelped. "My hands are wet, and I keep slipping!"

Rachel shifted, her knee perilously close to my groin. A fresh wave of icy water seeped into my jacket. At least her breath was warm against my neck.

Gritting my teeth, I mustered what little strength I had left, lifting her in an awkward, half-crumpled bench press and rolling her onto the snowy grass. Then, half-crawling, half-flopping, I dragged myself out of the puddle to join her.

She was already on her feet, shivering violently but moving. "We need to get inside. Now."

I didn't argue. Nodding stiffly, I stumbled after her, squelching my way into the warm lobby like a half-frozen zombie.

Wet and bedraggled, we left a trail of mud and melting snow behind us. Rachel urged me to go faster. "In the United States, between seven hundred and fifteen hundred people die from hypothermia each year."

"Not us," I said around my chattering teeth.

The owner—what was his name again? Gene?—entered through a side door, lifting a hand in greeting. But the moment he got a good look at us, his steps faltered, his brows drawing together in concern. "What happened to you?"

Rachel tightened her grip on my arm, steadying me as we trudged through the lobby. "The parking lot and sidewalk are a skating rink."

Gene's eyes flicked down to our soaked clothes, the trail of slushy water we were leaving in our wake. His expression shifted from confusion to alarm.

"I—I'll get our staff on that immediately." His voice wavered slightly as he pulled out his phone, already dialing.

"Twenty-five percent of ice and snow-related injuries happen in parking lots," Rachel muttered.

Gene's face paled. "Are either of you hurt?" His gaze darted between us, as if expecting one of us to collapse on the spot.

"You'd better hope not. Property owners are liable for any injuries or damages that occur on their property." She caught my hand and let me down the hallway to our room.

Gene wrestled the wet duffle off my shoulder. "I'll take this, and we'll wash and dry everything."

Rachel shivered. "Can you get my bag from outside? And wash the clothes we're wearing, too?"

"We'll take care of everything, and I'll have robes and food delivered to your room."

Gene led us down the hall to unlock our room with his master key, holding the door open. Once inside, Rachel pivoted and let the door close in his face with a loud bang.

"Take off your clothes," she ordered, walking stiffly into the adjoining bathroom.

I heard the shower turn on as I fumbled with the zipper of my soaked jacket. My fingers didn't seem to work properly. I tried pulling the tab, but it wouldn't budge.

Rachel returned, shrugging off her coat. She didn't hesitate, her eyes fixed on me as she said, "You have to get naked."

"I—I can't," I stammered, teeth chattering as I demonstrated my utter inability to unzip my jacket.

Without missing a beat, she reached over and unzipped it for me, dragging the soaked material off. Her hands were suddenly at my belt, then the button of my jeans, tugging the zipper down. I wanted to make a joke about shrinkage, anything clever to break the tension, but the words wouldn't form.

The jeans hit the floor with a soggy thud, puddling at my feet. My phone slipped out of the pile of clothes, and Rachel picked it up, her fingers grazing the cracked screen. She winced as she handed it to me.

It was dead, the screen a shattered mess. My thoughts flickered to Sunny and how she'd worry if I didn't call. And then there was Rachel's reaction when she touched my phone. What had that been about?

"You need to get in the shower," Rachel said, her voice cutting through my thoughts.

The next few minutes felt like an oddly uncomfortable game of *Simon Says* as she guided me through each step, stripping me of any lingering modesty. And finally, I was naked, standing in the bathroom, unsure of what had just happened but too cold to care.

The hot water hit me like a thousand tiny needles. I gritted my teeth until the warmth began to seep into my muscles, loosening them one by one. Just as I started to relax, feeling the tension melt away, I heard the shower curtain pull back.

Rachel stepped over the tub's edge, naked. Her peach skin was blue. Goosebumps covered her head to toe, and she shivered in the mist.

I could barely feel my fingertips, but I saw stars and heard Barry White crooning *Let's Get It On*. She adjusted the curtain, then stood with one arm covering her boobs and the other hand acting like a fig leaf.

"Come here," I said, shifting over so she could stand in the hot water. I gathered her close, my arms wrapping around her waist as the water warmed us both.

We stood, pressed together from hip to chest. Water sluiced over her hair, running down her back and restoring her healthy color. She relaxed, and her shivers ceased.

Her arms wrapped around my waist, and she rested her cheek on my shoulder. The heat between us grew hotter than the shower, and as my body warmed, it reacted to her. My cock thickened, pressing against her.

"Your... um..." She gestured toward my cock. "I thought you might be permanently damaged."

My whole body ached. I had bruises on top of bruises, and exhaustion made me feel slow, but I summoned a laugh. "I appreciate your concern for my future happiness, but I think my dick survived the trauma." I winced as I shifted. "Can't say the same for my dignity."

Rachel sighed and nestled a little closer. "Well, I couldn't just leave you to freeze. Men are twice as likely to get frostbite as women."

I huffed a laugh, running my hand over her wet hair. "Thanks for helping me."

She tipped her head up to look at me and got a face full of water instead.

Rachel sputtered, jerking back as water sprayed straight into her face. "Oh my God!" she gasped, swiping at her eyes. "You're taking up all the room in here, and I almost drowned."

I grinned, adjusting the spray so it wasn't hitting her directly. "That's what you get for standing in the splash zone."

She huffed, elbowing me as she turned away to grab the shampoo. But the second she reached for it, her foot slid out from under her.

She grabbed for the nearest thing to steady herself—me. Except I was bending to rinse off, and her panicked yank threw both of us off balance.

Rachel yelped as she toppled backward, dragging me with her. My elbow cracked against the shower wall. Desperately hoping not to crush her, I grabbed for the curtain. Big mistake.

With a horrible *ripping* sound, the shower rod came loose, the curtain wrapped around us like a plastic toga, and the next thing I knew, we hit the bathroom floor in a tangled, wet heap.

Rachel gasped. "Did we—? Are we—?"

Flat on my back, trapped under a mess of plastic and regret, I groaned. "We broke the damn shower."

Silence.

Then Rachel let out a single snort.

It was all over after that.

She burst into full, uncontrollable laughter, gasping for breath as she rolled off me, still half-wrapped in the curtain. "Oh my God, my klutz is rubbing off on you."

I sat up, shoving wet plastic off my face, and scowled at her. "This is not funny."

She clutched her stomach, wheezing through her laughter. "It's so funny. We made it through an ice storm just to get taken out by hotel plumbing."

I groaned again, rubbing my face.

But Rachel just kept laughing, her whole body shaking with it. I sighed, standing up and grabbing a towel, leaving her sprawled on the floor, still giggling like an absolute menace.

A knock on the door sobered her quickly.

"Is everything okay in there?" Gene's concerned voice filtered through the door. "I thought I heard a crash."

"We're fine!" we both called simultaneously.

"Great, great," Gene replied, his voice cheerful. "If you'd open the door, I have your robes and pizza."

Rachel squeaked in panic, dashing back into the bathroom, so I opened the door wearing a towel around my hips. Gene stood there with a tray, a medium cheese pizza on top, two glasses filled with ice, and a bottle of cola. He also had two fluffy white robes draped over his arm.

"Here you go," he said, passing everything over. "Please, let me know if I can get you anything else."

"Thanks," I said, closing the door. I tossed one of the robes to Rachel, before struggling into mine. "This pizza smells amazing," I said, inhaling deeply before the lights flickered.

Rachel stepped out of the bathroom in her robe, eyes wide. "Oh, please don't let the lights—"

Before she could finish her sentence, the room plunged into complete darkness.

Chapter 13

Rachel

What would you do if you had to share a bed with someone you secretly like?
a) Stay on your side and try to act normal (while overthinking every move).
b) "Accidentally" brush against them to see how they react.
c) Make a playful joke to break the tension.
d) Pretend to fall asleep... but secretly hope something happens.

Hot cheese, tangy sauce, and a chewy crust—the combination didn't sound like much, but as I bit into the slice, it tasted like the ambrosia of the gods. The warm, salty bite melted in my mouth, comforting me in a way I hadn't expected. I wasn't sure whether it was the pizza itself or just how desperate I felt for something to feel normal.

The snow wasn't letting up anytime for the foreseeable future. Keith and I huddled in thick, fluffy robes, the soft material almost making up for the cold still clinging to my bones. We'd tucked ourselves under the king-sized cream comforter, piling on extra blankets for warmth.

The pizza box rested between us on the bed, and the steam rising from it seemed to wrap the room in a cozy haze. The curtains were drawn tight against the cold draft. It felt like we were in our own little bubble, safe and warm. I finished off a slice and paused, considering taking another one.

"The average American eats forty-six slices of pizza a year," I mused.

Keith nodded, chewing silently. He took a swig of cola, the bubbles hissing as he swallowed. "Do you have any painkillers?"

"Yes!" I shot out of the bed, throwing the covers off and rushing to grab my purse. My feet brushed the rapidly cooling carpet, the chill creeping up my legs. The room would cool down fast without the heater working.

I dove back under the covers, surfacing with a tiny bottle of ibuprofen. "How are you feeling?"

He swallowed the pills with a grimace, then winked at me. "I've felt worse."

I rolled my eyes. "When?"

He stretched out a little, adjusting the pillows behind him. "I was in a car accident seven years ago. Another driver hit me head-on. I limped away with a broken leg and some nasty bruises from the seat belt."

"I'm glad it wasn't more serious," I said softly.

He passed the bottle back to me, then stretched out, sinking into the pillows while I swallowed a few pills myself.

The weight of the blankets felt strange, and I realized I wasn't shielding myself from the cold. I was hiding, building walls like I always did, but Keith didn't ask for more—he didn't push.

I hadn't planned on ever being this close to Keith ever again, let alone sharing a bed like it was the most natural thing in the world. But somewhere between the snowstorm, the cold, and the way he'd handled everything with humor, I found myself letting go of my doubts. My tension faded enough for me to breathe.

"Do you want to sleep?" I asked, pulling the covers up to my neck.

"Not really. I'm just trying to get comfortable."

Pushing the covers down, I allowed vulnerability to wash over me. If he could change, so could I. "Comfort is a twentieth-century construct," I said, voice slightly amused. "Human comfort has never been more valued or taken for granted as in the last one hundred years. Things like air conditioning, fabric softener, fleece, and central heating have brought ideal comfort into all our lives."

Keith let out a long sigh. "Central heat would be nice right now."

I moved the pizza off the bed, setting it on the end table. Pulling my robe tighter around myself, I rolled over to face him. In the dim light, I could just make out the shadow of his dark eyes watching me.

Eye contact always felt awkward, intrusive, and I tended to avoid it at all costs. But tonight, the shadows gave me just enough of a buffer to relax.

"Talk to me," Keith murmured, shifting his head on the pillow.

My mind blanked instantly. Making conversation was definitely not my forte. "What do you want to talk about?"

He coughed, and my heart leapt into my throat. What if he became ill? "Do you have a fever?"

"I'm fine," he said, his voice a little rougher than usual.

My inner voice urged me to slide over and feel his skin just to make sure. "What if you need to go to the hospital? How would I get you there?"

"I don't need to go to the hospital, Rachel. But if I did, you'd call 911."

Wait... was his voice slurry? Had he hit his head when he fell? Should I call 911 to ask what they thought?

He rolled over onto his back with a heavy sigh. "I can practically hear the gears grinding in your brain. Talk to me. Tell me something no one else knows."

My mind felt like an empty void, a vast expanse of silence. Intriguing secrets and deep confessions? Definitely not in my wheelhouse. But I welcomed the distraction. Needed, even. Because if I wasn't fumbling for something to say, I'd be too aware of Keith beside me, the steady rise and fall of his breathing, the way the blankets cocooned us together like we belonged here. And that was dangerous.

My gaze kept betraying me, drawn to the V of his robe where smooth, warm skin met the soft fabric, the faintest trail of hair leading lower, disappearing beneath the folds as he relaxed back onto the pillows.

He was too tempting, but wanting him meant risking everything. I didn't feel brave enough for that.

I lay there in the quiet dark, rubbing my thumb between my fingers as one minute stretched into another. "I have a tortoise."

Keith chuckled softly, the sound like a warm breeze. "I've met Bolt."

I shrugged, the corners of my lips twitching into a small smile. "I can't think of anything."

"What's your favorite color?"

"That depends. In the natural world, I love blue, but if you're talking Crayola, it's a tie between *Tickle Me Pink* and *Inchworm*."

He chuckled, the sound low and warm, and the mattress dipped slightly as he shifted beside me. "You had that answer ready."

"Obviously. It's an important distinction."

His voice seemed closer now, his body just a breath away. "What is something you're really good at?"

I stared at the dark ceiling, my thoughts meandering like a muddy river. I could feel his breath in my hair, warm and steady. Tendrils of it brushed my skin, sending goosebumps skittering down my spine, pooling low in my belly, heat curling between my thighs.

"I don't know," I murmured, my voice thinner than I meant it to be.

Keith let out a thoughtful hum, his breathing sounded rough in the quiet. "Do you have any hobbies?"

I turned my head slightly, aware of how close we were, how his body heat seeped through the blankets, wrapping around me like a slow burn. My palms itched to touch him, to trace the line of his chest where the robe gaped open, but I curled my fist into my hip instead, willing myself to stay still.

"I read a lot." My voice was barely above a whisper, the quiet admission hanging between us, fragile and charged.

I turned my head slightly, the space between us shrinking, his warmth sinking into my skin like an invitation. The shadows around us felt deeper, wrapping around us. I knew I should filter my answer, say something neutral, but the fact that he actually listened loosened something in me.

"You told me you enjoy smut," Keith prompted me, voice low, careful.

I swallowed hard, my fingers gripping the blanket, unsure if I wanted to give him the truth. But the quiet space between us burned slowly. "Yeah, that's my favorite," I whispered, my face hot but not from embarrassment.

The mattress shifted again. Keith's voice, just a breath against my ear, deepened. "Tell me more." His words were an invitation, but something in his tone made it feel like a challenge, like he waited for me to cross the line.

A part of me hesitated, but a bigger part of me wanted to play along. The thought of letting go, of giving in to the growing tension between us, made my pulse quicken. The weight of his body just inches from mine as we lay side by side, the steady warmth of him, beckoned me, making me want to curl into him.

I shifted slightly, the blankets now tangled around us both, and I couldn't remember a time when I had felt this close to someone. The space between us seemed to shrink with every heartbeat. I was hyper-aware of every brush of his arm against mine, the faint scent of his cologne, something warm and woodsy, like sandalwood and cedar, mixing with the crispness of the night air.

The tangible pull between us called to me. Begged me to relax and play. "What do you want to know?"

The words hung in the air, hanging between us like a dare. The shadowy darkness around us gave me the courage to speak. "I enjoy reading books for women that include spicy scenes."

"How graphic are these spicy scenes?"

He was closer now, leaning in, the heat of his breath fanning my flushed neck.

"Very. Five chili peppers," I whispered, my heart starting to race.

"Five, huh?" His voice was a low murmur. My body vibrated with the hope that he would touch me. "And how do you feel while you're reading these scenes?"

My heart squeezed, but I responded, "I imagine I'm in the book. That I'm the character." I kicked my foot out from under the covers, letting it hang off the bed.

His lips brushed the shell of my ear, and I gasped. Was this pressure in my sternum a heart attack? Could I die from sexual tension?

His voice was low, rough around the edges, but managed to send another jolt through me. "Do you get aroused while you're reading?"

"I—what?" I swallowed hard, struggling to focus, but my body reacted to the question with another layer of heat spreading across my skin. It was the kind of question that should have made me pull back, but instead, I found myself lingering in the moment. Relishing it.

"Do you have any with you?" Keith's voice came soft, almost hypnotic, his lips brushing the sensitive skin behind my ear.

"No," I lied, even though my phone's reading app practically burst with them.

"Then make up one of your own," he murmured, his voice smooth and coaxing.

"I can't think when you—" A moan slipped from my lips as his teeth gently nipped at my neck.

I inched away from him, the warmth of his body slowly fading as I put a few inches of space between us. The cool air hit my skin, but it wasn't enough to clear the fog of desire clouding my mind.

"I'm cold without you beside me," he murmured, but he let me go.

Concern washed over me like icy water. Was his body temperature not regulating? Keith shivered slightly, his muscles tense. I quickly grabbed some extra blankets, spreading them over us.

"Tell me a spicy story, Princess. Something that'll heat me up."

"Well," I started, shifting in bed and pulling the blankets tighter around us, "there once was a girl who met a dragon shifter. At first, she's terrified of him, but her father's indebted to him, so she has to approach him."

Keith's eyes flickered with interest. "What did she look like?"

The heat rose in my chest as I continued. "Long brown hair, golden skin, a cloak that hugged her curves. She looked like someone who'd survived battles, strong."

Keith leaned closer, the warmth between us growing. "I'd rather imagine you instead in a short dress and stilettos."

I smirked. "Do you want the story or not?"

He grinned. "At least tell me if she has boobs like yours."

"Hush," I said, trying to stay focused. "Her name was Arilynn. She always thought she'd marry a human, have kids. Though she longed for adventure and—"

"A good lover with a long dick," Keith teased.

His fingers brushed mine, and I swallowed hard. How could his touch be both grounding and electric all at once? Then he laced our fingers together, and I didn't care.

I shook the thought away and pressed on. "One day, she found a cave with a mysterious creature. He's cloaked in shadows, but they talk about everything. His name was Keithren."

"A strong name choice, Princess." Keith chuckled, his fingers moving up to rub my neck. "But where are the chili peppers?"

I giggled, the sound escaping before I could stop it. His fingers dug into my neck, the pressure both soothing and incendiary, sending a wave of heat down my spine that left me breathless.

I swallowed and continued. "One day Arilynn's village was attacked by a dragon, and all of her family died. She ran to the cave to find Keithren but discovered an enormous sleeping dragon instead."

Keith pulled me back against him, his arm slipping around my waist, drawing me closer until my head rested on his chest. I could feel the steady beat of his heart under my ear. "He's the dragon," he murmured, his voice low and tight, sending a shiver through me.

"Yes," I whispered, my voice caught in the tension between us. "What part of dragon shifter did you not get?" I shifted slightly, my body still pressed against his, and the proximity made my pulse race.

"Did he burn down her village?" Keith asked, his voice dropping.

"No," I said, my voice steady despite the storm brewing inside. "He sensed her presence, smelled the smoke. Keithren could never let her know he was a dragon, but he couldn't resist taking her to his castle."

Keith's voice dropped to a teasing tone. "Does he lock her up in his sex dungeon?"

I snorted, the tension between us cracking for a moment. "No," I said, trying to shift under the covers. "She woke in a plush bedroom, surrounded by servants. But she grieved, and for days, she just cried."

He kissed the top of my head, running his fingers through my short hair. "Was she alone?" he asked, his voice low, almost possessive.

I took a deep breath, trying to keep my thoughts straight. "She felt alone. But a constant presence haunts her the room. It's Keithren, though she doesn't know it. He watches her, keeping his distance, but she can feel him."

Keith's thumb stroked my arm gently, the touch so light, but it burned with a quiet intensity that mirrored the growing tension between us. "What was he waiting for?"

I hesitated, the question hanging in the air as his fingers lightly traced the length of my arm. Every touch from him made it harder to stay focused. "He's waiting for her to accept what he's offering. The protection, the love... but she doesn't know how to trust him, not after everything she's lost."

Keith's hand slid from my arm to my side, his touch deliberate and warm, as though testing the boundaries between us. "How does she learn to trust him?"

I swallowed hard, aware of the heat flooding my body. "When she finally sees his true form, and she realized she has nothing to fear, she knows him as more than just the creature."

Keith wrapped his arms around me, the hair on his arms tickling my chest where my robe had fallen partially open. "And when she finally lets him in?"

My breath caught in my chest, the tension building with every word, every inch that separated us. "They can be together in every way."

"What happens next?" he asked, his voice hoarse, like he was barely holding back himself.

I slowly turned to face him, my heart hammering in my chest. The story blurred with reality, the line between the two becoming dangerously thin. His steady gaze locked with mine, dark and intense, pulling me closer without a single word. I swallowed hard, the warmth of his body pressing against mine, and for a moment, it felt like we were the only two people in the world.

I took a deep breath, the tension wrapping around us tighter, and shifted just slightly, my body inching closer to his. "The slow burn ends, and the heat turns up the spice level," I whispered, my voice barely above a breath as I sought out his eyes in the darkness.

"Rachel?" Keith's voice was rough and uncertain, but I understood.

The need for control rose in me, sharp and insistent. Leaning forward, I sealed my mouth to his, my lips claiming his with an intensity that surprised me. I deepened the kiss, pulling him closer, our bodies pressed together in perfect alignment. Comfort and desire tangled together, each touch only stoking the fire that burned within me.

All that mattered was the heat between us, the wild rhythm of our kiss. I shifted, pushing up to meet his gaze directly. I'd finished playing it safe, done with the games. No more hesitation.

I slid my hand down his chest, feeling the heat of his skin under my fingertips. My touch was deliberate, slow, but with an edge of confidence I hadn't known I possessed. "If you want the rest of the story," I murmured, my lips just inches from his, "you'll have to keep up with me."

Chapter 14

Keith

What would you choose as your favorite make-out music?
a) *The One That Got Away* – Katy Perry (a bittersweet, longing-filled moment)
b) *Lover* – Taylor Swift (a slow, intimate reconnection)
c) *Come Away With Me* – Norah Jones (a tender, emotional atmosphere)
d) *Need You Now* – Lady A (a passionate, desperate reunion)
e) *It Feels Like the First Time* – Foreigner (an electric, nostalgic passion)

Whoever thought books could be great foreplay?

I sure as hell hadn't. Not until Rachel wove her storytelling spell around us, her voice soft and alluring, drawing me in until I didn't know where the story ended and we began.

Wrapped in blankets, warm and flushed, her lips formed each word with an intimacy that sucked me in and left me aching. Every flicker of her gaze, every breath between sentences, pulled me closer. The space between us had felt smaller, the air heavier.

I'd wanted to touch her, really touch her, and then she took charge and kissed me.

The tension between us crackled, alive in every brush of her tongue and shift under the blankets. The slow burn was killing me, but I wouldn't rush her.

I wrapped my arm around her, loving the curve of her hip and the dip of her waist. I splayed my hand against the small of her back, urging her body closer.

Her robe loosened. The softness of her breasts flattened against the soft hair on my chest. She shifted, moaning as her pebble-hard, sensitive nipples met my flesh. The sound of her pleasure ricocheted down my spine, straight to my balls.

My cock grew stiff. Had it only been a few hours ago that I'd been so cold, I wondered if I'd ever see it again? I thrust my hips toward her, the fabric of our robes parting. My cock eased against the apex of her thighs, barely touching the wet heat of her. Instinct screamed inside me to pull her leg over my hip and slid inside.

But something held me back.

It had been months since I'd felt Rachel this close, skin to skin, nothing between us, and the longing was a physical ache. I wanted to bury myself in her, to claim her, to brand her as mine in a way no one else ever could. But the time apart hadn't just been about distance. It had been about reflection.

I needed more than casual sex. More than stolen nights and a hundred rules that kept me from getting close to anyone.

I wanted Rachel. Her social awkwardness and facts for every topic. Her intelligence and the way she lit up when talking about something she loved. I wanted the fire of her arguments, the softness she tried to protect, and the thoughtful way she saw the world.

If I had to be patient, I would be. Because this time, when I touched her... when I held in her my arms again, it wouldn't be just about desire.

It would prove I wasn't going anywhere. That we weren't just giving in to the magnetic pull between us. It had to mean more this time.

My voice was low when I spoke, the words heavy with intent. "Rachel, are you sure this is what you want?"

She hovered above me, her weight balanced on her palms against my chest. Her breathing had gone shallow, her lips slightly parted like she wanted to speak but couldn't find the words. I could feel the faint tremor in her fingertips where they pressed against my skin as her gaze searched my face.

Her silence was charged with tension, electric current prickling against my skin. My heart pounded, each beat fueling desire racing through my body. I clenched my fists against the sheets, resisting the urge to reach for her.

I lifted her off me and set her gently on the bed. "Princess, let's take a minute."

Rachel's breath came in shallow bursts, but no words emerged.

I rolled onto my back, the cold sheets seeping into my skin like icy fingers. The room felt cavernous, the faint crackle of the candle's flame amplifying the echo of everything left unsaid.

"Keith…" Despite the foot of space I'd put between us, she reached for me. Her small hand pressed against my shoulder. The bed shifted as she slid across the mattress until her hip met mine. We lay side by side, staring up at the moving shadows on the ceiling.

She sighed. "It's hard for me to talk sometimes."

"I understand."

She sighed, her fingers stilling against the sheets. "Trust is an issue with me."

I softened my gaze, my thumb still gently tracing her chin. "I know I've hurt you, and I'm sorry for that. But I'm not that guy anymore. I'm here because I want to be here, for you, and I'll do whatever it takes to show you I'm not going anywhere. We can take things slow, and I promise I won't hurt you again."

Her gaze flickered to mine, but she didn't speak. Instead, she leaned in, her lips brushing mine in a slow, careful kiss.

I cupped her cheek, my thumb grazing over her skin. "We'll do this your way. Do you want to establish some rules?"

She relaxed slightly, a small, almost imperceptible smile tugging at the corner of her lips. "Yes."

"Lay them out."

"Don't lie to me. Don't make promises you can't keep."

I held her gaze, letting her see the sincerity in my eyes. "Deal." Then I shifted back onto my pillow, giving her space while keeping my hand resting lightly on hers. "Rule two?"

She smirked. "Don't push me. Let me come to you."

I squeezed her hand gently. "Done and done. Anything you want?"

"I want everything," she whispered, so low I had to lean closer to hear her.

Heat pooled in my gut. "Everything?"

"Can we take a chance and see where this goes?"

I cupped her face with my palm, turning her head toward me. Nibbling at her lips, I said, "I'll follow you around like a lovesick puppy."

She snorted but kissed me back, a teasing smile tugging at the corners of her mouth. "I'll believe it when I see it."

I smiled into her kiss, my heart beating a little faster. Her words rang in my head like a challenge that I was more than willing to meet.

I kissed her neck. The steady beat of her pulse under my lips, a rhythm that echoed through my body. Her breath hitched, and I smiled against her skin, savoring the warmth, the closeness. Her hands tangled in my hair, pulling me closer as if the space between us was too much. Every inch of her felt like a temptation I couldn't resist.

Meeting her gaze, my thumb traced the curve of her jaw. "Are you sure about this?"

She looked at me, her eyes soft but steady, and nodded. "Yes."

Rolling onto my side, her body lined up with mine as we explored each other's mouths. Her sweet tongue brushed against mine, and I vowed to let her lead. To give her all the power.

The soft edges of her robe fell off her shoulder, exposing creamy skin. Trailing my lips over her cheek, I teased her ear with my teeth and tongue before moving lower. Skimming down her throat, I kissed the soft place where her heart pounded.

"I love your silky skin. The softness and the smell of your desire," my husky voice rumbled.

She shivered, the movement allowing one firm breast to peek out of her robe. Her body arched forward, silently begging for more.

Kissing across her collar bone, I nudged the fabric wider. My palm slipped between us to fondle her. Remembering how sensitive she was, I lifted the heavy globe, brushing my thumb over the peak.

She sucked in a breath, reaching for me blindly. "Keith..."

"What is it, Princess?" I asked, repeating the movement, relishing her reaction.

"I need more."

Bringing her with me, I rolled onto my back, lifting her to straddle my hips. The robe's sash fell open, and I skimmed my hands under it to slide it off her shoulders.

Rachel was a goddess. Her round bottom nestled on top of my hard cock. Her wet core beckoned me with honey sweetness as she planted her knees on either side of me and sat up.

"I love when you pick me up," she whispered. "I'm not too heavy?"

"Never. You're the perfect weight for my arms. Your curves are so sexy."

Her cheeks flushed a rosy pink as she let out a nervous laugh. "That's... sweet." She avoided my gaze, her fingers fidgeting with the hem my robe, the corners of her lips twitching between a smile and uncertainty. "I just—sometimes I overthink things, you know?"

I couldn't help but grin, the way her shyness only made her more endearing. God, she had no idea how beautiful she was, how perfectly she fit against my body. How could she think for a second she'd ever be too much for me?

"Hey," I said, tilting my head until our eyes met. "You don't have to overthink anything with me. You're not too heavy, too much, or too anything. Perfect."

Her shoulders relaxed, and she dropped her gaze, a faint pink coloring her cheeks as she bit her lip, clearly trying to hold back a smile.

"You know that blush? Definitely one of your best features."

She threw her head back, her hips moving as she let out a soft, exasperated laugh, clearly trying to hide the effect I was having on her.

Her laugh pushed me over the edge. Yanking her close, aligning our bodies together. Rubbing her slick warmth against my hardness.

"Keith, I—that's... so good."

"Are you close, Rach?" I asked even though I knew she was. Her rapid breathing and musky sent of her arousal told me all I needed to know.

Drawing her closer, I repositioned her. I wasn't ready to lose control of myself just yet. Guiding her forward, I kissed her breast, sucking her nipples into my mouth, using my tongue and teeth to pleasure her.

She leaned over me, and my hand slid between us to find her clit. Stroking her sensitive bud, I circled around and over it. She mirrored my movements with her hips, her breath ragged, sounds of pleasure escaping her lips.

Her body tightened as she reached the peak. Jerking hard, she gasped, her mouth coming down hard on mine as she came apart, ripples of pleasure shaking her to the core.

Swallowing her cries of satisfaction, I kissed her gently. Soothing her mouth with my tongue, sweeping my hands down her back to curl them under her bottom.

Rachel melted on top of me, breathing hard. Her pussy hovered just above my cock. Soft and wet, her inner lips brushed against me as she recovered. My dick ached to be inside her. It would be so easy to find my own release.

But for possibly the first time ever, that wasn't my goal. I wanted to be patient, to let her take the lead, even if it meant fighting the urge to push for more. Counting backwards from one hundred, I focused on clearing my mind, willing myself to think with my brain and not my body, but I forced my desire down. I wanted this moment to be hers.

We lay together. Her breathing quieted and she relaxed against me. Time ticked by slowly. I'd just reached forty when she lifted her head. "Aren't you...?"

I kissed her, sucking her bottom lip into my mouth. She tasted like honey and rich, dark chocolate, a decadent mix that left me craving more. I was addicted to her taste, sweet and irresistible, and the clean, fresh scent of her soap, like rain-soaked linen drying in the sun. Every sensation wrapped around me, pulling me deeper, until the rest of the world faded away.

She pulled away, blushing. "Keith, seriously. You should... you know."

"Fuck you?" I asked. Her breasts dangled in front of me, and I couldn't help scooping them up again. "Where's my naughty storyteller?"

Her eyes fluttered with pleasure as I teased the sensitive buds. "Are you going to fuck me?"

"I just want to make you feel good," I said as I brought her breasts to my mouth.

"Wait," she murmured, her voice soft but resolute. She pulled away, lying down on top of me. The robe fell away and we were skin on skin. "I want..."

Her words trailed off as she kissed her way across my chest, working her way down. Her mouth and tongue made a trail across my belly. My breath caught on a groan as she continued south.

Her breath brushed against my skin, warm and uneven, sending a shiver racing up my spine. My balls ached and my cock grew even harder. My heels dug into the mattress as she took me into her hand, squeezing and pumping.

"Rachel," I growled, not recognizing my own voice. "You don't have to..."

She looked at me, her eyes soft and sure, a smile tugging at her lips that felt like sunshine breaking through the clouds.

And then her mouth was on me. Her mouth tasted me from the bottom to top, lapping up the drops at the crown. Her hot mouth closed around me, sucking me deep.

A rough groan broke past my lips as I watched her, mesmerized by the beauty of her. My eyes crossed as she drew me deeper into her throat, the exquisite pressure of her mouth driving me mad.

My hands tangled in her short hair, tugging on the silky tresses. "I'm gonna come."

Her mouth popped off my dick. "I'm fine with that, or we could—"

I had her on her back in a second. My mouth fused to hers.

"Shit. I need a condom."

"I have some in my bag." She pointed to her purse on the table by the bed.

"Really?" I raised an eyebrow even as I dug through the bag.

She lifted a shoulder. "Just in case."

She took the packet from my hand, her fingers brushing mine before she tore open the pouch with deliberate precision. Rolling the sheath down my shaft with the utmost care, her head bent close, and I shuddered at how sexy she looked.

"Did you know there is a connection between gum disease and erectile dysfunction?" she asked as she admired her handiwork.

I barked out a painful laugh. "Good thing I brush my teeth."

Reclining against the pillows, her arms reached out to me, an unspoken invitation in the gentle curve of her movements.

I hesitated, my breath catching. What if I screwed this up, shattered this perfect moment with a wrong move? Or hurt her afterwards?

"Keith," she called softly, her voice wrapping around my name like a gentle caress, pulling me back to her. "I want you inside me."

The mental barriers that had been holding me back crumbled in an instant. The scent of her skin filling my senses, urging me to move faster. My mouth claimed her tongue as her legs twined around my hips.

"Please," she begged, arching up toward me.

Wet heat surrounded me, the sensation driving me to the brink. I drove into her. Her arms wrapped around my shoulders as she drank from my mouth.

We moved together, our bodies falling into a rhythm. Her knees grasped my sides, her heels digging into my buttocks. I thrust into her, finding the pressure spot that unraveled her.

She bit my neck, her sharp teeth egging me on. My balls tightened even though I knew it was too soon. The months without her left me too ready, too sensitive, too close to the edge.

I lifted my hips, my hand sneaking into her wet folds, circling her sensitive clit.

Rachel gasped. Her body froze for an instant before increasing her pace, meeting me stroke for stroke.

"You feel so damn good," I ground out.

"I love your body," she moaned.

The L-word. Not *I love you*, but a step to the side. I used to run from any utterance of love, afraid it would box me in, but now... I found myself liking it. It wasn't the pressure I'd assumed it would be.

I gave her clit another pinch, and her body pulsed around me. Her muscles squeezed tight, holding me deep inside her as she went over the edge.

A powerful wave crashed through me. The sight of her face, taut with passion, burned into my mind, each subtle expression, each breath she took, a memory I'd never forget as I followed her, lost in the feeling, every movement syncing with hers as if we were one.

Chapter 15

Rachel

What do you do when doubts creep in?
a) Ignore them—instincts are overrated.
b) Get quiet and introspective.
c) Explain them using a cause-and-effect chart.
d) Jump in with both feet, no sense wasting time.

The next morning, I woke to the soft, steady rhythm of Keith's breathing beside me. The room was cloaked in shadows, heavy curtains blocking out the light.

The sheets tangled around us, warm and heavy, their crisp hotel starch softened by a night of pleasure.

The curve of his jaw relaxed in sleep, his beard a rough shadow against the stark white pillow, the dark strands slightly uneven. His hair, usually tousled from running his hand through it, was now a true mess: flattened on one side, sticking up in soft waves on the other. His arm lay draped over me, heavy with sleep, his skin warm against mine.

Caught between the warmth of his presence and the quiet hum of my thoughts, I sank back into the pillows, their softness cradling me like the lingering traces of his touch.

Late last night, Keith had kissed me slowly, his lips warm and unhurried like a quiet promise. The moment had felt real. Important. Like something I could hold onto, even when everything else felt uncertain.

He'd held me deep into the night as we talked, our voices low and secretive, full of silly jokes and laughter. And for the first time, I let myself believe in them—not as distant possibilities, but as something real. Did that mean he was mine now?

My boyfriend?

The word felt foreign. Too simple to capture the emotion between us, the way he'd looked at me as if he were memorizing every breath I took, every curve of my body.

Despite wanting to stay wrapped in the cocoon of tangled sheets, two things pulled me away. I needed to pee. And I wanted to see the snow.

Slowly, I inched toward the edge of the bed, carefully lifting Keith's arm and letting it rest against the mattress. His warmth lingered on my skin as I untangled the blanket from around my legs and draped it over my shoulders before stepping toward the bathroom.

The small room was steeped in darkness, and I reached for the light switch, only to remember the power was out. Our phones were probably dead too. Under normal circumstances, being cut off would have sent me into a panic. But this morning, it felt strangely freeing. No buzzing notifications, calls, or messages pulling us back to reality.

Still snug with the blanket around my shoulders, I tiptoed across the room and peeled the curtain back to peer outside.

A thick layer of white blanketed the cars in the parking lot, softening them into rounded mounds. The street was untouched except for a few tracks left by early risers. A handful of people clomped through the drifts, breath puffing into the cold as they scraped their windshields. In the distance, a snowplow trundled past, its blade carving a path through the road with a low, metallic rumble. The beauty of it stole my breath.

"What's it look like out there?"

Keith's deep, sleep-roughened voice startled me so badly, I jumped, yanking the curtain closed. The light from outside disappeared, leaving me frozen by the window, my blanket pulled tightly against my chest.

"There's a lot of snow," I stammered, my voice shaky and high-pitched. My face warmed as I became hyper-aware of my nakedness beneath the warm fabric.

Keith rubbed his eyes, his hair mussed from sleep as he turned toward the blank alarm clock on the bedside table. "The power's still out?"

"Yep," I squeaked, my voice betraying the nervous flutter in my chest as I shuffled backward, scanning the room for my robe.

"Come here, Rachel." Keith's soft voice melted the butterflies in my belly, leaving a warm, fluttery ache behind.

He patted the bed next to him, pulling the covers back invitingly. His sleepy smile sent a fresh wave of heat to my cheeks. Helpless to resist, I tried to walk casually across the room, but the blanket wrapped around me tangled awkwardly around my legs.

"What's taking you so long?" Keith's amused voice teased, his tone light but enough to set my face ablaze.

"I'm coming!" I muttered, giving up on casual and hurrying the last few steps. I slid under the covers in a flurry, tucking my chilled feet against him as I snuggled up.

"Ack!" Keith exclaimed, jerking slightly away as my ice-cold toes brushed his legs. "Your feet are freezing."

"Sorry," I whispered, grinning against his chest as I pressed closer, soaking up his warmth. But I wasn't sorry—not even a little. Every inch of me buzzed from the heat between us, and I needed more.

His arm tightened around me, pulling me in despite the half-hearted complaint, his lips grazing my cheek before finding mine. "We need to warm you up," he murmured, his voice low and teasing, full of promise.

He deepened the kiss, his tongue stroking mine, and I melted into him, the chill of my skin forgotten in the growing heat between us. Pushing me back against the pillows, his hands trailed down my arms, leaving a path of warmth and shivers in their wake.

"You're still cold," he murmured against my mouth, his breath hot and sweet—but his lips were already pressing back into mine, like he had no intention of letting me go. "Better keep going…"

His fingers laced through mine, and he pressed our joined hands into the mattress on either side of my head. He leaned across me, the weight of him sending sparks dancing across my skin.

"Maybe you just like an excuse to manhandle me," I shot back, my voice breathless.

He grinned slow and mischievous, his dark eyes glinting with amusement. "You caught me," he said, his tone a mix of playful and sultry. "Do you mind?"

I pretended to consider. "I guess I can tolerate it… if you keep doing it just right."

His lips found my neck, tracing the sensitive curve, and I gasped, arching beneath him as his teeth grazed the delicate skin. One of his hands slid free of mine, traveling down my side in a slow, deliberate caress, the blankets falling back to expose my bare skin to the cool air.

"I'm starting to think this was your plan all along," I whispered, my voice trembling with half a laugh, half a moan, as his hand settled on my hip.

"Warming you up? Absolutely," he said, his voice rough with desire, the humor in his words softened by the tenderness in his touch. "You're impossible to resist."

Keith lowered his head to my breast. Nuzzling the plump flesh, he closed his lips on my nipple, laving it with his tongue before adding his teeth to increase the pleasure. I shivered, my body shaking with passion.

Shifting his weight and pressing me into the mattress, his hand smoothed over my side. "Still cold?" His voice was softer now, tinged with concern but threaded with playful challenge.

"A little," I lied. The heat of his touch had already chased away most of the lingering chill.

He hummed thoughtfully, his fingers tracing lazy circles along my hip. "Guess I'll just have to try harder."

Before I could respond, he released my hands and ducked his head under the covers, kissing his way down my body, his whiskers tickling. Nudging my thigh apart, he settled between them.

A puff of warm breath tickled my clit and my hips lifted. "Keith—" I started, but his lips silenced my words, his chuckle vibrating against my center.

His voice was muffled by the covers and the light kisses he placed on my sensitive skin. "It's for science. Heat transfer or something."

I laughed despite myself, shaking my head at his ridiculous excuse. "That's not how it works."

"Feels like it's working to me," he countered. Trailing his tongue along my folds, he parted them with his fingers.

All joking ceased, his touch sending a shiver through me. Laughter faded into soft gasps as he explored me slowly, learning what made me unravel, and savoring every second of it. His fingers slid deep inside me while he circled his tongue around my clit then sucked it into his mouth.

I teetered on the edge, sensation gathering. My hips arched toward him, an unspoken plea, begging him to send me spiraling over the summit.

His movements slowed, deliberate and maddening, keeping me suspended in that aching moment just before release. I let out a soft, frustrated whimper, my fingers clutching at his hair, holding him to me, my movements telling him I couldn't wait any longer.

He understood. Building up the pressure higher, my body responding to the rhythm he set. My breaths turned into gasps as the heat coiled tighter and tighter, as he watched me with hooded eyes filled with awe and something deeper, something that made my chest ache even as my body climbed higher.

"Keith—" His name left my lips on a desperate whisper. He set my body aflame, and when I thought the torture would go on forever, he sent me over the edge. My body came apart, pulsing with pleasure.

His big body crushed mine. "I have to be inside you, now."

"Yes," I nodded, my voice trembling with the weight of the moment.

"I should get a condom."

"No," I gasped as his brown eyes pierced my soul. "I want to feel you. Is that okay?"

"It's more than okay," he whispered. "You're the only woman I've been with in a year. I'm clean."

A year… that meant something, didn't it? Not just restraint, but choice. He'd been waiting for me.

My hands slid up over his shoulders, fingers pressing into his skin as I held on. "I'm on birth control."

He closed his eyes, taking a deep, shuddering breath and pushed into me with a powerful thrust. His hips retreated then thrust again. My knees bent, my legs wrapping around him as I met each movement.

It was a wild, crazy mating—fierce, unrestrained, and completely out of control. Every touch, every movement, we clashed with need and want in a raw, unspoken language only the two of us understood.

It was terrifying and liberating.

I'd spent my life orchestrating every detail, trying to control every possible outcome. But this? This was like stepping onto a stage without a script, free-falling with no safety net.

I felt alive.

Keith wasn't just an unpredictable variable. He was steady, solid, safe. As his hands traced over my skin, his touch almost reverent, I felt the tight grip I kept on my world loosen.

This was freedom.

Freedom to let go, to trust this man. Keith met my intensity with his own, his hands firm as if he knew exactly what I needed, exactly what I craved.

I arched into him, my body moving of its own accord, untethered by logic or fear. His name became a litany on my lips, with each whisper, gasp, or cry, and I felt myself breaking free of the walls I'd built so carefully around my heart.

And when I exploded, when he shouted my name, everything melded into light and sensation. I didn't feel like I was falling. I felt like I was flying.

***

The hum of the heater kicking on broke the stillness, a soft beep from the clock marking the return of power. I blinked at the red digits glowing faintly in the shadows, their steady march forward a reminder that time hadn't stopped.

Cuddled warm against Keith, his arm draped across me in a way that felt both protective and possessive, I couldn't help the slight sinking in my chest. The world would intrude on our fragile bubble.

Soon, I'd have to untangle myself from his warmth and face all the uncertainties that waited beyond these walls. There were still so many questions, so many lingering doubts I wasn't sure how to address.

And then there were the practicalities: retrieving our clothes from Glen, figuring out how to get home in the aftermath of the storm. The thought of dealing with all of it felt overwhelming, and I didn't want to let this moment slip away.

Keith's stomach growled loudly, breaking the comfortable silence. I couldn't help the giggle that escaped. I turned my head to look at him. His face relaxed, but the glint in his eye turned sheepish.

"Did you make that sound, or was it a bear?" I teased, poking his side.

"Very funny," he muttered, pulling me closer. "A man needs fuel after a night with you." His grin remained unrepentant, and the way he looked at me sent a familiar warmth coursing through me.

"Oh, so this is my fault?" I teased back, arching an eyebrow.

"Aren't you hungry?" His stomach growled again, echoing his question.

"Well, we don't exactly have a kitchen here," I reminded him. "Unless you're planning to raid the vending machine downstairs."

He grinned. "Think they've got those tiny bags of chips? Maybe some questionable granola bars?"

"Only the finest five-star cuisine," I said with a smirk, my fingers idly tracing circles through the hair on his chest. "Funny, though—I seem to remember someone acting *very* above vending machine snacks just two nights ago."

He matched my grin. "Okay, okay. I'm a pretentious ass. But in my defense, I hadn't just worked up an appetite like this."

His hand caught mine, stilling my movements. "I could call Glen. I wonder if they have room service?"

I gave him a look. "With the power just coming back? Good luck."

Keith sighed dramatically, flopping back against the pillows before reaching toward the blankets around me. "Guess I'll just have to eat you instead."

My cheeks flamed as I grabbed the fabric. I smacked his shoulder. "Keith!"

He laughed, catching my wrist and tugging me down until I pressed against him, his nose brushing mine. "What? It's true," he said, his grin softening into something warmer. "You're the best thing I've ever tasted."

"We should get up," I murmured, though my body had no intention of moving.

His lips trailed over my cheek. "Why?"

Because I was falling. Because everything felt too good, too easy, and that scared the hell out of me. I needed space to think, to breathe. Keith nibbled on my ear, my mind racing to come up with a response. Instead of forming a coherent sentence, I said, "Because... uh... gravity?"

Keith pulled back, one eyebrow quirking upward. "Gravity?"

"Yes!" I scrambled to sit up, nearly kneeing him in a very delicate area in the process.

"Whoa." Keith caught me by the waist, lifting me slightly to avoid disaster.

Unable to stop my mouth from running, I blurted, "We're defying it or something, and that's bad. Very bad. Physics and... science... and stuff."

He chuckled, reaching out to steady me as I teetered on the edge of the bed. "Rachel, are you having a stroke?"

"No, I just—" My flailing hand knocked over a half-empty soda can on the nightstand. It tumbled to the floor with a dull clatter, its contents mercifully contained. "—I'm fine!"

Grabbing the can as if it were some sort of shield, I felt my cheeks burn as Keith smirked, his amusement obvious.

Before he could say another word, a sharp knock echoed through the room.

"Good morning!" Glen's cheerful voice boomed through the door. "You two decent in there?"

Clutching the soda can like a lifeline, I froze, my eyes darting around the room. Where was my robe? Tangled in the blankets or somewhere on the floor?

Keith groaned, dragging a hand through his messy hair. "Depends on your definition of decent," he muttered under his breath.

"Keith!" I hissed, smacking his arm and scrambling off the bed. My foot caught on the edge of the blanket, and I nearly toppled over. "Don't tell him that!"

"Give us a second, Glen. We'll be right there," Keith called, completely unbothered.

I was drawn to the sight of him standing naked in all his unfiltered glory. The light caught his muscular frame, highlighting the smooth curve of his shoulders and the strong lines of his chest. Large bruises blossomed in blue and green on his hip and shoulder from yesterday's fall. His hair stuck up all over his head. Was his beard longer than it had been yesterday? He looked like a rugged mountain man. I felt my stomach flip.

Keith rummaged through the bed, finally pulling out a robe. He tossed me a smirk that only made my heart race faster. "You okay?" he asked.

I forced myself to focus on anything but him. "Uh, yeah. Fine. Totally fine," I said, my voice a little too high-pitched as I wrapped my blanket tighter around myself.

Glen stood in the hallway, balancing a tray piled high with the delicious, mouthwatering scent of pancakes and eggs. "Howdy, folks. Hope y'all slept well. I thought you might be hungry."

"That's kind of you, Glen." Keith smiled, accepting the tray with that easy charm that always seemed to make everything feel a little less complicated.

"Your clothes should be ready in about an hour," Glen said eagerly. "I'm not sure where you're headed, but the plows are out. The highway should be clear."

"That's great news," I exclaimed, though my words felt hollow compared to the tension building in my chest.

"Do you think you'll be checking out then? Or should I extend your stay, lovebirds?"

A sharp ache gripped my heart as if leaving this room would be unbearable. I glanced at Keith. His bare feet, robe fitting just right, balancing the tray like we had all the time in the world. Here, we were just us. No schedules, no pressure, no pretending.

But Keith's busted phone lay face up on the table by the door, its cracked, dark, and lifeless screen a stark reminder of the reality we were avoiding. He glanced at it, his expression tight.

And I knew reality was about to pop our bubble.

"We need to head home," Keith answered, staring down at his phone. His finger hovered over it for a second before he let out a frustrated sigh and tossed it aside.

My stomach twisted. It was a painful reminder of the things we couldn't outrun. Old wounds didn't heal overnight, and I couldn't shake the feeling that, once his phone was back in working order, he'd leave.

Chapter 16

Rachel

How would you prefer to spend a snow day?
a) Stay in bed all day, preferably with someone to keep you warm.
b) Make spiked hot chocolate and see where the cozy vibes take you.
c) Have a pajama party with your besties.
d) Warm your cold toes against a hard man.

The first thing I noticed when I woke up Monday morning was the stillness. No cars, no voices, no hum of life beyond my window. Just silence, thick and unbroken.

I hurried out to the living room in my pajamas, and there it was. A thin blanket of pristine white, softening the sharp edges of the world and muffling everything beneath it.

It had snowed in Marchfield.

For a moment, I just stood there, letting the quiet sink into my bones. It was the kind of morning that begged for coffee and old sweaters, curling up on the couch, and pretending the rest of the world didn't exist.

Last night flickered through my mind. A cold rain mixed with sleet started falling just as Keith pulled into my driveway. We'd sat in his truck for a moment, reluctant to leave the cocoon of warmth.

"Guess this is goodnight," he'd said, his voice low and rough, his hands resting loosely on the steering wheel.

I nodded, my hand on the door handle, though my heart wasn't ready to leave. "Goodnight, Keith."

His lips quirked into a half-smile. "I wish I could stay."

I felt the flush creep into my cheeks, but I couldn't help teasing him. "Stop acting like it's some noble sacrifice to go home. You're just afraid Barb will catch leaving in the morning."

He laughed softly, shaking his head. "One hundred percent. It's a school night, princess. Do you want to explain to your students why you look like you haven't slept in two days, or should I?"

"Fair point," I admitted, my mouth curving into a reluctant smile.

His grin softened, the teasing fading into something more serious. "But if it wasn't..."

I looked away, my chest tightening under the weight of what he didn't say. A tiny voice of self-doubt whispered, did he regret not staying, or feel relieved he didn't have to?

"If it wasn't," I said, my voice quieter now, "I'd probably ask you to stay."

Keith exhaled slowly, then leaned in, brushing his mouth against mine in a brief, fleeting touch. It wasn't enough.

I leaned back, my heart heavy with the thought of him leaving. What if it fades away? What if we're just a moment, nothing more?

I pushed open the door before I could second-guess myself any more. The sleet stung sharp against my skin, biting at the exposed parts of me. Already regretting this, already wishing I could stay a little longer, but there was no turning back now.

Keith pulled my luggage from the trunk as I fumbled with the keys to unlock my door. Before I could step away, his hand stroked my arm, then pulled me into him. His lips brushed mine in a kiss that was slow and deep, like he was trying to imprint the moment into my memory.

It wasn't just a goodbye; it was a promise, or maybe an unspoken plea. I could feel it in the way his hands tightened around me, in the way he lingered, as if he, too, didn't want to let go. But then he pulled away, and the cold outside felt even colder.

After he left, I tried to convince myself this felt better. Simpler. Cleaner. I pretended the ache in my chest was indigestion.

Now, my phone buzzed on the charger in the kitchen, yanking me out of my thoughts. Work emails, probably. But when I grabbed it, Keith's name lit up the screen.

I hesitated, thumb hovering over the notification. A stupid thought crawled into my head before I could stop it. Was his name lighting up someone else's phone right now too?

Why had that thought even crossed my mind? I trusted Keith. I did. But trust and certainty weren't the same thing, and doubt had a way of sneaking in through the cracks.

9:30 AM
Keith: The univarse gave us another snow day to recofer from our last one.

I stared at the message, my finger hovering over the screen as my heart twisted. "Univarse" and "recofer." The spelling mistakes stood out, but instead of feeling amused or judgmental, I felt a pang of something closer to understanding.

Keith never tried to hide his dyslexia, but he didn't exactly put it on display either. For him to send this message, knowing it might not be perfect, meant he hadn't overthought it. He'd just... written to me.

My thumb traced the edge of my phone as I reread the words. I could almost hear his voice, casual and warm, like the snow outside didn't matter nearly as much as letting me know he'd thought of me.

9:31 AM
Me: It's barely more than a dusting.

9:35 AM
Keith: In Marchfield? Same as 10 in NY.

Suddenly, I wanted to see him. The thought hit me like a wave, sharp and insistent, pulling me out of my carefully constructed solitude. I wondered if he'd want to see me too, or if last night had been enough for him, a neat ending to a messy story. Could I ask him? Would it ruin the fragile balance we'd managed to find?

Was I being ridiculous? Desperate? Or was this just... real?

My fingers hovered over the keyboard, my chest tightening. My fingers flew over the keys before I could chicken out.

9:40 AM
Me: What are you doing today?

The words stared back at me, heavy with everything I couldn't say. I hesitated for one breathless moment before hitting send, the sound of the message swooshing off into the void making my stomach twist.

Now all I could do was wait. And hope.

9:44 AM
Keith: Gym. See u aftr? @ 2?

I stared at the screen, my heart tripping over itself. His response sounded casual, yet something about it felt like an answer to all the questions that haunted me.

I swallowed hard, the rush of relief and nerves colliding in my chest. He wanted to see me. I typed my response and hit send before I could second-guess myself.

9:45 AM
Me: Yes. I'd like that.

And then it struck me. I needed help. I wasn't sure how to navigate what was happening between Keith and me, and I'd never been good at figuring these things out on my own. I needed perspective. People who weren't caught up in the middle of it, who could see things more clearly than I could through the fog of my own emotions.

I opened the group text with Val and Audrey and typed:

9:50 AM
Me: Emotional crisis! Can you come over?

I stared at the message for a moment, heart pounding. Writing it out made it real in a way I hadn't allowed it to be yet.

9:52 AM

Audrey: I'm still in my jammies, and I have to bring Liam.

9:53 AM
Val: Why are y'all up so early? It's a snow day!

9:54 AM
Audrey: Rachel needs us.

9:55 AM
Val: Or does she need coffee?

I laughed at Val's response, but it was true. I needed coffee.

9:58 AM
Me: Wear your PJs. See you in an hour.

By the time Audrey and Val pulled up together in Audrey's silver mini-van, I'd brewed a large pot of coffee and given Bolt his greens, his basking light on full blast. He sleepily munched on collards and blueberries before heading back to his cozy bed for a much-needed nap.

The clock on the microwave blinked 10:52 AM. I had three hours to get my emotions in order before Keith came over.

Dressed in warm flannel pajamas with the words *Shy Girl, Naughty Thoughts* across the front, I opened the door to help Audrey in with Liam, all bundled up in his car seat.

Barbara waved from her back door, and I motioned for her to come over. Her face lit up, and I bet she would bring more of those ridiculous penis cookies. Val and Audrey would definitely love those.

"Thanks for coming over," I said, stepping aside to let them in.

Val unbuttoned her puffy black coat, revealing candy apple red flannel pajamas underneath. Across the front, in bold letters, it read: *Hot Girl. Off Switch Not Included.*

Audrey raised an eyebrow. "Did Evan buy those for you?"

"My mom bought them." Val smirked. "Let's see yours."

Audrey peeled off her coat, revealing blue and white plaid pajama pants and a top emblazoned with bold white letters: *Take Me As I Am.*

"Like it," Val approved. "Is there coffee?"

"Of course," I said with a grin, gesturing toward the carafe on the kitchen counter.

Before anyone could react, Barbara swung the door open and breezed inside, no invitation necessary. Her snow-white hair was wrapped in a daisy-patterned silk scarf, and she carried a covered tin like it held the meaning of life.

"Good morning, girls!" she chirped, all warmth and good intentions. "I brought snacks. Thought you might need a little something sweet to go with all that coffee."

Val shot me a look, one brow arched.

"Barbara, these are my friends Val and Audrey," I said quickly, waving a hand toward her. "Barb is my landlady, friend, and incessant busybody."

The older woman shot me a mock glare, though her grin never wavered. "Don't listen to her. I'm a delight." She held up a tin of cookies like a prize, but I barely registered it. My gaze darted to the clock—11:05 AM.

Audrey stepped forward, Liam snoozing in his car seat. "I'm Audrey, and this is my plus-one, Liam."

Val passed Audrey a cup of coffee. "I'm Val. And what kind of snacks are we talking about?"

Barbara winked as she set the plate down. "The kind that'll make you laugh and maybe blush. Let's just say I hope you're not too shy."

My mouth dropped open. "You didn't bring edibles over at eleven in the morning, did you?"

"Oh stop," Barb shushed me. "I save those for after five."

Val lifted the foil, revealing the infamous penis cookies. She burst out laughing, while Audrey choked on her coffee.

"Oh, I like her," Val declared, helping herself to one. "Barbara, you're my kind of people." She took a bite of her cookie, grinning wickedly. "Okay, Rachel. Spill. How was your adventure with Mr. Tall, Dark, and Distractingly Handsome?" She sank down on my sofa with a sigh and kicked her snow boots off.

Audrey smirked as she cradled a now-stirring Liam in the easy chair. "You made us drive through the snow, risking our lives. This better be a great story."

Barbara, who was already on her second cookie, came around the counter with her own coffee, eyes sparkling. "Ooh, there's a tale here. I can smell it."

Audrey leaned in, her eyes wide with excitement. "So, tell us everything. Did Keith let you drive his truck?"

Val, sipping her coffee, smirked. "Did you share a bed? Or did you stick with the just friends act?"

Barbara grinned, her voice low with mock seriousness. "There's gotta be some juicy details."

Heat rushed to my cheeks. I wanted to talk about Keith. I really did. But the second I tried to put the memories into words, it felt too raw, too exposed.

The clock blinked **11:26 AM**.

Time was flying by. My pulse hammered in my ears. If I couldn't get the words out now, I'd have to face him with nothing but scrambled thoughts and a stomach full of caffeine and panic.

Val's sharp gaze followed mine to the clock, then back to me. "Tick-tock, Rach."

Barbara clucked her tongue. "Nothing good ever came from rushing."

My heart clenched. I'd sent out the SOS—now I had to follow through before time slipped away. If I could just get the words out, just ask the right questions, these women could help me. Every second of silence was a second closer to facing Keith unprepared.

"Okay, fine. But I'm not giving you all the details. You'll just have to wait for my memoir."

"Oh, please," Val said, her tone dripping with mock disbelief. "You disappeared with him for three days, came back late without a word to us, and you expect us to believe nothing happened?"

Audrey draped a blanket over her shoulder, a knowing smile tugging at her lips as she loosened her top to breastfeed Liam. "We're here to support you, not judge you. But we are going to need details. Especially if they're juicy."

Barbara chuckled and leaned closer. "Sweetheart, I'm in my eighties. You're not going to shock me. Spill the tea."

Cradling my own mug like a lifeline, I shifted from one foot to the other. "It's just... complicated."

Val snorted. "Of course it's complicated. Everyone says women are high maintenance, but it's really men. Now, start at the beginning. Did he make a move on you in the truck?"

"You're impossible," I said as I sank down onto the floor, picking up Bolt and holding him in my lap.

Liam made soft slurping sounds as he ate. Audrey softened. "Seriously, Rach. We're not trying to pry. We just want to make sure you're okay."

"Well, that's a joke," I said, with a laugh as I gathered the courage to continue. "We got stuck in the snow, had to share a room, and then...."

The room stilled. All eyes locked on me.

"Wait, wait—don't hold out on us, Rach! Details!" Audrey leaned in, her grin wide and mischievous.

I cleared my throat. "It was cold and the power went out, and, well, we had sex."

Val's jaw dropped. "Wait, what? I figured he'd hit on you, but—"

Barbara whooped and shoved a penis cookie into my hand. "Oh, sweetheart, now we're talking. Don't skimp on the details."

Audrey tapped a finger against her coffee cup, studying me like a scientist might examine a worm. "Was it better or worse than the first time?"

Barbara perked up, setting her drink down with an eager thud. "I wish we had a whiteboard and markers."

"A Venn diagram, right?" Val shot her hand up for a high-five.

Barbara smacked her palm against Val's with a satisfied grin. "Exactly. We could chart emotional growth versus sheer hotness factor."

A Venn diagram? Really? My cheeks burned. I was in uncharted territory, still trying to figure out my life. And they were turning it into a school project?

11:52 AM. Time kept slipping forward, and I still didn't know what I'd do when Keith got here.

Val snatched my romance novel journal off the end table and flipped to a blank page, tapping her pen against the margin. "You told us the closet was frantic, out-of-control heat. How about his time?"

Barb fanned herself dramatically. "Young love is so hot." She leaned back, a wistful look crossing her face. "I remember when my husband and I couldn't keep our hands off each other." She winked. "Ah, the good old days."

Audrey snickered, and I, still trying to hide my smile, finally gave in. "Alright, alright, enough with the nostalgia trip." She shifted uncomfortably in her seat. "It felt different. Less rushed. More..." I trailed off, cheeks burning.

"More what?" Barbara waggled her brows.

I exhaled, getting to the root of my fears. "Emotional. He says he's changed. That he hasn't slept with anyone in a year."

The room went quiet for a moment. I could feel all three of their gazes on me, waiting. I shifted uncomfortably, suddenly feeling exposed.

Audrey was the first to break the silence, her voice light but thoughtful. "Well, that's... interesting. I mean, people change, right?"

Val tapped her pen against the notebook. "Let's break it down, Rach. What was Closet Keith like?"

I thought back to that night, the heated rush of the moment, the way he'd been all about the physical, no strings attached. "Casual, all hands, no promises." The words left my mouth before I could stop them, and I could feel the weight of them hanging in the air.

Barbara sighed, leaning back in her chair, her eyes glazing over slightly as if daydreaming. "I wouldn't say no to some of that."

"And Snowstorm Keith?" Audrey's gaze turned gentle but probing, as if she could see through me and into the heart of what I struggled with.

I took a deep breath, trying to steady myself. The memory of the night in the snowstorm was still vivid, the soft laughter, the quiet moments between us that felt real. "He let me make the rules and set the pace. He made me laugh. We cuddled."

Barb raised an eyebrow, the corners of her lips curling into a sly grin. "Sounds like Snowstorm Keith might have more substance than Closet Keith."

Audrey's eyes gleamed. "What happened when you got back?"

I hesitated, the memory of his kiss at my door flashing through my mind. "He kissed me goodbye."

"And?" Val pressed.

I sighed. "And this morning, he texted that he wanted to see me later."

Audrey nodded. "How does that compare to Closet Keith?"

He'd casually swiped through dating apps while I was in the bathroom, completely unaware.

Out loud, I said, "I saw him on the dating apps." I winced as the words left my mouth. "It felt like I'd never be able to trust him again."

Barb leaned forward, her eyes narrowing. "Hmm, I guess it's time I see if Keith is worthy of my girl. Don't worry, I've got some top-notch investigative skills." She grinned. "I'll scope him out to make sure he's not hiding any skeletons…"

Audrey waved a hand dismissively. "He's changed. He's checking in, making plans like a man in a relationship." She leaned forward, eyebrows raised. "So why are we here, Rachel? Why send out the SOS?"

I exhaled, my fingers tightening around my coffee mug. "I don't want to be stupid about this," I muttered, avoiding their gaze.

Barbara gave me a sidelong glance, a glint in her eyes. "You're not stupid, Rach. But if you want my expert opinion, I'd suggest you let me do some research. See if he passes the Barbara Test."

Val nodded smirking. "We've got you. Let us help."

"He says he deleted the apps, but he gets calls all the time, and he steps out to take them. At first, I convinced myself I didn't care, but now... I wonder. I'm not sure I can keep pretending I don't notice." I chewed my lip, thinking. "I want to trust him, but how can I when his phone keeps pulling him away?"

Val leaned back in her chair, tapping her fingers thoughtfully. "Have you talked to him about it?"

"No," I answered, my voice tight.

Barb leaned in, her eyes narrowing. "You've got to have that conversation, Rachel. You've got to trust yourself enough to ask the hard questions. And trust him enough to tell you the truth."

I wrapped my hands around my coffee mug, letting the heat seep into my palms and chase away the chill creeping into my chest.

Keith might think he wanted me now, but what if he got bored or frustrated when the novelty wore off? My ASD and anxiety would never go away, and he would get tired of it... and me. I wasn't sure my heart could take another crash.

Audrey must have noticed the flicker of something in my expression because she reached over, squeezing my arm gently. "Hey. You okay?"

I nodded, pasting on a small smile that I hoped looked convincing. "Yeah, just trying to untangle the emotional spaghetti in my head, no big deal."

Audrey's expression softened, but before she could press further, I latched onto the nearest distraction.

Liam had dozed off on Audrey's shoulder, his little footie pajamas stretched snug across his bottom. His fingers twitched occasionally, a small repetitive motion. "So, how's Liam? He looks bigger every time I see him."

Audrey's face lit up, the kind of glow only a proud mom could manage. "He's not sleeping great at night, so it's been a little rough, but Oz is a champ. He gets up with him half the time."

Val grinned, leaning over to tickle Liam's tiny foot where it peeked out of his blanket. "He's adorable, Audrey. Totally worth the sleepless nights."

Audrey snorted. "Easy for you to say. You get to sleep eight hours and wake up looking like a Pinterest board."

"Pinterest board?" Val scoffed, flipping her hair dramatically. "More like 'before' picture in a dry shampoo commercial. But go on, tell me how perfect I am."

Barb smiled, leaning back with her coffee. "Sweetheart, if you're the before, I don't even want to think about what the rest of us are."

Val grinned, tossing her hair "Good hair genes and an unshakeable sense of style. It's a burden, really."

Audrey rolled her eyes. "Yeah, it's a real tragedy. Val's hair gets its own spotlight, and the rest of us just exist in the shadows. Anyway..." She turned to me, her tone shifting. "How's Yona holding up at school? I'm dying to know if she's already questioning all of her life choices."

Barb chuckled. "If she's smart, she'll bribe the kids with snacks. Works every time."

Val grinned. "Or threaten them with detention."

12:12 P.M. Less than two hours left.

I laughed, but it was forced. "She's doing fine, actually. The kids like her, and she's surprisingly good at keeping things under control. No bribes or threats necessary."

The conversation swirled around me, but my thoughts were miles away, racing back to Keith.

How should I act? What if we had sex again? Did that signal we were taking things further, or just a repeat of the mess we'd already started? Was he my boyfriend now?

I forced myself to focus on their voices, but the urgency in my chest didn't let up. Time ticked down, and I had no idea how to handle what came next.

Audrey sighed, though a smile tugged at her lips. "They'll all cry when I come back. The Wicked Teacher of the West."

My throat tightened. What if Keith was coming over to break up with me?

"Please," Val said, rolling her eyes. "You're their favorite, and you know it."

What if he's already moved on? The thought made my stomach churn.

"Favorite? I've seen the memes they've made about me," Audrey retorted. "Last year, they photoshopped me onto a wanted poster and taped it to my classroom door."

I tried to force my mind back to the present, but all I could see was his face, his hands, his voice. What if I'd read it all wrong?

Barb chuckled, chiming in. "Sounds like a promotion to me. At least they know who's boss."

12:45 P.M. Less than an hour now, and I was running out of time. I shifted uncomfortably in my seat, desperately trying to shake off the thoughts spiraling in my head. I needed them to go.

I forced a smile, trying to sound light. "I, um, think I need to get ready before Keith comes over."

Audrey raised an eyebrow but didn't argue.

Val gave me a teasing look, though her eyes softened with understanding. "Listen, you've got this. Just be honest with him. You're not obligated to have all the answers right now." She leaned in a bit, her voice softer. "And whatever happens, don't let the fear of messing up stop you from taking the leap."

Audrey carefully tucked Liam into his car seat, draping a soft blanket over him as his tiny head lolled to one side in sleep. She glanced up, her expression turning mischievous. "Speaking of telling people how you feel…"

Val groaned, already anticipating where this was headed. She held up a hand, her voice dry. "Don't start, Audrey."

But Audrey's grin widened, undeterred by the warning. "Oh, come on, Val. Have you figured out how you're going to do it yet?"

I blinked, glancing between them. "Do what?"

"Propose," Audrey said, practically bouncing in her seat. "She's been dropping hints about popping the question to Evan for weeks, but he's not taken the bait."

Val gave Audrey a mock glare before turning to me with a small smile. "I was waiting for the right moment to tell you, Rach, but yes, it's true. Remember how Evan wanted to marry me last year, but with my parents divorcing and all the drama, I just wasn't ready?"

"Yeah, I remember."

Determination flickered in her eyes. "Well, I'm ready now, but Evan won't take a hint, so I've decided I'm going to propose to him instead."

My eyes widened in awe. Val was so bold, so fearless in taking charge of her own happiness. "Do you have a plan?"

"Not yet," Val admitted. "But when I do, it's going to be perfect. I want it to be something he'll never forget."

Audrey leaned forward, her eyes gleaming. "I'm just saying, if it involves fireworks or a flash mob, I want in."

Val snorted. "You'll be the first to know. But no flash mobs. We're teachers; we can't afford to get arrested for public disruption."

Barb smiled wickedly. "Picture this: you show up at the door, dressed to the nines, holding a sparkly rock in one hand and two tickets for a weekend getaway trip. Then you look him dead in the eyes and say, 'I'm done waiting. Here's the ring. Make it official.'"

Val raised an eyebrow, clearly entertained. "Not a bad idea, Barb. I might just do that."

Audrey grinned. "See, Rachel? This is why we all need a wise mentor with penis cookies our lives."

Barb winked, her youthful energy undeniable. "You're welcome, darlings. When's the next club meeting?"

Chapter 17

Keith

What would you do if your friends barged in when you had romantic plans?
a) Play it cool and pretend nothing was about to happen.
b) Give them the death glare until they take the hint and leave.
c) Whisper a promise to pick up where you left off—later, with interest.
d) Invite them to stay... but make sure they know exactly what they interrupted.

I had a plan. Get a good workout in, then swing by Rachel's to pick up where we left off yesterday morning.

I grabbed my keys and checked the time. **11:15 AM**, plenty of time to be at Rachel's by two.

It had only been a night, but I already missed her. I didn't just want her. I wanted to be with her. To spend a quiet afternoon with her and hear her laugh. To remind her that whatever this was, it was more than I'd ever wanted before.

The doorbell rang.

It was followed by a sharp knock. Impatient. Persistent.

Damn it. I had a bad feeling about this.

I opened it to find Bobby, Oz, and Evan standing there, grinning like fools. They were loaded down with enough sandwich fixings and chips to feed an army.

"Yo, man! We brought the goods!" Bobby declared, holding up a bag of chips like she'd just won an award.

"What the hell is all this?" I asked, raising an eyebrow as she pushed past me.

She kicked her boots off inside the door, and the others followed suit like a damn invasion force.

"Poker night," Oz said, stepping into my living room without so much as a glance for permission. "Only earlier since it's not even noon. We're taking over your space."

"Yeah, you've got the only table big enough for us," Evan added, flashing a cocky grin as he peeled off his coat. "And room for the food, too."

Jaw loose, I stood there. They'd caught me off guard.

"Guys, I'm heading out," I started, jingling my keys.

"Uh-uh, nope," Bobby cut me off, smirking. "You've got hot gossip, and we're here as your supportive friends. To listen and tease you." Her words were light, but serious.

"And interrogate," Oz added, cracking his knuckles.

Evan nodded, his eyes serious. "Yeah, man. We just wanna make sure your head's on straight."

Bobby flopped onto my couch, legs stretched out like she owned the place. "We love Rachel. So, if you're messing around..."

I let out a deep breath. Of course, this wasn't just about annoying me. They were here to protect Rachel. And, damn it, I respected that.

I checked the time. 11:35 AM. I'd give them an hour, before kicking them out.

I exhaled through my nose, forcing a grin as Bobby dumped the chips onto my table like a dealer at a casino. "Fine. But I'm calling it now—I'm winning, and you're all out of here by twelve-thirty."

Oz smirked. "We'll see about that."

Evan scowled at him. "We've got all afternoon."

I clenched my jaw. Not if I could help it. I needed them in and out, fast. Rachel was waiting.

Tension built in my chest, coiling tighter with every passing second. I needed to go to the gym. I needed the burn, the sweat to sort out my emotions.

Oz slouched in the chair, arms crossed over his chest, his brow furrowed as if permanently annoyed by the world. The five o'clock shadow on his face made him look tired and grumpy.

His mood was the perfect distraction. I grabbed a bag of chips. "You alright, man?"

Oz yawned. "Liam isn't sleeping great, so I'm just here for the intimidation and a nap between hands. You know how it goes with the newborn sleep schedule."

Bobby raised an eyebrow. "Babies are just like the military. Everything's regimented, everyone's on edge, and the minute you think you've got a plan, the whole damn thing falls apart."

Oz chuckled. "Except now, it's not an enemy you're dealing with; it's diapers and endless crying."

"Shame," Bobby teased. "You were always the life of the party."

"Still am," Oz shot back with a grimace. "But the party's quieter these days."

"Yeah, I totally agree," I said, nodding as I grabbed another chip. "Raising Sunshine was a full-time job—hell, more than full-time, if that's even possible. It wasn't just about keeping a roof over her head or getting her to school on time. There's no room for dating or hookups when you're a single parent."

Now that Sunny was getting her master's, I felt lonely. The house turned too quiet, and there was no one to talk to. A hole formed in my life, and I hadn't realized how big it grew until Rachel.

My focus drifted back to the clock. 11:57 AM. Time slipped through my fingers. "What's up with Val lately?" Bobby interrupted my thoughts, her voice cutting through the buzz of the kitchen. The guys had set up the game and were now making sandwiches. The smell of deli meats and bread made my stomach twist a little.

Evan's thoughtful gaze landed on Bobby. "What do you mean?"

She shrugged, slapping mayo on a sub roll. "She's been different lately."

Evan said, tapping his finger on the table. "Huh. I thought it was just me. It's almost like she's waiting for me to figure something out."

Oz slapped a giant sandwich on a plate. "You sure you're not just missing the signals, man?"

"Maybe she's trying to get you to pop the question," I snickered.

Evan sighed. "Last year she said she'd let me know when she was ready."

Bobby punched him in the shoulder. "Maybe that's what she's doing."

I tried to focus on the conversation, but all I could hear was the ticking of the clock, each second pulling me further from Rachel.

12:07 P.M.

The urgency built in my chest, a pressure I couldn't shake. I wanted to let her come to me, but I wasn't sure I had that patience. And what if I read everything wrong? What if this was just a fling to her, and I was already too deep? Every tick of the clock felt like a countdown to something—what exactly, I wasn't sure.

"What are you gonna do?" Bobby asked, her eyes sharp as she fixed me with a look that told me I wasn't off the hook. Evan ran a hand through his hair, his face a mix of confusion and realization. "I guess... maybe I need to take the hint. I want to marry her. But the pressure of a surprise engagement is rough."

Oz nodded slowly, his tone serious. "Yeah, I get it. But sometimes, you just have to... take the plunge. No perfect moment. Just... go for it."

Bobby laughed, her voice teasing. "Says the man who orchestrated a proposal that people still talk about to this day."

Oz dealt the cards. The game began, and we settled into a rhythm... of them harassing me.

"Alright, Keith," Evan said, leaning back in his chair as he studied his cards. "I hope you're not planning to fold every round."

"Keith's poker face is so bad, it's like he's holding a neon sign that says, bluffing here!" Bobby added with a smirk, grabbing a handful of chips.

I rolled my eyes, tossing a chip into the pot. "Fuck off."

Evan laughed "Keith, you might as well hand over your wallet now and save us all the time."

"Don't worry, Keith," Oz said, his voice edged with sarcasm. "If you screw up this hand, we'll just blame it on you trying too hard not to break Rachel's heart."

Shaking off the threat, I said, "Let's see how long you all keep running your mouths when I take this pot."

"You're talking a big game for someone who hasn't mentioned how the weekend went with Rachel," Evan said, leaning back in his chair.

Bobby eyes darted toward me with a smirk that immediately put me on edge. "Yeah, spill it. Did you two spend the whole time talking about curriculum strategies, or did things get... extracurricular?"

I groaned, tossing a chip into the pot. "You guys are worse than middle schoolers."

"Don't dodge the question," Bobby scolded. "Details, Payt. We want details."

"There's nothing to tell," I said, though my pulse betrayed me, quickening at the memory of Rachel's laugh, her hesitant smile, the way she'd looked as I plunged deep into her body and she came apart in my arms.

I looked at my watch again. 12:15 PM. I need to hurry these guys up.

"I call," I said, my voice steady. I leaned back. "Let's see your cards."

Bobby's brows shot up. "Oof, bold," she muttered, setting her cards down face down, folding with a grin. "I'm out. Y'all can fight over it."

Evan gave a low whistle. "Now this is getting interesting." He pushed his cards forward and flipped them over. "Two pair. Queens and nines."

Oz's smirk faltered just a little. With a sigh, he tossed in his cards—king-high bluff.

"Seriously?" Bobby laughed. "That's what you were running with?"

Oz shrugged. "Had to try."

All eyes turned to me.

I turned over my cards with quiet confidence. "Straight."

Then Bobby let out a bark of laughter. "Well damn."

Evan pushed his chair back with a groan. "Unbelievable."

Oz narrowed his eyes but offered a nod. "Guess Rachel's not your only lucky hand."

We dealt the cards again and continued to play.

"So, what happened this weekend?" Bobby asked.

"Nothing to tell," I said, but the guys weren't buying it.

Oz leaned back with a smirk, folding his arms across his chest. "You're too much of a player for nothing to happen."

The hairs on my neck stood up. That wasn't fair. I wasn't that guy anymore. I'd changed. And it pissed me off that they were still giving me shit.

I slammed my hand on the table, frustration rising. "I'm not messing around, Oz. Rachel's different. This is serious."

"Prove it," Oz said, leaning forward with a raised eyebrow, his arms crossed over his chest.

"Fuck you," I growled, throwing my cards down and storming away from the table. I spun on my heel, glaring at them. "You want proof I've changed? You just have to open your eyes. Have any of you seen me with a woman besides Rachel in the last year?"

Frustration boiled over, my fists clenched at my sides. "You think I've been playing some game with Rachel? That I'm just fucking around? I'm not. I've worked my ass off, trying to be better, trying to do right by her. And if you can't see that, then maybe you're the ones who don't get it."

Oz's grin was gone. "You're right, man," he said finally, his voice quieter. "But you hurt her bad last year."

I nodded, my jaw clenched. "I won't mess this up again."

Evan raised an eyebrow, a chuckle bubbling up in his chest. "Sounds like he's sincere."

"Looks like our boy Keith's finally grown up." Oz smiled.

"I called it!" Bobby crowed, almost too satisfied. She motioned to Evan and Oz with her palm up. "Y'all owe me ten bucks."

I glared at them, but I couldn't suppress a grin. "You guys are the worst."

"Our resident Romeo wants to settle down." Bobby smirked as she collected the cash. "I knew you'd fallen in love."

My stomach dropped. Love? The word hit me like a punch to the gut. I wasn't ready for that.

"I—I'm—" I cut myself off. Was I in love? The question kept circling in my head, buzzing like a damn fly I couldn't swat away. No. I couldn't be. It was too soon.

I checked my watch. **12:47 PM.** Time was up.

"Thanks for the vote of confidence, Bobby," I muttered. "Now, you guys need to leave."

Bobby smirked. "Hit a nerve, did we?"

"Get out." I pointed to the door.

They chuckled but didn't argue, packing up their stuff and filing out with the smug satisfaction of a job well done. As the door clicked shut behind them, I ran a hand through my hair, exhaling sharply.

Forget the gym. I needed to shower, pull myself together, and get to Rachel's. No waiting. No second-guessing.

It was time to prove I wasn't the idiot I'd been last year. I could be there for Rachel and show up when it mattered.

But love? That was a whole other story.

The thought of it made my chest tighten. Could I be in love with Rachel? We'd only just started to figure things out again. A month ago, she'd hated me, and since then... it had been a whirlwind of fighting and figuring out how to teach together. We needed to try to find a balance between what we were and what we could be.

Love felt like a hell of a leap. But I knew that I couldn't walk away.

Chapter 18

Keith

What would you do if a sweet, well-meaning older lady cockblocks you?
a) Sigh deeply, accept your fate, and tell yourself it wasn't meant to be.
b) Pretend you can't hear her over and casually slip away.
c) Charm her with a compliment and a little small talk before making up an excuse.
d) Enlist her help! Who better to vouch for you than a sweet older lady?

Because I was nervous, I decided to walk to Rachel's to calm down. The air smelled sharp and crisp and my breath puffed small clouds with each exhale. The streets were quiet, most people staying inside to avoid the biting cold.

Marchfield was a charming patchwork of architecture and styles. The houses weren't cookie-cutter, each one telling a story of its own. Several stately Victorians stood side by side, their wide porches dusted with a thin layer of snow, railings edged with icicles glinting faintly in the pale winter sunlight. A few were already been decked in holiday greenery, their tall windows framing holiday candles.

Nestled between the Victorian homes, a warm, inviting Craftsman house caught my eye. Its low-pitched roof and deep eaves wore a blanket of snow, while the brick chimney puffed out soft curls of smoke that dissolved into the icy blue sky.

My boots crunched through the thin layer of snow on the pavement as I made my way toward Rachel's, leaving a trail of prints behind me.

I turned into the driveway of Mrs. Bartlett's mid-century modern home, its clean, angular lines a striking contrast to the more traditional styles nearby. The flat roof was lightly dusted with snow, and the large floor-to-ceiling windows offered a glimpse of a cozy interior, the glow of a fireplace flickering inside. A simple concrete pathway, framed by low shrubs capped in frosty white, led to the front door, where a modern wreath of twigs and berries hung.

Behind the main house, Rachel's carriage house stood like its smaller sibling. Similar in design, it looked like a scaled-down version of Mrs. Bartlett's home, its flat roof and wide windows perfectly mirroring the mid-century aesthetic. A warm light spilled out from its windows, pooling softly onto the snow-covered lawn and giving both buildings a welcoming charm.

The red door of Rachel's apartment glowed like a beacon through the winter dusk. The soft crunch of snow beneath my boots felt oddly satisfying as I pictured Rachel inside, maybe curled up with a book or working on lesson plans. My pace quickened, my focus narrowing on getting there, on seeing her, on the way she'd smile when she opened the door.

"Keith, dear!"

The familiar voice made me stop mid-step, my shoulders tensed as Mrs. Bartlett peeked her head out of her door. Bundled in a thick knit scarf and a puffy coat that swallowed her small frame, she stepped out of her house and waved.

She looked tiny and frail. Not at all like the cheery, robust women I'd met before. Her small hand clutched the doorframe for support.

"Could I trouble you for a moment?" she asked, her voice tinged with that unmistakable mix of neighborly warmth and Southern charm that left no room for a polite refusal.

I forced a smile, glancing toward Rachel's place. The walk had taken longer than I expected, and it was already two-thirty. Too damn late to be offering assistance.

I didn't have time for this. Not today. Every moment here was one I could have spent tangled up naked with Rachel. And another minute she had to convince herself I wasn't worth the risk.

But Mrs. Bartlett had that unmistakable grandma energy, the kind that made ignoring her impossible. So, I stayed, even as the clock worked against me.

"Of course, Mrs. Bartlett," I said, stuffing my gloved hands into my coat pockets to hide my reluctance.

"I've been decorating for the holidays, and I was hoping you might put the lights up on my house? Holiday lights make everything more cheerful, don't you think?"

"Of course, Mrs. Bartlett, I'd be happy to help."

Because nothing says freezing my ass off on a ladder sounds like a great use of my day off from school.

Reluctantly, I followed her Inside. The house was warm and smelled faintly of cinnamon, like she'd been baking earlier. The strings of lights were in a cardboard box, tangled and knotted.

As I loosened them, testing each strand to see if it worked, Mrs. Bartlett hovered nearby, chatting about everything from the weather to her bridge club. I tuned her out, nodding and making sounds of affirmation occasionally. How long was this going to take?

"I understand those cookies I gave you may have spiced things up during your trip," Mrs. Bartlett said with a sly smile as I untangled the last cord. "Not that I'm fishing for details, but I do love a good romance. Did the sugar work its magic, or do I need to add more spice next time?"

Her words hit me like a snowball to the face, and I blinked. Was I getting grilled by and eighty year old woman?

"You know, my husband and I were married almost fifty years. We raised three boys and taught them to be good men who didn't waste time when they found someone worth keeping."

Damn if that didn't feel like a direct hit. I forced a chuckle, shifting the lights in my hands. "Sounds like they had a hell of a role model."

Mrs. Bartlett smiled, clearly pleased with herself, before nodding toward the open garage. A metal ladder leaned against the wall, surrounded by neatly stacked boxes of decorations, all waiting for their moment to shine.

I positioned the ladder securely against the side of the house and climbed up to begin attaching the lights to the gutters. The wind was bitter, stinging my face, but I slipped off my gloves to make the work easier.

Mrs. Bartlett gave the ladder a firm shake, testing its stability. "Don't worry, dear, I've got you." Her small hands rested on the rungs, but her voice took on a wistful edge. "I look out for my sweet Rachel, you know. She's like the daughter I never had, but she pretends she doesn't need anyone. And if you hurt her, Keith, well—" She patted the ladder. "I might just forget to hold this steady."

Her tone was light, but the warning landed all the same.

I looked down at Mrs. Bartlett, trying to hide the way her words made my chest tighten. "Don't worry, Mrs. Bartlett. I'd never hurt Rachel. I've got a thing for *not* ending up in a hospital... or in a feud with anyone who bakes cookies as good as yours."

Mrs. Bartlett chuckled. "Good answer, dear. But this isn't about me or my cookies. Rachel doesn't let people in easily, but when she does, she gives them a hundred percent. She's awkward in ways most people don't understand, and it's hard for her. She cares about you, even when she tries to pretend she doesn't. You hurt her last spring, Keith. I won't stand by and let that happen again."

"I swear, I'm trying to make it right this time," I muttered, feeling like a kid caught sneaking in after curfew—ashamed and unsure if I even deserved another chance.

Seconds kept ticking away, and the pressure in my chest only grew. *Rachel's waiting,* I reminded myself. *Every minute I spend here is another minute I'm pushing her away.* I couldn't help but steal a glance at my phone—**3:15 PM**. Urgency clawed at me, gnawing at the back of my mind.

When I finally finished, I climbed down one last time, shaking out my hands to get the feeling back. Mrs. Bartlett took in the display with a satisfied smile.

"Well... it'll do," Mrs. Bartlett said, arms crossed but the corners of her mouth twitching like she didn't want to smile. "Thank you for taking the time."

Her words hung in the air, but I barely heard them. I was already mentally five steps away, my thoughts locked on Rachel and the conversation we still needed to have.

Before I could form a response, the unmistakable sound of boots crunching on snow interrupted us. I turned just as Rachel came into view, bundled in a puffy coat and scarf, her cheeks flushed from the cold.

"Barb, are you putting Keith to work?" she teased, her eyes sparkling as she looked between us.

"I sure am," Mrs. Bartlett replied with a grin. "He's got good, strong arms for decorating."

Rachel raised an eyebrow, her lips quirking. "I wouldn't know. He's never offered to hang my lights."

"I'll add you to my schedule," I replied with a grin.

Rachel laughed, the sound warm enough to cut through the icy air. "I thought you weren't coming."

I felt the tension in my shoulders as I stepped closer, trying to keep my voice steady. "I got held up by this sweet old lady. And about two hundred feet of twinkle lights."

Her laugh lingered in my chest, making it hard to focus on anything but the way she smiled, the way her eyes twinkled in the low light. It melted the tightness around my ribs that had been there all day.

Every moment with Rachel felt like a step closer to something I couldn't quite name. I wasn't sure if I was ready for it, but I also wanted to be.

"All done here, Mrs. Bartlett. Lights are up, and your house looks like it belongs in a holiday catalog."

"Call me Barb," she said with a sly grin. "I should be the one thanking you. Rachel, don't let him slip away without some hot chocolate. He's earned it... I suppose."

As the older woman disappeared inside her house, Rachel tilted her head, studying me. "So, you hang Barb's lights, but I have to pay you in hot chocolate? I see how it is."

I shrugged, stuffing my hands in my coat pockets. "I like you more than Barb the Merciless."

Rachel's laughter followed me as we headed toward her house, the red door glowing like a promise.

Inside, I peeled off my boots and jacket and shoved my cold hands into my pockets, feeling the chill of winter slowly ease away. Rachel's home radiated comfort, like stepping into a hug. A thick carpet covered the floor, muffling my footsteps as I took in the warm, earthy tones of the walls and the soft glow of lamps scattered around the room. The cozy sofa and mismatched chairs, piled high with knitted throws and cushions, invited me to sit and stay a while.

In the corner of the room, four or five boxes were stacked high against the wall. Each was labeled BOOKS, but the smaller words beneath them swam together in a blur, the categories slipping out of focus just as quickly as I tried to read them.

My eyes shifted away and landed on the plush bed beneath the heating lamp, where Bolt lounged lazily, looking every bit the picture of reptile contentment.

"Bolt has the right idea," I said, nodding toward the little guy. "No snow or ladders. I might have to start taking notes."

Rachel shot me a grin from the kitchen as she poured steaming drinks into mismatched mugs. "You're welcome to try, but I don't think I have a heat lamp big enough for you."

"Figures. Bolt gets the VIP treatment, and I'm stuck defrosting in a dark corner." I smirked, wandering toward the sofa, tempted by its cozy allure.

She walked over, balancing two mugs in her hands. "Hot chocolate with extra marshmallows for the hero."

I took the mug, letting the warmth seep into my frozen fingers, but the moment I caught her smile, something in me shifted. Without thinking, I set the mug down, leaned in, and pressed my lips to hers.

Her lips curled into a playful smile. "Your hands and lips are freezing."

I grinned and reached for her. "Well, it's our tradition to take a shower together to warm up." I forced a dramatic shiver. "Quick, get naked." I leaned in closer, letting my lips hover just above hers.

There was an undeniable warmth in her eyes. "Oh, is that our tradition now?" She chuckled, closing the distance between us. "Well, who am I to argue?" And her lips finally met mine.

The kiss was slow at first, tentative, as if we were both trying to figure out if this was real, if it was the right moment. But the tension in the air melted, and I pulled her closer, deepening the kiss.

When we finally pulled away, her eyes were bright, lips slightly swollen from the kiss. "Better?" she whispered, a little breathless.

"Definitely," I replied, my thumb brushing over her lower lip. "Though, you might have to help me warm up a few more times tonight."

She laughed again, leaning in for another kiss. "You're lucky I like you, Keith."

"Come here," I said, my voice low, tugging her gently.

Her laughter was soft and surprised, but it faded as she settled against me, her legs draped over mine and her hands resting lightly on my shoulders. My fingers drifted to the hem of her sweater, brushing against her skin.

"Keith," she moaned before letting out a sharp shriek. "What are you—?"

I couldn't help the grin that spread across my face as I tickled her, just enough to make her squirm. "Oh, nothing," I teased, gently tightening my grip to keep her from escaping.

Her glare was half-hearted, her cheeks flushed as she swatted at my chest. "No tickling is now on my rules list."

"I've broken all the other rules," I said, leaning in closer, my breath brushing against her ear. "Might as well break this one."

Before she could protest, I slid my hands to her back, pressing my palms flat against the fabric of her sweater. She yelped again, laughing as she wriggled but didn't pull away.

"You menace!" she huffed, though her smile betrayed her.

"And yet, you're still sitting on my lap," I shot back, my grin widening.

She fought back a smile, so I let my fingers trail a little lower, testing her resolve. I brushed a kiss against the corner of her mouth, then another, softer this time, until she sighed with pleasure.

"You're the one with the rules," I murmured, my voice low and teasing, as I leaned in closer, the heat between us intensifying. "But you're breaking them just as fast as I am."

Her eyes narrowed despite the spark of amusement in them. "You're lucky you're cute."

"Cute?" I repeated, arching an eyebrow. "I think I'm more dashing than cute."

She tilted her head, pretending to consider. "Fine. Cute and tolerable. Don't push it."

Laughing, I kissed her again, loving the feel of her in my arms, warm and laughing despite my antics. "I can't seem to stay away from you, Rachel."

Her cheeks flushed, but her gaze held mine, unguarded and curious. "Maybe I don't want you to."

My fingers brushed along her side, tracing the hem of her sweater. "Yeah?"

She shivered, but her lips curved into a slow, wicked smile. "I don't."

I leaned in, my hand sliding up her back as I kissed her. She let out a startled breath and then sighed, her lips warm and teasing against mine.

When her fingers tangled in my hair, all restraint slipped away. All I could feel was her. She fit perfectly against me, making quiet little sounds as I deepened the kiss. My hand slid under her sweater, brushing over her skin, exploring, until my fingers grazed the curve of her breast.

Her lips parted, and I took the invitation, savoring her taste, the way she responded to every movement, like we'd been doing this forever. It was intoxicating, her warmth, her softness, the spark of something deeper pulling us closer.

When we finally broke apart, her cheeks were flushed, and her eyes locked on mine with a mix of want and mischief. "Keith," she said, her voice low and urgent. "Maybe we should relocate. Somewhere warmer. With fewer windows."

My heart skipped a beat, and heat surged through me. "Are you inviting me to your bedroom, Ms. Bright?"

Her grin widened. "I don't know. Are you accepting the invitation?"

"Absolutely," I said, already shifting to stand and scoop her up when the shrill ring of the wall phone cut through the air like a cold gust of wind.

Rachel glanced at the screen and groaned, burying her face in her hands. "You've got to be kidding me."

I let out a breath, chuckling as I reached for the phone on the coffee table. "Who is it?"

"It's Barb." Rachel winced, snatching the phone out of my hand. "She's the only one who ever calls on that phone."

"Don't answer. We're not here." I barely had time to close the distance between us before the damn phone rang again.

Rachel sighed, muttering, "She knows I'm home," before picking up.

That woman had a sixth sense for ruining a good moment. It had to be on purpose.

Did she think I wasn't good enough for Rachel? Wouldn't be the first time someone underestimated me. Or maybe she was just one of those people who enjoyed meddling for sport. Either way, she had impeccable timing.

She hung up, and I leaned against the sofa, smirking. "I'm guessing she wants to thank me for my ladder acrobatics?"

Or chaperone me and Rachel.

"She insists on feeding us as a thank-you. Early supper in fifteen minutes. Bring your appetite, and a high tolerance for questions." Rachel sighed, flopping onto the sofa.

I grinned, leaning down to kiss her forehead. "Well, guess it's not the worst way to spend the night. But just so you know..." I let my hand slide down her arm as I whispered in her ear. "I'm holding you to that invitation later."

Her cheeks flushed, but the sparkle in her eyes told me she wasn't opposed to the idea. "You'd better."

***

Barb's house exuded a cozy charm, the kind that made you feel like you'd stepped into a holiday postcard from decades past. The air smelled of cinnamon and pine, and every corner was adorned with vintage Christmas decorations. The table, set with an eclectic mix of Christmas dishes, looked like it had been pulled from a family heirloom collection. A centerpiece of flickering candles and pinecones cast a soft, golden glow, their light dancing across the room.

She bustled around the kitchen, wearing an apron and setting out what looked like enough food to feed a small army. "Sit, sit!" she called, waving us into chairs at the table. "I don't get to entertain much anymore, so you'll have to humor an old lady who likes to spoil her guests."

I glanced at Rachel, who was already suppressing a smile as she took a seat beside me. "Old lady, my foot," Rachel teased. "You run circles around half the people in town, Barb."

Barb gave her a mock-glare. "Flattery won't save you from taking leftovers home, young lady." She turned her attention to me with a pointed look, her hands on her hips. "Keith, how do you feel about ham?"

"Love it," I replied easily, though I could already feel the weight of her scrutiny. "Smells incredible."

Barb beamed, but there was a sharp edge to her smile. Setting down a platter of ham and sitting across from me, Barb's sharp eyes gleamed. "Keith, Rachel tells me you're a teacher. What subject?"

"Special education," I said, passing the homemade rolls to Rachel. "I co-teach inclusion classes with Rachel."

I could feel Barb studying me, like she was turning me over in her mind, looking for cracks.

"The kids definitely keep me on my toes," I added, catching the little smirk Rachel tried to hide.

Barb nodded, setting down her fork. "And where are you from originally?"

Casual question... on the surface.

Was she trying to figure out if I was Rachel Material or digging for reasons to warn her off me? It was hard to tell. The polite smile, the measured tone. It could go either way.

I kept my expression easy, like I didn't notice the sharpness behind her words. No way was I giving her the satisfaction of seeing me squirm.

"Born and raised in Charleston, South Carolina," I said, meeting her gaze. "But I've been in Marchfield for a while now. It feels like home."

Barb hummed, clearly mulling that over. "Do you have family around here?"

"My sister, Sunshine, is getting her master's in social work at Old Dominion. Mom died when I was twenty-four and Sunshine was nine, and it's been just the two of us for a long time." I glanced at Rachel. "But I've got a good community here. It's a great place to be."

Barb's eyes darted between us. "You raised your sister?"

I nodded, keeping my tone light even as I braced for whatever Barb was fishing for. "Yeah. I couldn't let Sunny go into foster care. She deserved better than that."

Rachel reached under the table and squeezed my hand. "And you made sure she got it."

Barb's eyes narrowed slightly, like she was recalibrating.

Was that a point in my favor or a strike against me? Some people saw it as admirable. Others assumed it meant I came with baggage. Hell, maybe both were true.

"And how did you and Rachel meet?" Barb asked, her sharp eyes sparkling with curiosity. "My Rachel has a way of keeping people at arm's length. She's not exactly the easiest person to impress."

Her words hung in the air, and I couldn't help but glance at Rachel. She was staring down at her plate, her cheeks tinged with a rosy flush that had nothing to do with the chilly weather outside.

I let out a short laugh, more out of disbelief than amusement, and set my own fork down with a deliberate clink. "With all due respect, Barb, I think Rachel's got plenty of reasons to keep people at arm's length." My voice came out sharper than I intended, but I didn't care. "And if she's not easy to impress, that's because she learned the hard way that some people are assholes."

Rachel's head snapped up, her eyes wide, but she didn't look away.

"She's smart enough to know who deserves a place in her life and who doesn't," I continued, leaning forward slightly. "And for the record, I didn't win her over with some grand gesture or smooth talk. We spend every day in a classroom together. We've seen each other at our best and our worst. So yeah, I worked for it, but not because Rachel's difficult. Because she's worth it."

Barb's eyes narrowed, but there was something unreadable in her expression, like she hadn't expected me to push back. Good. Let her sit with that for a second.

Rachel cleared her throat, her voice quiet but firm. "I don't need you to vet him, Barb."

"Well, I'll be," Barb said, her voice a little lighter. "He's got some fire in him. Maybe I should be trying to impress you."

Rachel rolled her eyes, reaching for her drink. "Are you done yet, or do you need his blood type, too?"

The conversation shifted after that, with Barb entertaining us with stories about her holiday mishaps over the years, including the time she accidentally brought spiked eggnog to church and served it to the choir.

I could see why Rachel adored her.

As we helped clear the table, Barb caught my arm and gave it a squeeze. "You made quite an impression, Keith. But if you hurt Rachel again, I'll string you up with those Christmas lights."

I grinned, nodding. "Rachel has lots of friends who love her. You'll have to get in line."

"Just doing my due diligence," Barb said breezily, but there was no mistaking the gleam of satisfaction in her eyes. She began piling food into Tupperware with a practiced efficiency, then added tins of cookies on top for each of us. "Now, Keith, it's seven-thirty, and you should run along home. Tonight's a school night."

Before I could protest, she ushered us out the door, the sound of the latch clicking behind us like the period at the end of a sentence.

The cold air bit at my face as Rachel and I walked the few yards to the carriage house. Rachel shot me a grin, stepping closer. "About that invitation..."

I crossed my arms, flicking a glance toward Barb's window, where the curtain might have shifted just slightly. "We can't," I said, voice low.

Rachel frowned. "Why not?"

"She's watching us," I muttered, jerking my chin toward the kitchen window.

Rachel rolled her eyes. "Keith, I'm a grown woman," she said, stepping into my space, her voice half-exasperated.

I huffed, glancing back at the house. "I know, but... it would be weird."

Rachel let out a soft laugh, shaking her head. "You're ridiculous."

"Am I?" I shot back. "I think I'm being smart. That woman has eyes like a hawk."

"Fine," she said, her tone all false surrender, but then she reached for me, fingers curling in the front of my jacket. "This will have to do."

Before I could process what she meant, Rachel rose onto her toes and kissed me.

Heat shot through me, a sharp contrast to the frigid night air. My hands automatically found her waist, holding her close, the scent of her skin, the softness of her lips, the warmth of her body against mine all driving one undeniable fact home—I didn't give a damn who was watching.

But then I did.

Shit.

I tensed, just enough for Rachel to notice. When she pulled back, her eyes sparkled with amusement. "You're seriously still thinking about Barb right now?"

"I—" I exhaled, frustrated with myself and my traitorous self-preservation instincts.

Rachel smirked, clearly delighted. "You're cute when you're paranoid."

I scowled. "I'm not paranoid. I just know that if we stand out here too long, she'll be outside with a flashlight, demanding to know what my intentions are."

Rachel's laughter was warm, teasing. "Fine. Go home, Boy Scout."

I sighed dramatically, taking a step back. "You're really enjoying this, aren't you?"

"Oh, absolutely." She winked. "Goodnight, Keith."

I groaned, turning to go, but not before casting one last glance at the window. Damn Barb.

Chapter 19

Rachel

What would you do if your enemy is now your lover?
a) Pretend you're still at odds, just to keep things interesting.
b) Keep it a secret and relish the thrill of getting one over on everyone.
c) Enjoy the tension but secretly wonder if they're playing you.
d) Embrace the chaos and let passion take over, no holds barred.

The first day back at work after a snow day was a special kind of terrible. The kind that made me question my life choices and wonder if it was too late to change careers. I was gritting my teeth before the first bell rang, anticipating the kind of chaos only middle schoolers could conjure after a day of sledding, video games, and not a single thought about school.

Keith strolled in just before the kids with two coffee cups and a grin plastered on his face. "Morning, Rach. Ready for round one?" He passed me a cup, leaning casually against the desk as if the storm wasn't about to hit.

"I was born ready," I replied, watching the first wave of students shuffle in, leaving trails of slush and mud across the floor. "You're helping with cleanup."

"Deal," he said, taking a long sip of his coffee like he was gearing up for battle.

The room filled quickly, the tang of wet wool and teenage energy saturating the air. Backpacks spilled open, and I caught glimpses of crumpled papers, half-eaten Pop-Tarts, but zero signs of Friday's assignment.

"Wait, there was work?" Sawyer asked with a wide-eyed with innocence that I wasn't buying. Keith, standing by the door, raised an eyebrow and shot me a look that screamed, *Here we go.*

"I didn't see anything online," Emily added, despite the fact that the assignment had been emailed, posted, and, for good measure, written in giant letters on the whiteboard.

Keith leaned closer to me and whispered, "Only two and a half hours until lunch."

"Plenty of time to write my letter of resignation," I whispered back.

Keith stifled a laugh, shaking his head as he straightened up. "Don't worry, I'll help you make it convincing. Just let me know if you want dramatic or downright pitiful."

I returned my attention to the class. The groans began when I asked everyone to login to the class portal.

"Mine's dead!" Gennie announced like it was breaking news, holding up a dark screen.

"It was at fifty percent last week!" Marquis added, their tone accusing.

My lone charging cable became the center of a minor war, students jockeying for position like they were competing in a reality TV show.

Keith stepped in, clapping his hands. "All right, people, it's just a charger, not a golden ticket. Form a line, or no one gets to use it."

The kids groaned but obeyed, shuffling into something vaguely resembling order.

As the noise finally died down to a low hum, Sawyer leaned back in his chair and threw out the inevitable: "Can't we just do something fun today? We just had a snow day."

A chorus of agreement followed, with murmurs of "movie day" and "game day" rippling through the room.

I forced a smile, gripping the edge of my desk like it was a lifeline. "Fun," I muttered under my breath. "Sure. Let's call this fun." And with that, I picked up the dry-erase marker, turned to the whiteboard, wracking my brain for how to make the poetry lesson more fun.

By the time my last class was halfway through, my head pounded like a marching band had taken up residence behind my temples, and my patience dangled by a thread. A tiny muscle in my left eye twitched with maddening persistence, a constant reminder that I was one more "Can I go to the bathroom?" away from completely losing it.

"Sawyer, please sit down," I said, guiding him back to his seat for what felt like the sixth time. "Let me see your poem."

"Poetry's dumb, Ms. Bright," he grumbled, crossing his arms defensively. "No offense."

"Some people think music is just poetry with a beat," I suggested.

Sawyer paused, his face scrunching up like he was trying to solve a particularly tricky riddle. "Like... rap?" he asked cautiously.

"Exactly," I replied, seizing the opportunity. "Rap, country, pop."

He tilted his head, considering this. "So, like... could I write a rap instead of a poem?"

"Sure," I said, smiling.

Sawyer's pout faded as a spark of interest lit his face. "Okay, but can it be about something cool, like superheroes?"

I nodded, suppressing a grin. "Superheroes, aliens, video games—whatever speaks to you, Sawyer. Just make it yours."

Keith leaned over from where he was helping Emily, grinning. "Bet you could even rap about how dumb poetry is."

Sawyer's eyes lit up at the challenge. "Oh, I'm gonna. And it's gonna be awesome."

I watched Sawyer's hand fly across the paper, his usual disinterest replaced with something that looked like real effort. It was the first time all year I'd seen him actually engage with the assignment.

Job well done, I thought, allowing myself a small, satisfied smile.

Before I could move on to the next student, the unmistakable sound of a key turning in the door's lock sliced through the air, snapping me out of my small victory.

Principal Kline entered, his polished shoes clicking against the floor as he straightened up with his master key in hand. Dressed in his usual suit and tie, his iPad was clutched firmly in the other hand.

I could already feel my stomach tighten. The last thirty minutes of school were always the worst for observations, yet here he was. Fantastic.

Tommy's hand shot up, and before I could even acknowledge it, he blurted, "Can I go to the bathroom?"

I glanced at his desk, the blank paper mocking me. Walking over, I knelt beside him, trying to keep my voice steady. "Let's get some work done first, Tommy."

Mr. Kline, who had wedged himself into a desk at the back of the room, was already typing furiously on his iPad. Was I imagining the judgment radiating off him as he silently observed?

"But it's an emergency!" Tommy whined, his eyes wide with exaggerated urgency.

I pinched the bridge of my nose, swallowing the urge to roll my eyes. The last thing I needed was bathroom drama under

Kline's hawk-eyed scrutiny. "In a minute," I said, keeping my voice calm but firm. "Let's get an idea for your poem first."

Behind me, Mr. Kline's fingers tapped on his tablet, the steady rhythm sounding like a countdown to disaster.

"I can't wait that long!" Tommy blurted, his voice loud enough to turn a few heads. The other students perked up, their attention shifting like sharks catching a whiff of blood in the water. It was only a matter of time before things spiraled.

"Fine," I relented with a sigh, waving him off. "But you owe me a stanza when you get back."

"Yes, ma'am." Tommy's tone was appropriately contrite, but the devilish grin spreading across his face made it clear he'd won this round.

As Tommy bolted for the door, Mr. Kline leaned in, his voice low but no less intrusive. "Could you forward your lesson plan, please? I need to confirm how the objectives align with this activity."

"Of course," I replied, forcing a tight smile while glancing across the room at Keith. He caught my eye, and I gave a quick nod toward the clock, then the agenda on the board. Hopefully, he'd pick up on the silent message: wrap it up in ten minutes and move to the exit ticket before things got too far off the rails.

With a few hurried taps, I sent the principal the email while trying to quell my anxiety. Observations meant performance reviews, and it didn't seem fair that one visit might be the difference between a glowing evaluation and a year of nitpicking feedback. It wasn't just about the lesson. It never was. It was about proving I could manage the class, the curriculum, and keep composure, all while under the microscope.

A knock on the door signaled Tommy's return. I hurried over to him to determine that he delivered on that promised stanza. He wrote for a few minutes, then handed me the paper with a triumphant smirk. Sure enough, his poem was all about me.

Ms. Bright is always on me
She's meaner than a snake
And when I want to pee
She always makes me wait.

Reading it, I wanted to laugh. At least it rhymed.

Out of the corner of my eye, I saw Mr. Kline stand up and make his way to the back of the room, settling next to Emily. Why does admin always choose the least prepared students to talk to? Emily was sweet, no doubt, but she spent most of her time daydreaming or drawing in her notebook. If Kline asked her to explain the learning target, I already knew the blank stare she'd give him.

I held in a groan, trying to focus on keeping the rest of the class on track while silently bracing myself for whatever Emily might, or might not, say.

Keith and I wrapped up the lesson, directing the students to complete their exit tickets on their laptops while we moved through the rows, collecting their poems.

My thoughts were scattered as I sifted through the papers, my eyes scanning the verses about friendship, love, and school lunch. Sawyer's rap about hating poetry was pretty amazing.

Keith's calm good humor got us to the end of the day even as my nerves buzzed from Mr. Kline's silent judgment at the back of the room.

When the bell rang, the students bolted. Their chatter quickly faded into the hallway, and I let out a small sigh of relief. But it didn't last long. Mr. Kline lingered by the door.

My stomach tightened, a familiar knot of anxiety forming as I braced for whatever critique or task he had in store.

"I understand the conference ended early because of the snowstorm," Kline said. "But I'd like the two of you to present anything you learned to the faculty during the teacher in-service day before winter break."

The vague expectation of "presenting anything you learned" made my mind race. What had I learned at that weekend, aside from the fact that Keith had a great ass and the sexual stamina of a Greek god?

"A training on the day before Christmas break?" Keith winced. "That sounds a little Scroogy, don't you think?" Keith was cracking jokes while my stomach churned. Couldn't he see this was no laughing matter?

The principal shrugged. "You can buy some cookies and make hot chocolate. It'll be fine."

I forced myself to maintain a neutral expression. It would not be fine.

"Okay," Keith said, and I did a double take.

Unbelievable!

He'd agreed—again—to do something I wasn't on board with, so I had to follow suit. Forcing a tight smile, I nodded.

When Mr. Kline finally left the room, I glanced at Keith, who was casually leaning against a desk like we hadn't been handed a professional landmine to navigate.

"So," I said, crossing my arms. "Do we start with the snowstorm or the part where we got stranded and I saw your dick?"

Keith chuckled, the sound light and easy, like this was all some inside joke I hadn't caught up to yet. "Relax, Rachel," he said, his voice warm but teasing. "We've got this."

"Do we?" I asked, my tone sharper than I intended. I immediately felt a pang of guilt. Keith didn't deserve to be on the receiving end of my stress, but his teasing infuriated me.

"Come on, Rachel," he said, softer now. "You're the most organized person I've ever met. If anyone can make this look easy, it's you."

I wanted to believe him. "Me? The person who freezes up whenever she speaks in front of a group of adults?" I said, folding my arms.

Keith stepped closer, his expression shifting to something more intimate. He took my hand and leaned down to brush a kiss across my lips. "We're a team, remember? I'll handle the talking if you want. I'll make the slide show, and you can put in the text. And impress everyone with those charts you love so much."

I couldn't help it—I laughed, the sound surprising even me. "Charts, huh? That's your idea of wowing the faculty?"

He grinned down at me, clearly relieved to see me cracking. "Absolutely. Everyone loves a good bar graph. I'm telling you, Rachel, we'll be legends."

I shook my head, but the tightness in my chest eased just a little. "Fine," I said, leaning into him, letting his confidence carry me for a moment. "But if we bomb, I'm blaming you."

"Deal," he said with that easy grin, the one that made everything feel lighter than it was. "In fact, why don't we grab some dinner together tonight and sketch out our presentation?"

"Oh." The word slipped out before I could stop it, and I instinctively jerked back, my gaze darting to the clock. "I can't. I've got plans tonight. In fact, I need to leave. Right now."

Keith's eyebrow lifted, his curiosity immediate and unmistakable. "Plans?"

I turned away, fumbling for my bag. My fingers were clumsy as I started grabbing what I needed off the desk, trying not to look at him.

I could feel his gaze, sharp and probing, burning a hole through me. I tried to steady myself, but the heat in my cheeks was already betraying me.

"Rachel." His voice, low and insistent, made my heart skip. It was like he was pulling me out of my own head. "Are you trying to make me jealous?"

"What? No—" I stammered, my words tripping over each other. His question hit me like a bucket of cold water. Jealous? Why would he be jealous? My stomach did a flip at the thought.

"Then what are your plans tonight?" he asked, his tone charged with something I couldn't quite place. Curiosity? Disappointment? Or something else entirely?

I couldn't help but feel frustrated with myself for not catching the nuance in his voice, for not being able to tell if he was joking or actually jealous. This constant guessing game, trying to decode expressions and tones, was exhausting.

"It's trivia night," I said, the words coming out in a rush.

His expression flickered for just a moment before his grin returned, but it didn't quite reach his eyes this time. "Trivia night, huh?" he said, the teasing note in his voice a little more subdued.

I nodded, feeling suddenly exposed, like I had to explain this too. "I told you about Quiz Pro Quo. I do it every week. You know, to unwind."

Keith's gaze lingered on me, his eyes narrowing just a fraction. "Sounds fun." He took a half step closer, his body language shifting just enough to make me acutely aware of how close he was to me. The air between us felt different, heavier, like the conversation had taken a sudden, unspoken turn. "Can I come?"

Something in his voice made me wonder if we were still talking about Trivia Night. It wasn't just the question. It was the way he said it, low and smooth.

My breath caught in my throat as he leaned a little closer, sending a shiver of pleasure down my spine. I tried to mask the strange flutter in my chest, but it was there, radiating from somewhere deep inside me, and I couldn't quite shake it. Was I imagining this? Was this just another one of those moments where my feelings didn't line up with reality?

Get a grip, Rachel.

"Sure," I said, forcing the words out before my mind could process them. "Do you want to play or watch?"

His voice dropped low and husky. "I'll watch tonight." He leaned in, his eyes darkening as he added, "But don't think I won't be enjoying the show... especially with you in the lead."

Chapter 20

Keith

What would you do if your partner is the trivia master?
a) Let them take the lead and secretly enjoy watching them.
b) Play it coy and let them think they're winning—until you surprise them with the right answer.
c) Tease them with *oh-so-close* answers, just to watch them get flustered.
d) Challenge them to a *personal* round of trivia—where the stakes are much more... intimate.

Barrel was one of my favorite hangouts. It had the kind of cozy, worn-in charm that made it feel like a second living room for the locals. The walls were a deep, weathered red, covered with framed black-and-white photos of Marchfield during its heyday. String lights crisscrossed the ceiling, casting a warm golden glow that softened the edges of everything and everyone.

A long wooden bar, scarred with decades of stories, spills, and elbow marks, flanked by rows of mismatched stools. Behind it, shelves lined with liquor bottles gleamed under soft backlighting, while a chalkboard listed the rotating local craft beers on tap in sloppy handwriting.

Barrel's back room, usually reserved for pool and darts, had been transformed into the trivia zone for the night. Tables and chairs were crammed into the space while the trivia host perched on a high stool on a makeshift stage. The air was thick with the smell of fried food, spilled beer, and just a whisper of sawdust, a comforting scent that seemed ingrained in the place.

Every so often, faint, rhythmic thuds from the ax-throwing room next door punctuated the hum of conversation, lending an odd but fitting soundtrack to the bar's rustic vibe. Overhead, country music twanged softly from speakers mounted high on the wood-paneled walls, but it was hard to hear over the cheers and bursts of laughter from the trivia crowd.

The whole space felt alive, buzzing with energy. One table erupted in groans as they missed a question about a 90s sitcom.

The Trivia Master repeated the question. "What beloved 90s sitcom was adapted into a Russian version titled *The Voronins?*"

Rachel's team leaned in, huddling together for a quick moment before she slapped the buzzer.

"Quiz Pro Quo?" the host joked, raising an eyebrow.

"*Everybody Loves Raymond,*" Rachel replied confidently.

"Correct."

Rachel's table celebrated another point with a round of high-fives, and the host's voice crackled over the mic, announcing the next question.

Rachel's team was eclectic, but I'd been impressed when she introduced me. Maggie, Ben and Raj had different skills, but together, they were an unpredictable mix of expertise, quirks, and unrelenting determination.

After an hour or so, it became clear that Rachel's team was going to win because Rachel was a trivia assassin. She was cool under pressure, relentless with obscure knowledge.

When the final question came—*What was the original name of Istanbul?* —she didn't even let her teammates deliberate. She grabbed the mic and said, "Byzantium," like it was the most obvious thing in the world. "And after Constantine moved in, it was more like *Constant-in-total-disrepair.*"

It took me a full three seconds to catch the joke. Maybe four. By the time I snorted, she was already celebrating the win.

Now, leaning against the bar, drink in hand, I tried to play it cool while keeping my eyes on her. Not that I had a choice. Rachel had this gravitational pull. Her wild hand gestures, a quick, almost mischievous smile that lit up her entire face, and her short, carefree hairstyle tousled and messy made her look like the human equivalent of a tornado. A beautiful, brilliant tornado.

I sipped my beer, shaking my head as she mimed what I could only assume was her team's glorious victory. Her laugh cut through the noise, big and unapologetic, and I swear, the whole room dimmed around her. She had this way of being in her own orbit, completely unaware of how stunning she was.

"Man, you've got it bad," I muttered to myself, still watching Rachel as she half-danced, half-paraded around the bar with a plastic trophy that looked like it came out of a claw machine.

My phone buzzed in my pocket. I pulled it out and saw Sunny's name on the screen.

"Hey, everything okay?"

A sniffle. Not a good sign.

"I hate it here."

I pushed back from the bar, angling toward a quieter corner. "What happened?"

"Dr. Solna is hates me. She gave me a D on my last paper. She treats me differently from all the other students."

"Did you talk to your advisor?"

Another sniffle. "Yeah, but she just said that Solna sees potential in me and wants me to work harder, but I'm already pulling my hair out. Maybe I don't belong here."

My chest tightened. "No one ever went through a master's program and said it was easy. You're almost to the end of the semester. Stick it out."

"But that D will ruin my average. If I do bad on the exam, I'll have to retake the course."

"So, treat this like a social work case. Interview the professor. Figure out what makes her tick. Ask open-ended questions like,

'How does it make you feel to crush my GPA like a bug under your academic boot?'"

That got a small huff of laughter. "Pretty sure that would get me another D."

"Okay, fine. Maybe ease into it. Hit her with the strengths-based approach. Tell her you deeply admire her ability to find flaws in your work that no other human eye could detect."

Sunny snorted. "Yeah, that won't sound sarcastic at all."

"Good point. Maybe just cry. Professors hate that."

She let out a real laugh this time. "I love you."

"I love you, too."

She sighed. "I just wish I didn't feel so alone."

"You're not alone, Sunny. You've got me. And you'll find your people, I promise. It just takes time."

Across the bar, Rachel's laugh rang out. I glanced over just in time to see her waving the trophy in the trivia host's face, clearly debating the cultural significance of a movie featuring gremlins in Santa hats. My lips twitched.

"Are you out?" Sunny asked, her voice sharper.

"I'm at trivia night."

"Oh my God, you're with *her*, aren't you?"

I hesitated. "What?"

"Rachel."

I pinched the bridge of my nose. "I'm supporting a colleague."

Sunny made a skeptical noise. "Uh-huh. Sure. Look, I'll be okay. Go stare at her some more."

"I wasn't—"

She hung up before I could finish the lie.

I exhaled, slipping my phone back into my pocket. When I turned back, Rachel caught my eye from across the room and grinned, holding up the trophy like she'd just won the Stanley Cup. I raised my beer in a silent toast, and she sauntered over, her smile half-mischief, half-I-did-something-awesome.

"Good evening, Number One Fan," she said, leaning casually on the bar next to me.

Her cocky tone sent blood racing south. If shy, awkward Rachel was a turn-on, bold, swaggering Rachel set my senses on fire.

I barely had time to smirk before my phone buzzed on the bar. Rachel's gaze flicked to the screen just as I flipped it over, ignoring the message.

"Who was that?" she asked, her tone light but her eyes sharp.

"Sunny," I said, watching her closely.

She tilted her head, like she was trying to figure me out. "You usually answer when she calls." There was an edge to her words, a question buried underneath. She didn't believe me? Or maybe she didn't trust herself?

There was something she wasn't saying, some truth hiding just beneath the surface. And I wanted it. Needed it. I wanted to know if she was testing me, or if I was just another part of her puzzle she hadn't figured out yet.

"I just talked to her, and..." I said, leaning in slightly, my voice low. "I'm a little... preoccupied."

Rachel's eyes flickered, her fingers tightening around the trophy like it was the only thing holding her steady. "Oh?" she asked, her voice tight.

What was happening? She avoided my gaze, freezing me out. I tilted my head, narrowing my eyes. "What's wrong?"

Rachel shifted on her feet, clearly uncomfortable. Then, she finally spoke, her voice quieter. "It's just... Sometimes I remember last year." She paused like the words were weighing her down, her gaze dropping to the floor.

Her words hit me harder than I expected. Guilt swept through me as I realized the sight of my phone brought back bad memories for her and how we'd never really talked about it.

I didn't blame her for being cautious, but it didn't stop the ache of wanting to pull her closer, to make sure we didn't fall apart again.

I leaned in, just enough for her to feel my breath on her skin, and let my gaze drop to her lips, then slowly pull back up to meet her eyes. "I'm not that asshole anymore, Rachel."

She sucked in a breath, and I caught the way her pulse jumped at the base of her throat. That familiar flutter that only made me want her more. "Show me," she demanded, her voice shaky despite her attempt at control.

I reached for my phone, but she shook her head. "No, show me how you feel about me."

"I want you. Just you."

I didn't hesitate. The tension between us had been building too long, and there was no denying it any longer. I pulled her toward me, my hands sliding around her waist as I kissed her fiercely, as if I were staking my claim. Not out of arrogance, but because I needed her. I wasn't going to let her slip away again.

She kissed me back with the same intensity, her hands tangling in my shirt. There was no more talking. No more pretending we weren't feeling what we were feeling. All that mattered now was the heat, the need, and the way we fit together like pieces of something we hadn't quite figured out yet.

The air around us had thickened. Her smile wavered for the first time all night, a brief flicker of uncertainty crossing her face. It was enough to make my chest tighten.

The tension between us was undeniable now, as thick as the warm air of the bar. It pulsed, almost like a rhythm, a dance only we knew. I leaned in, just a little, instinct taking over, drowning out the noise of the bar. Her breath caught, eyes flickering up to meet mine—wide, uncertain, but there was something more in them.

I didn't stop.

Closing the space between us, my hand brushed lightly against hers where she still held the trophy, and then, in one fluid motion, I kissed her.

Her lips were softer than I'd imagined, but not delicate. There was a strength there, an intensity that matched the undercurrent of tension that had been building between us all night. The kiss was quick, but it hit me with the force of a freight train, an unspoken question answered in the press of my lips to hers.

For a split second, I thought she might pull back, but she didn't. Instead, she slipped the trophy into her pocket and gripped my shirt as she kissed me back, and the world narrowed until it was just us.

My voice sounded rough when I whispered, "Come with me."

Her eyes searched mine for a heartbeat, and then, without another word, she threaded her fingers between mine.

Leading her through the crowded bar, we passed the tables of people who were too caught up in their own worlds to notice us slipping away.

We reached the back hallway, the dim lighting casting long shadows along the walls. I paused for a moment, just breathing her in, the sweet smell of her skin. My heart pounded harder, faster.

Then I pulled her toward the utility closet at the end of the hall, the door creaking as I pushed it open. The space was small, cramped, barely enough for both of us to fit.

The soft click of the door closing echoed in the silence that settled between us. Her back bumped the smooth surface as I stepped closer, her breath mingling with mine, and I could feel the heat rising, thick with anticipation.

I could feel the pulse of desire in my chest, racing and unpredictable. The energy between us had shifted, and I couldn't wait any longer. "I can't wait, Rachel. I need you," I murmured, my voice low, raw with longing.

"Yes, Keith. Please."

The distance between us vanished as I reached for her, hands trembling with anticipation. I lifted the hem of her maxi dress to her waist, fingers brushing along her soft skin as I traced the curve of her waist. She gasped lightly at the touch, and I could feel the shiver of pleasure run through her body.

The room seemed to grow smaller, the noise of the world fading into the background as I gathered the material, pushing it higher. My heart thundered, the urgency rising with each beat, but there was something else there too that made me want to savor every second.

I fell to my knees, yanking her panties down, spreading her wide, and driving my tongue and fingers into her heat. Hooking her leg up over my shoulder, I delighted in the tangy sweet and spicy smell of her, sliding my fingers into her wetness as her body jerked around me, pulling me deeper. Time stopped, and her body tensed, tighter and tighter with each brush of my tongue.

Her pleasure fueled mine, sending waves of heat racing across my senses. Her hands tore at my hair, her nails scratching my shoulders. A soft gasp that escaped her lips as she came, her body arching taut.

I stood, fumbling my pants until my cock was free.

"Rachel, I need you."

"Yes," she moaned, her mouth sliding across mine, her teeth nipping at my lips.

Keeping her back braced against the door, I lifted her hips. Her legs wrapped instantly around my hips, and I growled rough and harsh in her ear as my cock thrust deep inside her.

My mind went blank. The feel of her arms and legs wrapped around me. Her hips moving with mine as I ravished her. I buried my head against her neck as my balls squeezed tight.

The intensity between us was undeniable, but it wasn't just the physical. It was something more. The way she leaned into me, the way her hands found their place on my skin, the way she responded to every movement. It was like we were speaking in a language that was all our own, one that didn't need words, just touches and whispers and the shared rhythm of our hearts.

Every moment was electric, charged with a raw kind of intimacy that made the world outside feel like a distant memory. And in that space, with her in my arms, it felt like nothing else mattered but this connection, this shared understanding of what each of us needed.

My climax washed over me. Thrusting deep into her triggered her own pleasure, and I thought I'd die from the joy of her.

When I finally pulled back, her eyes were soft and dreamy, and there was trust in the way she looked at me. After all these months of trying to win it back, an undeniable sense of accomplishment filled me. I felt like doing my own victory lap.

Chapter 21

Keith

What would you do at a holiday-themed escape room?
a) Propose—it's so romantic.
b) Concentrate on the puzzles—you want to WIN!
c) Secretly flirt with your lover.
d) Disappear behind the sleigh for a kiss.

The escape room was tucked away in an old building that creaked under the weight of years and smelled faintly of cinnamon and pine. A string of twinkling lights framed the door and cast a soft glow over chipped paint and frosted windows. Above it hung a glittery red-and-green banner that read: *Santa's Workshop: Can You Save Christmas?*

I hadn't volunteered for this. No one had, really. But Val insisted we needed holiday memories or some bonding crap like that. So, after a hundred group texts and zero discussion, we were expected to save Santa in under sixty minutes.

Still, I'd offered to drive—specifically so I could take Rachel home afterward. Trivia night had been... satisfying. Jokes, flirting, and then that moment in the closet when things got heated in all the right ways. But after? We hadn't had time for real conversation or clarity.

But now, I needed to know where we stood, what she was thinking, and if she'd committed to giving me a second chance.

When Oz and Audrey's car pulled up, Rachel slid out of the back seat. She waved when she saw me and started toward me with a smile, but I saw it—that careful distance in her posture, the tension in her shoulders.

Whatever this night turned into, I wasn't letting it end without saying what I needed to say.

I stepped closer. My hand grazed the small of her back, a subtle touch, just enough to steady her without making it awkward. "You good?"

She hesitated, her eyes flicking over the entrance again before she forced a smile. "I just... didn't expect it to be so... festive." She waved a hand at the over-the-top decorations, the fake snow covering everything and the giant nutcracker standing in the corner like it was about to come to life.

I chuckled softly, the sight of her trying to push through her anxiety making me want to protect her, even though I knew she wouldn't let me. "It's definitely a lot. But I'll make sure you don't get locked in a toy chest or anything." I flashed a grin, hoping to break the tension a little.

Her laugh was small but genuine, and I saw her shoulders relax just a fraction. "Yeah, okay. No toy chests. Got it."

Val's voice rang out, bright and teasing, "Come on, you guys!"

We turned to see her waving from the door, bundled in a red coat and tall black boots. Beside her, Evan stood, looking every bit the leader with his clipboard in hand.

Inside, we signed our waivers and stepped through the ridiculously festive decorations. I spotted Bobby and Mel near the hot cocoa stand, chatting with Yona and Han Carges, Marchfield's Spanish teacher.

When they ushered us into the first room, I couldn't help but let out a low whistle. It looked like someone had taken every Christmas cliché and cranked it up to a thousand. Fake snowflakes dangled from the ceiling, a roaring fireplace was painted on the wall, and in the corner sat a tree with a pile of presents. The centerpiece was Santa's sleigh, glowing reins and all, toys spilling out like it was real.

"Find Santa's sleigh keys!" someone called out, and a countdown clock started ticking.

Nearby, Han edged closer to Yona as they inspected a grouping of large candy canes. Val, ever the leader, noticed and called out, "Han! Did you find something?"

"Nothing yet," he answered smoothly. He shot a warm smile around the group, his easy confidence contrasting with Rachel's nervous energy.

"Yona, stop eating the candy canes and help us find the sleigh keys," Val teased, and Yona rolled her eyes dramatically before tossing the candy stick aside with a sigh.

"Fine, but only because I want to win," Yona muttered.

I turned to Rachel, watching her face as she squinted at a reindeer statue. Her fingers were tapping restlessly against the side of her leg, a clear sign she was feeling anxious. "You've got your *why-did-I-agree-to-this* face on."

She raised an eyebrow, but I could see her trying to push through it. "I don't have a face for that."

"Oh, you absolutely do," I teased, leaning in a little closer, hoping to lighten her mood. "And it turns me on."

She shot me a quick, almost-too-brief smile. "Everything turns you on."

I shook my head, taking her hand in mine. "Only you."

Evan's voice cut through the moment, loud and enthusiastic as he clapped his hands. "Let's go! We're saving Christmas, people!"

Val appeared at my shoulder. She linked her arm with Rachel's, practically dragging her toward Audrey, Mel, and Yona.

Val nudged Rachel, her voice light with excitement. "You're the trivia queen. We need your brainpower."

Rachel adjusted her coat, gripping the edge like it was the only thing keeping her grounded. "Okay." She squared her shoulders, and I knew she'd be okay. She was always tougher than she thought.

The game was simple: solve riddles, find objects, and win. Rachel's mind excelled at it. She zeroed in on the details, her expression calm, even though I could see her brain racing behind those eyes.

Val handed her the scroll, and I couldn't look away as Rachel's fingers traced the red-and-gold ribbon before she unrolled the paper. She read the riddle aloud: "I'm a symbol of cheer, both grand and small, I hold hidden treasures but reveal none at all. I shimmer and shine, yet I'm fragile, take care, you'll find me up high, not just anywhere."

"It's an ornament," Yona called, dashing toward the tree.

The others set off, fumbling through the decorations with no real purpose. Audrey hummed along with the music as she searched through a pile of fake presents.

But Rachel didn't rush. She stood thinking, then scanned the room. Her sharp eyes processing every detail.

I followed her gaze to a small display shelf, tucked behind a glass case. There, gleaming among vintage ornaments, something metallic sparkled.

"Found it," Rachel said, her voice lighting up with excitement.

"Good catch!" Val praised her.

Rachel's lips curved into a smile and the sparkle returned to her eyes.

Bit by bit, a rush of warmth settled in my chest that had nothing to do with the room's holiday lights. My heart kicked up, hard enough that I felt it in my throat.

She brushed her hair behind her ear, and it was the most beautiful thing I'd seen all night. Suddenly, everything felt sharp and real. I couldn't shake the thought that I might be falling for her.

Evan reached up, carefully lifting the ornament from the shelf. As he did, his fingers brushed against Val's.

My thoughts flicked to Rachel, standing nearby, her expression neutral, though I could see the subtle way her eyes followed every movement.

Val turned the ornament over in her hands, her face lighting up with that unmistakable spark of excitement. "Alright, let's see if we can figure out the next one." She reached for the scroll, untied the ribbon, and unrolled the paper with a flourish.

"To love is to trust, to laugh, to grow. But what really makes it work is letting go. When two hearts meet and vow to stay, they seal it forever in their own way."

"You know," Evan's voice was soft, but full of sincerity, "I think I know this one." His gaze never left Val's face. "I think this riddle is about us, and the journey we've taken together," Evan continued.

And then, without warning, Evan dropped to one knee.

"Val," Evan's voice was thick with emotion, low and full of weight. "You told me to wait, and I did, but over the past few months, something's changed. I feel it in the way you look at me. Will you marry me?"

The room seemed to hold its breath as Val's finger pressed gently to his lips, a playful look in her eyes. "Don't move."

She darted off toward the pile of presents, rifling through them with purpose. A moment later, she returned, holding a small black jewelry box, her hand trembling just enough for me to notice. "I told you I'd let you know when I was ready. Will you marry me, Evan?"

My eyes snapped to Rachel, and everything else faded.

I'd never met anyone like her. Someone so carefully layered, like she wasn't sure how much she could give, or maybe just didn't trust that anyone would want it. But I did. I wanted everything about her. Her awkward vulnerability and the way she saw the world in ways I could never dream of. I exhaled sharply, trying to push the feelings down, but they were unstoppable.

The room erupted into cheers, hands clapping, voices overlapping in excitement. Val's face was flushed, a shiny engagement ring catching the light as she grinned at Evan.

A crackling voice broke through the speaker in the ceiling. "Congratulations, Evan and Val. Consider having your wedding at our venue with a ten percent discount."

Silence. A stunned, almost reverent pause before laughter erupted. But my heart was still trying to catch up, my brain scrambling to process more than just the proposal.

"Christmas can't be ruined on my engagement day!" Val declared, snapping us back into the moment. "Let's win this, people!"

Evan laced his fingers through hers, grinning at the rest of us. "You heard her! This holiday isn't going to save itself."

People scattered, diving into puzzles, pulling levers, working against the clock. The room buzzed with energy, but I barely registered it.

Rachel moved through the crowd, sharp and focused, her eyes scanning the room with that quick, clever way she had of seeing things others missed. Her steady determination and the quiet way she pulled people together, made sense of the world.

I swallowed hard, the weight of emotion pressing down on me. Tightness squeezed in my chest.

I loved her. I loved Rachel.

The realization knocked the breath from my lungs. I had no idea when it happened. There was no pinpointed moment, but it was undeniable and completely terrifying.

Because loving her wasn't enough. I had to prove it, too.

Jingle bells interrupted my thoughts. Cold, wet, artificial snow landed on my face and neck.

They'd cracked the final puzzle with three minutes left on the clock.

Santa was saved. Christmas was restored. The room whooped in victory.

And I had a mission.

I needed to show Rachel what she meant to me. Something big enough, real enough, that she'd know, really know, that I wasn't going anywhere.

Chapter 22

Rachel

What would you do to prove you're all in?
A) Saying I love you first and hoping they say it back.
B) Making a grand gesture that shows you see and understand them.
C) Dropping subtle hints and waiting for them to figure it out.
D) Letting your meddling friends push you together.

The glow of the dashboard lights lit up Keith's face as he drove, his hands gripping the steering wheel tightly. The energy had settled into something quieter, more awkward. More... *us.*

I exhaled slowly, pressing my fingertips into my thighs. The escape room had been overwhelming. My skin still prickled from the sensory overload, my brain sluggish after filtering it all.

I'd held it together by hyper-focusing on solving puzzles. But now in the aftermath, a deep, bone-weary exhaustion gripped me, and I was ready to get home.

Keith cleared his throat. "So, that was fun."

"It was," I agreed, watching the streetlights blur past. "Especially when you tried to brute-force open that last lock."

He scoffed, his fingers tapping against the wheel. "Hey, logic is overrated. Sometimes you just gotta shake things until they open."

I smirked, my stomach flipping at the easy banter, but the warmth of it couldn't quite smooth out the awkward energy between us. Keith had hovered closer than usual tonight, his hand lingering on my back and clearing his throat like he was trying to say something but couldn't force it out.

He coughed lightly. "I, uh..."

I arched a brow. "You, uh... what?"

My first instinct was to laugh. I was the awkward one, not him. Seeing him hesitate, struggle with words—it flipped something in my chest, something both terrifying and thrilling.

His hands tightened on the steering wheel, his arms tense. "Rachel, I, uh... Maybe we should wait to have this conversation when I'm not driving."

A prickle of anxiety crawled up my spine, my brain immediately running through every worst-case scenario. He didn't want me anymore, and he was ending it. My pulse pounded in my ears as I tried to keep my breathing steady.

"You'd better pull over. I'm worried."

Keith exhaled sharply, dragging a hand through his hair before nodding and flicking on the turn signal. "I'm sorry, Rach, I'm fucking this up."

He pulled into the nearly deserted lot beside Wicked Roasts Coffee, the *Closed* sign buzzing faintly in red neon, casting a soft, eerie glow across the dashboard. Overhead, a single streetlamp flickered, stretching long, restless shadows across the cracked pavement. The engine settled into a low hum as he shifted into park, but his hands stayed locked on the wheel, fingers tightening until his knuckles turned white.

I reached over, my hand settling on his arm, feeling the tightness beneath the fabric of his hoodie. "Tell me like pulling off a Band-Aid. Quick and clean."

He cleared his throat, staring out the windshield. "We haven't, um, talked about this thing between us."

I furrowed my brow, the words catching me off guard. "Thing?"

He hesitated, looking over at me with a mix of confusion and another emotion I couldn't place. "Yeah. The, um, relationship."

My heart skipped a beat, a lump forming in my throat. Panic rising in my chest, threatening to swallow me whole. I blinked rapidly, trying to keep myself together, but the uncertainty hung in the air like a heavy fog. "Are you breaking up with me?"

He cursed under his breath, shaking his head vehemently. "No, God no. I told you I was fucking it all up."

"So, what are you saying?" My fingers tightened on my seatbelt, feeling the sharpness of my own breath.

Clearly wrestling with whatever was on his mind, he scrubbed his palm over his face, letting out a deep sigh. "God, I suck at this." He glanced at me, then quickly back at the road, as if looking at me might make things worse.

I couldn't help but laugh, though it came out strained. "Yeah, you do. But I'm sure you'll figure it out."

He shot me a sheepish look, half-smiling, but it didn't reach his eyes. "Can't you just read my mind?"

I rolled my eyes. "I'm a terrible psychic." Tapping my fingers nervously on my knee, I continued, "You know, the first recorded psychic was a Greek named Pythia, and she was considered the oracle of Delphi. People would travel for miles just to hear her prophecies."

Keith gave me a sideways glance, a mix of confusion and amusement dancing in his eyes. "Are you telling me you're not an ancient Greek oracle?" He raised an eyebrow, clearly trying to lighten the mood.

I couldn't help but laugh at the absurdity of it all. "Well, if I could predict the future, I wouldn't be sitting here, waiting for you to talk to me." I gave him a pointed look, hoping he'd just hurry up and say it already.

Keith shifted in his seat, his leg bouncing nervously beneath the dashboard. His eyes caught mine. "Well, if you could read my mind, you'd know that since our trip to Charlottesville, I've been half in love with you."

I froze. My breath caught in my throat, and I felt the weight of his words sink into the pit of my stomach. I glanced over at him, trying to gauge if this was some sort of joke, but he was looking at me seriously.

Was this really happening? *Half in love with me?*

My heart hammered in my chest. I needed to know if he was serious, or if this was just another one of those complicated things that I was hopeless at. I tried to keep my voice steady, though it cracked slightly when I spoke. "Half in love with me?"

Keith shifted in his seat, fingers drumming an erratic rhythm against the steering wheel. "I don't know what the hell I'm doing here, Rachel," he said quietly. "I just know I'm halfway gone over you, and it's scaring the crap out of me."

I couldn't help but swallow hard, the weight of his confession sinking in. My stomach twisted, but not in the bad way, the nervous way. It was like a mix of excitement and fear—of something real. I leaned back in my seat, trying to process everything he'd said, my mind still racing.

"Okay," I said, my voice softer now, a little unsure. "So, you've been... half in love with me. And now you want to... what? Be my boyfriend?" The word boyfriend felt strange on my tongue, like I was back in middle school, dreaming for a boy to sweep me off my feet.

Keith glanced at me, his expression softer. "Yeah, I want to be your boyfriend." He exhaled sharply, like he was bracing for rejection.

Silence between us stretched, my thoughts jumbling together in a way that felt almost dizzying. I pulled in a shaky breath. "You know, for someone who says they're bad at this, you're doing pretty good."

He half-smiled, the corner of his mouth twitching up. "I've been practicing."

I couldn't help but laugh. "Yeah, I can tell."

Keith smiled, "I haven't been someone's boyfriend since eleventh grade." His smile faltered for a second, but then he leaned back in his seat. "Look, I'm not trying to rush anything, Rachel. I know you might not be in love with me."

My heart did that stupid little flip again, but I held my ground, keeping my arms crossed tightly across my chest. "What if I'm half in love with you, too?"

He hesitated, his eyes softening as he looked over at me. "I'd say what can I do to convince you to be completely in love?" He took a deep breath. "A relationship with me won't be perfect because, hell, I know I'm going to screw it up somehow." He sighed, shaking his head.

I swallowed hard. "What happens if I screw it up? Because we both know that's likely to happen."

Keith chuckled softly, shaking his head. "I guess we figure it out together."

The sincerity in his voice hit me like a wave, making my chest tighten. I wanted to believe him. I really did. But I couldn't shake the nagging doubt in the back of my mind. What if I wasn't enough for him? What if I couldn't keep his attention?

He leaned closer, and my breath caught. I shoved my doubts into the back of my mind, my heartbeat pounding louder in my ears as he closed the distance between us until his lips met mine.

I kissed him back, my doubts unraveling with every brush of his lips against mine. His hand found my cheek, gentle and sure, anchoring me in the moment.

And just like that, something shifted—quiet and certain—as if my heart had already decided.

I wasn't just falling for him. I already had.

Chapter 23

Keith

What would you do if your partner took you roller-skating?
a) Hold onto them for balance, pretending you're not totally out of your element.
b) Playfully race them, hoping you can keep up and maybe even win.
c) Fall into their arms on purpose, making it *really* hard for them to resist you.
d) Get a little too close while trying to show off your moves, turning the rink into a private dance floor.

The smell of pepperoni pizza and sweaty skates hit me the second I stepped into the roller rink, as sharp and overwhelming as a slap to the face. Overhead, a giant disco ball spun lazily, scattering fractured bits of light that danced across the polished floor and flickered on the walls. Multicolored string lights dangled from the ceiling, blinking along with a Taylor Swift remix blasting through the speakers, the bass rattling my chest.

Kids zipped past in varying states of confidence. Two eighth-grade boys were locked in a high-stakes speed duel, weaving dangerously around their slower classmates. Meanwhile, a pack of sixth-grade girls clung to one another like a human chain, shrieking every time one of them teetered on the brink of disaster.

"Keep the laces tight, Sawyer," I called the rapscallion as he wobbled away from the skate rental counter, arms flailing like a baby bird trying to take flight.

He shot me a thumbs-up, immediately lost his balance, and slid down the wall in a heap. To his credit, Sawyer laughed it off, pushing himself upright and skating away.

Marnie McQuistion, the teen living teacher, came over to stand beside me. And we surveyed the roller-skating mayhem together.

"I can't remember having that much energy," Marnie chuckled, glancing around the rink.

I didn't reply. My attention was fixed across the rink, where I spotted Rachel skating with a group of students. Her cheeks were flushed, and the changing lights made her hair shift from green to red, making her look like a middle schooler herself.

Marnie followed my gaze, her grin widening. "Paging Keith. Earth to Keith. Word on the street is you and Rachel have been spending an awful lot of time together. Should I be updating my Marchfield staff romance bracket?"

"You've got a bracket? That's concerning," I said, raising an eyebrow.

"Gotta supplement the retirement income somehow." The cheerful, redhead sighed, but her eyes were sparkling. She was one of the sweetest teachers at school, but she had a talent for gossip, and she kept the breakroom far more entertaining than it had any right to be.

Rachel skated by, waving. I waved back despite Marnie's hawk like observation. I could stand here all night, just watching her, and it still wouldn't be enough.

Marnie's eyes widened as she leaned back, crossing her arms. "Well, would you look at your face! I'll have to make some adjustments to my predictions. Does Rachel know she's been added to your bracket?"

I gasped in mock shock. "You're nosey," I shot back.

Emily hobbled up with one skate on and one off. Her glasses were sliding down her nose, and she looked like she was about cry. Holding it up, I saw the broken lace. "Can you help me, Mr. Payt?"

"Sure thing," I said, shooting Marnie a smirk, relieved to have dodged her questioning.

As I threaded the lace through the eyelets, I stole a glance at the rink. The music had shifted to *All I Want for Christmas Is You*, and in the center, a group of kids was belting it out—off-key, off-rhythm, and somehow still louder than the speakers.

I handed the skate back to Emily, who beamed like I'd just saved her life. "Thanks!"

"No problem," I said, giving her thumbs-up.

Skating off the rink, Rachel rolled over to grab a water bottle from the counter next to me, twisting off the cap with a flick of her wrist. Tilting her head back, she took a slow sip, her throat moving with each swallow. A drop escaped the corner of her mouth, trailing down her flushed skin before she wiped it away with the back of her hand. Her eyes flicked to mine over the bottle, amusement dancing in them, like she knew exactly what she was doing.

"Enjoying yourself, Mr. Payt?" she asked, her tone teasing as she came to a stop in front of me.

I crossed my arms, smirking back at her. "I didn't realize roller-skating was your hidden talent."

"I was a Girl Scout. Got my roller-skating badge when I was, like, nine. Total pro."

I smirked. "Impressive. I think I was still falling off my bike at nine."

Rachel tilted her head, smiling, her expression making my stomach do an unexpected little flip. Her eyes sparkled under the rink's shifting lights, and that smile, equal parts challenge and mischief, was impossible to ignore. "So, when are you getting out there?"

I blinked, caught off guard. "Out where?"

"On the rink," she said, gesturing dramatically at the swirling lights and skating frenzy behind her. "You know, skating."

"I don't skate."

"What? Never?"

"Yup. Never."

She crossed her arms, smirking. "You're chaperoning a skating party and you don't skate?" Tilting her head, she gave me a dramatic, doe-eyed look, her voice taking on a wistful lilt. "But I always wanted to skate with my boyfriend."

I sighed dramatically. "Fine." Squaring my shoulders, I took a pair of skates and followed her over to the chairs. "But if I break my leg, I'm blaming you." But beneath the teasing, something warmer settled in my chest. If she wanted to skate with her boyfriend, I wanted to be the guy who laced up and made it happen. I wanted to give her everything—even if it meant risking total humiliation.

A few minutes later, I'd run out of time. Rachel skated closer, eyes dancing. She gestured toward the rink. "The floor awaits."

Together we rolled across the carpet, and I foolishly thought skating wasn't that hard. But when we stepped onto the slick surface of the rink, my feet immediately forgot how to function.

"Whoa!" My arms pinwheeled as my skates slid out from under me. I stiffened, gripping the wall like my life depended on it. Rachel grabbed my arm, steadying me before I could completely wipe out.

Around us, kids zipped by, whispering, pointing, and offering their unsolicited skating wisdom.

"Lean forward, Mr. Payt!" Emily called helpfully. "You're gonna fall backward!"

"Thanks, Em!" I shot back, trying to sound grateful rather than terrified.

Sawyer skated past, throwing out a dramatic warning. "Keep your knees bent, or you'll wipe out!"

"Great. Just what I need—tips from the peanut gallery," I muttered under my breath, flailing until my hands found Rachel's shoulder.

"You're doing great!" she said, way too cheerfully.

"We obviously have different definitions of that word." My feet moved in every direction except forward.

Rachel just grinned, clearly enjoying my struggle. Normally, she was the one who felt awkward, who needed saving. I wanted to be the one who had it together, but right now, I was just trying to survive.

Then my skates betrayed me completely. My legs buckled, and like a slow-motion car wreck,

I

    started

      to

        fall...

...only to be caught by Rachel. Her arms wrapped around me, strong and steady, pulling me against her before I could crash onto the unforgiving hardwood.

Her warmth seeped through my jacket, her breath fanning against my cheek as she held me upright. All that existed was the feel of her hands gripping my arms, the steady rise and fall of her chest. I never wanted her to let go.

"I love you." The words burst out of me louder than I had intended, hanging in the quiet space between songs. The next track kicked in, but it was too late.

Everyone around us screeched to a halt. Kids stopped mid-glide, eyes going wide. Someone let out a romantic sigh. I suspected it was Marnie.

Rachel stiffened in my arms. Her lips parted, and for the first time since I'd met her, I saw real, unguarded surprise on her face.

And then the dawn broke, and she was smiling like the sun. "I love you, too."

For a moment, I just stood in her arms, taking in the way the rainbow of light made her look even more beautiful. Her eyes sparkled, and that smile of hers made me feel like I was standing on the top of a mountain. This was it. Everything clicked.

But before I could find the words to tell her, a chorus of giggles shattered the moment.

"Are you guys, like, boyfriend and girlfriend?" one of the girls called, her high-pitched voice teasing, while the others tried to stifle their laughter.

I rolled a bit away from Rachel, wobbling unsteadily on the skates, to face the curious eyes of students and teachers alike. But I held her hand. "Yup, and I'm the luckiest guy in town."

Chapter 24

Rachel

What would you do if his old flame texted?
a) Act casual, but keep a close eye on how he responds.
b) Pretend it doesn't bother you, but secretly start plotting your response.
c) Play it cool, then subtly make your presence known in the background.
d) Confront him head-on, making it clear that you're the one he should be focusing on now.

The carriage house smelled like cinnamon when Keith and I bustled in after the roller-skating event, breathless and tangled together in the doorway. The cold clung to our coats, but the heat between us burned hot.

He barely got the door shut before I was tugging at the zipper of his worn leather jacket, desperate to get closer. Shoving it off his shoulders, it dropped to the floor. I fumbled with mine, but his hands were there, pushing it past my shoulders, his mouth chasing mine.

"Finally, alone," he murmured against my lips, his breath warm despite the winter chill still clinging to his skin.

"And nowhere else I'd rather be," I whispered, my fingers curling into his sweater as I pulled him deeper into the apartment.

Keith's hands slid under the hem of my sweater, his fingers tracing the dip of my lower back, slow and deliberate.

I shivered at his touch, pressing in closer. "Seriously, do your hands live in a snowbank?"

"It's the theme of our relationship," he said with a grin as I slid my hands up his back, tugging him against me.

I laughed, breathless. "Why is that both tragically inconvenient and weirdly addictive?"

Keith chuckled, his voice low against my neck. "At least I'm not bruised and muddy this time." His lips brushed my jaw, soft and slow, like a promise stretched out in heat.

He didn't rush, letting my skin warm his fingers as he explored, his thumbs pressing gentle, teasing circles that sent shivers up my spine. Every brush of his skin against mine tightened the coil of anticipation low in my stomach, making it impossible to focus on anything but the way he felt, the way he *always* made me feel like I was treasured, savored, *loved*. I shivered at his touch, arching closer.

"I love you, Rachel." His voice was low and rough, those precious, new words, sending a spark straight through me. He pulled back slightly, his forehead resting against mine. "I should probably be a gentleman and ask if you want me to stay."

I rolled my eyes, pulling him closer by the collar of his jacket. "Keith, you can stop pretending to be a gentleman."

His grin was pure mischief. "Oh, thank God."

Loving the feel of his laugh, deep and warm, vibrating through me, I pressed closer, feeling the solid warmth of him. His lips found my jaw, the spot beneath my ear, trailing heat with every slow, teasing kiss.

My hands slipped beneath his sweater and traced along his lean ribs. He exhaled sharply, his muscles tensing beneath my touch, and then he was lifting me, carrying me toward the couch without breaking the kiss.

I saw movement from the corner of my eye as Bolt plodded along the floor silently and paused near Keith's boot on his endless quest for snacks.

"Watch out," I called, laughing. "Tortoise on the move."

He froze instantly, eyes wide as if Bolt were a threat of epic proportions. "What? Where?"

I grinned as he carefully sidestepped Bolt, like he was navigating a landmine. "Good thing you've got your boots on. He might've mistaken your toes for a snack."

"No thanks, Bolt." Keith grinned, lowering me to the sofa. "But I wouldn't mind if you bit my toes."

Before I could respond, his lips were on mine, deep and slow, pulling me into the kiss. His hands slid up my sides, thumbs brushing the edge of my bra, sending a shiver through me. The teasing lightness of his words melted away as the kiss deepened, the heat between us growing undeniable. Keith kissed like he had something to prove—like he was making sure I felt every ounce of his love.

I curled my fingers into his hair, tugging just enough to make him groan, and he pressed me harder against the door, his body solid against mine. My knees were already unsteady, my breath catching in my throat as his lips moved to my neck, his hands wandering in ways that made my brain go static.

A shrill ringtone shattered the moment.

Keith swore under his breath, dropping his head to my shoulder as I let out a frustrated groan.

I pulled back, frustration bubbling up in my chest. Of course. His phone. My mind raced with memories of coming out of the restroom to find him scrolling through dating apps.

I'd tried to push past my knee-jerk reaction, but I couldn't stop myself from tensing as that familiar, nagging doubt crept in again. The one that whispered I'd never be enough for him.

His breath hitched, but then his phone rang again. "It might be Sunny. She's driving home tonight for winter break," he muttered, pulling it from his pocket.

I forced a sigh, hoping it was Sunny. Hoping it was anything that didn't stir up a gnawing insecurity inside me.

"Keith," I murmured, trying to ignore the tightness in my chest and the worry that I couldn't compete with the women in his past.

"I don't recognize the number. Must be spam."

But before I could relax, the phone buzzed again. This time, it was a text. His eyes flicked over to the screen. His shoulders tensed and he frowned.

He didn't say anything for a moment, just stared at the phone in his hand.

And I knew.

I realized he was decoding the text, but I couldn't help asking, "Who is it?"

He stared at the phone for a long time as he struggled to decode the text. "It's... someone from my past."

I felt my heart sink as he tilted the phone towards me.

8:49 PM:

1(757) 555-6969: Hey, Keith. It's Joy. Been thinking about you lately. Want to reconnect?

The words stung like a slap, the sudden rush of jealousy and insecurity threatening to drown me. I leapt up, trying to stop the whirlwind of thoughts racing in my head. Slow the pounding of my heart, but I couldn't quite steady my breath. What if he was just settling for me until someone better came along?

Keith's expression was soft as he tried to reassure me. "She's not in my contacts. I didn't reach out to her," he said, his voice calm and steady, like I was a nervous animal he had to soothe.

The walls closed in, the weight of my own mind pressing down on me. My anxiety flared as thoughts bounced in rapid-fire circles.

Turning to him, I murmured, "I can't keep doing this."

Keith's eyes widened, a mix of confusion and concern flooding his face. "I'll block her. I'll do whatever it takes, Rachel. You have to know that I'm serious about you. I love you."

He was saying everything I needed to hear, but it didn't untwist the knot in my gut. His promise felt like a Band-Aid that would cover the wound in my heart but never heal it. I wanted to believe him. I did believe him.

But the nagging fear was too much. I'd never be enough. He loved me now, but it wouldn't last. And when he left, I'd be broken.

"I just..." My voice trembled, and I hated myself for it. I hated that I couldn't silence the panic. "I don't know if I can be what you need without constantly wondering if I'm enough."

His face softened, but the silence between us was suffocating. "Rachel..." He took a step forward, but I stepped back, shaking my head, unable to let him get close.

"I can't do this now, Keith." The words felt raw and jagged as they spilled from my mouth, and for a moment, I regretted them, but I couldn't take them back. "I need... I need space."

He opened his mouth, but no words came out. His frustration was palpable, that made me feel even worse. He hadn't done anything wrong this time, but I was still pushing him away, and I hated myself for it.

"I need you to go," I said again, my voice breaking.

Keith's jaw tightened, his shoulders sagging. The hurt in his eyes was too much to bear, but this was the only choice I could make.

He didn't argue. He just nodded slowly, a sad smile tugging at the corner of his mouth. "Okay. I'll go. But don't shut me out, Rachel. Please. I know we can figure this out." He shrugged on his jacket. "I love you, Rachel."

I buried my face in my hands, trying to hope the tears at bay until the door clicked shut behind him.

Chapter 25

Keith

What do you plan for your grand gesture?
a) Write a heartfelt letter, then hope they don't lose it in the trash.
b) Plan a surprise date and pray they don't figure it out too soon.
c) Set up a quiet moment and hope your nerves don't ruin it.
d) Organize a spectacle.

I parked my truck behind Sunny's Nissan, and yanked out my phone, Joy's message blinking up at me, a stark reminder of how fucked up my life was.

Hey, Keith. It's Joy. Been thinking about you lately. Want to reconnect?

I stared at the message, frowning. I couldn't even picture this woman—the name stirred nothing. Just static from a time I didn't want to revisit. With a quiet sigh, I tapped over to the block feature and let my thumb do the rest, sending her back to the past where she'd always belonged.

Frustration burned inside me. I'd really tried to show Rachel how much I wanted to be with her. But in the end, all the promises in the world couldn't prove to her that I'd changed. That she was the only one for me.

I could still feel the weight of her words, her voice trembling when she told me to leave.

I need space.

I'd wanted to demand that she listen to me, that she see what was right in front of her. But I knew it would only make things worse.

Slamming the door to my truck, the cold air cut through me as I trudged to the front door. What the hell was I supposed to do now?

Every light in the house was on. The steady thrum of music pulsed through the walls, so loud it felt like it was coming from inside my head. I stood there for a moment, hands in my pockets, debating whether I should just turn around, get back in my truck, and drive away.

Before I could, the front door swung open. Despite the freezing temperature, Sunshine ran out barefoot, wearing nothing but skimpy shorts and a tank top. She threw her arms around me.

"I'm home!" she said, grinning ear to ear, her long blonde hair flying around her face.

I smiled in return, but fatigue weighed on me like a thick coat. My jaw was sore from clenching it, and my shoulders ached from the effort of keeping my frustration inside.

I ruffled her hair and pulled back slightly, my hand still resting on her shoulder. "Hi," I said, trying to keep the cheer in my voice, but it was hard.

Sunshine leaned back, her quick eyes scanning my face. "Come inside and tell me about your day."

She ducked into the warm house, and I followed woodenly, searching for something easy to talk about. "How was the drive home?"

"Good," she answered, her voice light but then she turned to face me, her expression sharpening. "What's going on with you?"

She could always read me better than anyone. She knew the subtle shifts in my energy, the way I carried myself when my mind was elsewhere. No matter how I tried to hide my emotions, she could always see through the cracks in my mask.

I sank into the couch, rubbing my face with both hands. "I... I fucked up," I muttered, my voice raw.

Sunshine raised an eyebrow. "What else is new?" She perched on the arm of the couch next to me and gestured for me to continue.

"My past finally caught up with me," I muttered. I could still feel the sting of Rachel's words, the look on her face when she asked me to leave.

Sunshine frowned, sitting up straighter. "What'd you do?"

I sighed, running a hand through my hair as frustration bubbled over. "It's not what I did, it's who I was. You know, I did a lot of dumb shit, but I've moved on in the last year. Yet, every time I take a step forward, something from that past shows up and..." I trailed off, the weight of it hanging in the air. I could feel her watching me, waiting for me to continue.

"Rachel doesn't trust me," I said quietly, almost more to myself than to her. "Every time my phone rings, she worries I'm trolling for women or something."

Sunny's expression softened, but there was steel in her voice. "That's not fair. You've shown up, Keith, again and again. She sees that, even if she's not ready to admit it yet. Just... keep being steady. She just doesn't know how to stop bracing for impact."

I shook my head. "I love her and she loves me. I want her to see me for who I am."

She leaned back. "If she doesn't, she's a fool."

"But I'm always one mistake away from losing her."

"I know," she said, her voice softer now. "Don't give up."

I exhaled sharply, leaning back in my chair. "I'm not giving up. I just... need to do something."

Sunny gave me a small smile. "Show her you're serious, that you're willing to fight for her."

I stared at her, processing her words.

"Didn't your friend, Oz, do a performance on the field? Maybe you could do that?"

"Rachel would hate that," I said immediately, knowing deep in my bones that Rachel was too private for a grand gesture like that.

"Okay, something more intimate," Sunshine mused. "What about something here at the house?"

"Maybe. But what?" I leaned forward, elbows on my knees.

Sunshine shook her head. "She needs to feel like there's room for her in your world—not just in your heart, but in the day-to-day stuff. The plans. The hard moments. All of it." She tucked her legs under her and rested her chin on her fist. "What does she like to do?"

"Room, huh?" I dragged a hand over my face again, thinking of all the little details I'd collected about Rachel without realizing I'd been storing them away. "Hazelnut coffee, donuts from Pat's, and romance books."

Sunny's grin was immediate, eyes sparking with amusement. "She's a fellow smut lover. I knew I liked her." She nudged my leg with her foot. "Maybe you could buy her a new tablet."

I shook my head before she even finished the sentence. "She likes paper books. She's got bookshelves and boxes of them."

An image of Rachel flashed through my mind. Curled up in her oversized chair, lost in a book, her fingers absently toying with the edge of a page. I could see her forehead creased as she was deep in thought, and the way she bit her lip when she hit an emotional part.

Sunshine studied me, her smirk softening into something warmer. "What if you made her a bookcase?"

The idea landed with more force than I expected.

And that's when it hit me—I had space for Rachel. Not just in my life, but in my house.

I'd been circling ideas for the attic for weeks. An office, maybe. Expanding the master suite. But none of it ever stuck. A library, though. A quiet, sunlit space filled with shelves for all her books? That felt right.

I stood, rolling my shoulders as the idea took root in my mind. "I can do better than that."

Sunshine arched a brow. "Tell me more."

I didn't answer right away. Instead, I grabbed a flashlight from the kitchen drawer, nodding for her to follow.

Wood creaked under our feet as we climbed up the attic stairs. Dust hung thick in the air, illuminated by a single, weak overhead bulb. Boxes were stacked haphazardly along the walls, remnants of previous owners, their labels faded and curling.

I leaned against the wooden beam, looking around the dusty attic. "What if I turned the attic into a retreat for Rachel? Her space. A place where she belongs. Where she can disappear when life gets too loud."

"This isn't exactly what I pictured when you said retreat," Sunny said with a grin, giving the ceiling a skeptical glance. "But I get what you're going for."

I pointed along the far wall. "Right here. I could put in bookshelves. Rows of them, all different sizes, to fit the space. A mix of high ones and low ones, like... like they're a part of the place. Books of every size, color—her favorites, but also books she hasn't discovered yet."

She nodded, following my line of sight. "You could even build shelves so the room itself becomes part of the story."

"Exactly," I said, already imagining it in my mind's eye. "It'll feel like the room's alive, breathing stories in every direction. And over here," I pointed to a small nook by the window, "a wooden desk, maybe an antique. It's gotta be the kind that feels worn in, like it's been around forever but still functional. She can write there or sit with a cup of coffee."

Sunny stepped over to the spot and ran her fingers along the edge of the floorboards. "I like that. That's a good spot for a desk. Then what? Some seating?"

I smiled, knowing exactly what I wanted. "Armchairs. Big, overstuffed ones. One by the window, and another near the desk. It'll be cozy, something that pulls you in."

"How about a chaise lounge?" she asked. "And some floor lamps."

"Nothing too bright. I want it to feel like a secret. Like she's walking into her own personal world." I ran a hand across the floorboards, lost in thought for a second. "It'll take a lot of work. It needs insulation, the electricity needs to be up to code, and a million other things."

Sunny was silent for a moment, then gave a slight smile. "I love it, and she will, too."

I nodded, turning to look at her. "I want her to feel like she's the center of everything in this room. Like nothing else matters but her comfort. Nothing else but her peace."

Sunny met my eyes, her expression worried. "It's gonna cost a lot."

I took a deep breath, trying to steady myself. "Mom had a life insurance policy. It wasn't much, but I invested it, and it's grown. I was going to give you half when you finished college. But this is what I've been saving mine for."

Sunny gave a slow nod, her expression thoughtful. "You've always taken care of me, Keith. I don't know how you've managed to do it all, but I've always felt like you had my back. Mom would be proud of you. And she'd love that what she left us is going toward something that means so much to you." She paused, her smile growing. "It's the perfect grand gesture."

Chapter 26

What would you do to find your inner power?
a) Embrace your flaws and hope they turn into "quirky charm" in the end.
b) Take a deep breath, channel your inner confidence, and fake it until you make it.
c) Call your bestie for a pep talk, then strut out like you own the place.
d) Dive into what scares you, because who needs comfort zones anyway?

Hours blurred together as I sprawled on my couch, surrounded by stacks of romance novels as I packed them into boxes. My coffee table was a graveyard of empty mugs and crumpled tissues. The TV droned quietly in the background, some reality show I wasn't watching.

I couldn't stop thinking about Keith. My mind, stuck in an endless loop, replayed his words and actions over and over. His past, the women, the fear that he might slip back into old habits.

And then I'd hear him say I love you. And I'd cry because I wanted to believe him. I wanted to feel secure in his love, but how could I? I was me, and Keith was... Keith. His past, his habits, the doubts made it impossible to trust in something so fragile as love.

When Barb knocked on my door around ten, she took a long silent look at me and pushed her way inside. Her arms were loaded with romance novels. She wore warm, comfortable patterned leggings and an oversized sweater.

"Sweetheart," she sighed, setting the books down on the coffee table. "You look like you lost a fight with a box of tissues—and the train that brought them to town."

I nodded, not trusting my raw voice after hours of sobbing.

"Well, nothing heals a broken heart like smut." She plopped onto the couch beside me, tucking her legs under herself and diving into the bag of books. "Now, let's see what we've got. Have you read this one?" She held up a book with a minotaur and a half-nude woman on the cover. "It comes highly recommended."

I eyed the cover. "Recommended by who? Someone with... very specific tastes?"

Barb grinned. "Listen, I don't judge what gets people through their lonely nights. But if you're not feeling this one, how about we talk about the one with dragons we finished last week?"

Normally, I'd roll my eyes and let her distract me with plotlines and her latest book boyfriend obsession. But even Barb's endless enthusiasm couldn't pull me out of my misery.

I shook my head, tears welling up. "I'm done with romance, Barb. I put all my books up for sale last night on Marketplace."

Barb's eyes widened in disbelief. "No! You've been building that collection for years!" She shook her head.

I let out a shaky breath, crossing my arms over my chest. "I'm not kidding. They're all up for sale. It's all a fantasy. The idea of happily ever after... it's all just... not real. Not for me."

Barb stared at me for a long beat, her expression one of shock mixed with confusion. Then, without another word, she grabbed her phone and started typing out a text. "Alright. This is bad. I'm calling in reinforcements."

"What?" I asked, my voice slightly panicked. "Who?"

"Audrey and Val."

I blinked, trying to process.

Despite my inner despair, I couldn't help but raise an eyebrow. "How did you get their numbers?"

Barb looked up from her phone, a grin spreading across her face. "Are you kidding? Audrey gave them to me the last time we all hung out." She paused, her fingers still typing away at lightning speed. "How about a manicure? You'll feel like a brand-new woman in no time."

I let out a frustrated sigh. Why did people always feel like I needed fixing? What if a brand-new me wasn't any better?

But Barb sent the text, already plotting my transformation with Val and Audrey. I wanted to protest, to say I wasn't ready for this, but part of me responded to her energy.

"You need this, Rach. Trust me." Barb flashed me a determined look.

It seemed I didn't have much of a choice, but I protested anyway. "Barb, I don't need a manicure. I just need a shower and some sleep."

"I'm not taking no for an answer. I'm calling Margie at the salon, and the girls will meet us there."

I didn't have the energy to fight her. "Fine. I'll hop in the shower."

This was a distraction—a way to avoid the bigger problem in my life. At first, I told myself that it was pointless. But the more I thought about it, the more going out started to feel like something I needed. And as much as I hated to admit it, excitement to do something just for me sounded fun.

***

The scent of eucalyptus and lemongrass lingered in the air, mixing with the faint hint of acetone as Audrey, Val, Barb and I lounged in oversized chairs, our hands resting on plush towels while the nail technicians worked their magic. Soft instrumental music played overhead, the sound of water trickling from a nearby fountain adding to the peaceful ambiance and making worries melt away.

Too bad mine clung like ugly nail polish.

I'd scrubbed at my feelings, tried to file them down into something manageable, but the truth was raw and jagged beneath the surface. I'd told him I loved him, and I'd meant it. And yet, the second I saw that text from his ex, every ounce of certainty shattered like a glass bottle of polish on tile.

Love didn't mean people didn't betray you.

I clenched my jaw, watching as the technician carefully swiped another layer of pink polish over my nails, smooth and flawless. I wished emotions worked the same way. That I could just add on a layer of defense, hide the cracks, and make myself normal.

But no amount of polish could cover up my problems. I was never going to be easy. Never going to be the kind of woman who instinctively knew how to navigate life without overthinking everything.

What if one day, Keith woke up and realized I was too much—too rigid, too literal, too caught up in a world that made sense only to me? Would he reach out to a woman like Joy?

A warm, steady hand settled on my hand, pulling me back before I could spiral further. I blinked, my breath catching as I realized Barb had covered my fingers with her own, keeping them still so the technician could paint the last coat without my fidgeting ruining it. The gentle pressure reminded me I wasn't alone.

Val let out a dramatic sigh, her head lolling to the side as she fixed me with a look. "Okay, time to talk about the elephant in the nail salon."

I stiffened, eyes locked on the pale pink polish being applied to my nails. "I'm fine."

Barb didn't even bother pretending to believe me. "Are you?"

My stomach twisted. "I have a right to be upset."

Val arched a brow. "Absolutely. If one of Evan's exes texted him, I'd probably have a mini meltdown, too. But, Rach... you're running on zero sleep, selling your romances, and worrying about worst-case scenarios."

My jaw tightened. Logically, I knew that my thoughts had spiraled, so intensely, that by the time Keith tried to explain, it was already too late. My body had gone into survival mode. But knowing it and stopping it were two different things.

Barb exhaled slowly, her fingers drumming against the arm of her chair until the technician gently stilled her hand. "My instincts told me you could trust Keith this time." She frowned, her voice quieter now. "If I was wrong... then I let you down."

Barb wasn't wrong. Keith was kind and patient, and he'd never once made me feel like I had to be anything other than myself. But that's the problem, isn't it? He understood how my brain worked, but I was terrified he'd eventually decide it was too much.

I swallowed hard, staring down at my hands. This was why I'd kept my autism to myself for years, afraid of what people would think. I couldn't handle them treating me differently, seeing me as fragile or broken. But sitting here now, hearing the worry in their voices, I wondered if keeping it from them was just another way I'd been trying to protect myself. Another layer of armor.

I swallowed hard. "I don't have a lot of experience with men. And I—I just panicked. I couldn't breathe, and I shut down before I got hurt."

Barb lifted an eyebrow. "And how's that working out for you?"

I pressed my lips together, the truth thick in my throat. "It sucks."

Val leaned back, a satisfied smirk curving her lips. "Good. There's still hope."

Audrey's gaze softened. "You can be scared, Rach. But don't let fear make your choices for you."

The nail technicians finished and slid fresh mugs of tea in front of us. The fragrant blend of chamomile, lavender, and honey calmed me. I wrapped my fingers around the warm cup, letting the heat seep into my palms, as I tried to steady my thoughts.

"There's something I haven't told you guys... something I've never said out loud, but you may have guessed. I'm... I'm on the spectrum."

The silence that followed was deafening. The air in the room thickened, and I could barely breathe through the weight of it.

The fear of their judgment, of their disappointment, gripped me harder than I expected. My heart raced in my chest, my fingers twitching, unsure what to do with myself.

Barb's expression softened, and she reached out to squeeze my hand. "Oh honey, that doesn't change anything. You're still you."

Audrey leaned forward, her smile warm and reassuring. "Exactly. You're our Rach, just with a little extra depth. If anything, it just explains why you're so damn smart and always one step ahead of the rest of us."

Val nodded. "Honestly, I always thought you were secretly a genius. This just confirms it. It's no big deal, Rach. We're here for you, no matter what."

"Does Keith know?" Barb asked.

I nodded, but the knot in my stomach tightened. "Yes. But I'm scared he'll get overwhelmed. That he'll realize I'm too much or too broken to handle."

Val reached over and gave my hand a quick squeeze. "Keith's not the type to walk away because you're different. He knows what it's like to struggle."

Audrey nodded in agreement, her voice steady and firm. "Val's right. And you know what? You've got more strength than you give yourself credit for. You've been doing this, being you, your whole life. If Keith can't handle that, then he's not the one. That's on him, not you."

A sense of clarity washed over me. Maybe I had spent so long worrying about what might happen that I hadn't considered what was already in front of me. Keith knew me. And he'd still said he loved me.

His phone, the other women. He'd promised he was over them. But I kept using them as a barrier, convincing myself that I had to compete with them. When, in reality, they were just dusty remnants of his past.

I didn't need to make excuses or hold back. If Keith loved me, he loved all of me: the quirks, fears, and everything else. It was time for me to stop being afraid of what might happen and accept what was right in front of me.

Taking a deep breath, the knot in my stomach loosened just a little. "You're right," I said, more firmly than I expected. "If Keith really cares about me, then he'll accept me as I am, just like you did."

Barb smiled softly, her hand still resting on mine. "Exactly. And if he doesn't, then we'll squash him like the cockroach."

The four technicians cheered from where they stood by the desk, clearly listening to the whole story. One of them clapped, another whistled, and someone tossed a stress ball in the air like they'd just won a prize. The energy in the room shifted—lighter now, full of relief and a hint of celebration.

Val stretched her legs from her chair with a grin, her eyes sparkling with mischief. "We deserve something a little more indulgent now. Who's up for a shopping spree?"

Audrey's eyes lit up. "Are we talking about Classic Curves down the street? I've been dying to try on their winter collection."

Barb grinned. "Count me in. I need something new for a Christmas party at the senior center next week."

"Let's go," I said, standing and shaking out the last of the tension in my shoulders.

Moments later we were down the street and entering Classic Curves. The shop felt warm and inviting, the soft lighting casting a cozy glow across the racks of clothing. The scent of vanilla and citrus teased my senses, and an upbeat tune floated through the space. My friends dashed from rack to rack, chatting excitedly as they grabbed sweaters and dresses.

I ran my fingers over soft fabrics, admiring the colors and textures, but nothing felt like me. The fabrics were inviting, but I couldn't make a choice. Clothes didn't speak to me the way they did to many women. I'd take a book over shopping any day.

Audrey sidled up beside me, a knowing grin on her face. "Find anything you like, Rach?"

"Not really," I muttered.

She hummed thoughtfully and began pulling a few pieces from the rack.

She held up a copper and gold sheath dress with a grin. "Oh, Rachel. This is your lucky day. This color is perfect for you."

Barb adjusted her glasses and looked over. "You'd look amazing in that dress."

Val, deep in a pile of oversized sweaters, glanced up. "You're not leaving here until you find at least three outfits that make you look and feel great."

I laughed, half in disbelief, half in gratitude. "You guys are seriously going to make me try this on, aren't you?"

"Yes!" Audrey said with a mischievous grin, shoving clothes into my arms. "Let us spoil you a little. You deserve to walk out of here feeling incredible."

I tried on the copper and gold dress Audrey had picked out first. The fabric slid smoothly over my skin, fitting me perfectly.

I looked in the mirror, and for the first time in a long while, I didn't second-guess what I saw. The woman staring back was beautiful. I was beautiful.

When I stepped out, the room went silent.

Barb blinked a few times, clearly surprised. "Wow, Rachel. That's... wow."

Val squealed. "I love it! You're a woman who knows exactly what she wants and is out to get it."

I looked at myself again, the shimmer of the dress catching the light just right. I wasn't used to seeing myself this way.

"Could I wear this to school?" A spark of boldness flickered inside me. Maybe I could.

"To school or on a date. You'd look great either way," Val smiled, her eyes sparkling with approval.

"You look stunning," Audrey insisted. "This is you. No more hiding."

For once, the small voice in my head was silent. This dress was a statement. A reflection of a new me. Strong, confident, and unapologetically me. "I'll take it. This is my dress now."

My friends cheered, and Val tossed me a pair of boots, her eyes gleaming with excitement. "We're not done yet." She quickly added, "Try these boots with these jeans and this maroon sweater."

Forty-five minutes later, I walked out of the store in a soft cream-colored sweater, high-waisted jeans, and soft brown boots.

A few hours ago, I'd been weighed down by doubt, unsure of myself. But now, I wasn't just in my own skin, I owned it. And it wasn't about impressing anyone, least of all Keith. This was for me. I was ready to take charge and embrace every part of myself.

Chapter 27

Keith

You feel guilty. What would you do?
a) Go on a road trip to the wrong destination, end up stranded in a snowstorm, and share one bed with someone you *definitely* shouldn't fall for.
b) Fake being your best friend's partner at a wedding, only to be seduced by the best man, your office rival.
d) Apologize with an emotional letter but accidentally mail it to your boss.
c) Join a team-building retreat full of trust falls and improv games with your secret crush.

I ran my hand over the smooth wooden shelves, feeling the grain beneath my fingertips. It was finally coming together.

Sunlight streamed in through the skylight, casting golden patches of light over the soft, thick carpet, turning the dust motes in the air into tiny floating stars. The built-in shelves stretched from floor to ceiling, their rich mahogany finish gleaming in the afternoon glow, each one waiting to be filled with well-loved stories.

A cozy reading nook nestled in the far corner, complete with a cushioned window seat sat near the far end. Plush chairs, the kind you could sink into for an afternoon, were arranged near a low coffee table. The chaise lounge, like Sunny had suggested, pulled the area together.

The scent of aged paper and fresh wood lingered in the air, blending with the faint vanilla scent from a candle Barb had set on a side table. It was a place meant to be lived in, to be filled with laughter, quiet whispers, and the rustling of pages late into the night.

The attic had been transformed into a library.

Rachel's library.

Bobby and Oz reached the top of the stairs, still bickering, their voices bouncing off the attic walls. With a final grunt, they dropped the last two boxes onto the growing stack near Barb, who made a note on her clipboard. She arched a brow at me, then exchanged a knowing look with the others.

I owed Barb more than I could say. She was the one who'd helped me track down Rachel's books on Marketplace and buy them without her catching on.

"I gotta say, Keith," Bobby said, brushing dust off her hands, "we told you not to screw things up with Rachel."

"Warned you," Oz corrected, stretching exaggeratedly like the effort of carrying boxes had nearly killed him. "Multiple times. Pretty sure Barb even gave you the third degree."

"I did," Barb said, matter-of-factly, checking another box off the list. "And a well-organized, well-researched lecture on not being an idiot."

I let out a short laugh, but it didn't reach my chest. A stone had rested in my gut since last Friday night, since the moment Rachel looked at me like I'd betrayed her.

Joy's text had ruined everything.

One message. And Rachel had believed the worst of me.

While I'd directed contractors, carpenters, electricians, and cleaners twenty-four hours a day, I'd spent the last week reliving the way her face had closed off, how she'd told me to go. I hadn't known what to do to fix the hurt in her eyes, so I left.

At school, I stayed quiet and waited. Hoping she'd open up and talk to me. Instead, there was a new edge to her voice, a crisp professionalism that made every interaction feel measured. No more inside jokes, no more lingering glances.

Rachel didn't hesitate before brushing past me or look up when I walked into the room. Her laughter was reserved for the students and not me. She wasn't cold, exactly. But she wasn't mine anymore either.

I could sense that she was different, too. In obvious ways—her new manicure, the soft sweaters, all of that was new. But it was more than that. She had a new confidence in the way she carried herself. She moved with purpose as if she'd figured it all out, but I wasn't in the loop.

I wanted to believe finishing the library would fix all our problems. That once she saw what I'd done, she'd realize what she meant to me, and she'd love me again. But I wasn't sure.

Sunshine's footsteps were light on the stairs. When she stepped into the attic, cradling baby Liam against her shoulder, the tension in the room shifted. Liam let out a sleepy cry, his tiny fingers yanking on the fabric of her shirt. "Somebody woke up on the wrong side of the pack-n-play."

Oz turned with a smile for his son. "There's my little man," he murmured, reaching out to take the baby, brushing his hand over Liam's downy head.

The room quieted for a moment, softened by the sight. Something about the way Oz held his son hit Keith harder than he expected. He looked away, jaw tight, then spoke quietly, almost to himself.

"I love her. I love her, and she's scared of me. Not because I'd ever hurt her, but because she can't trust in us. How do I fix that?"

Barb set down her clipboard with a sigh. "Keith," she said, her voice gentler now, "Rachel just needs time."

Sunshine hugged me, her eyes full of understanding. "She's working through her own stuff."

My throat felt tight. I wanted to believe them. I really did. But the doubt had been gnawing at me for days, carving out a hollow space in my chest.

"She's different now." The words slipped out before I could stop them. I let out a rough breath and scrubbed a hand over my face. "What if she realizes I'm not what she wants and just walks away?"

Oz bounced the baby on his hip. "Keith, man, don't be a dumbass."

I shot him a glare. "Thanks for that."

He shrugged. "Rachel told you she loved you. She's pushing back because she thinks she cares too much."

Bobby nodded. "You told her you loved her, and you're giving her time. Sometimes that's all you can do."

Sunshine gave me a small smile. "If you're worried about her trusting you, maybe you try trusting her."

The words settled deep. I swallowed hard, nodding. I wasn't sure what came next, but I knew one thing. I wasn't giving up.

Barb clapped her hands together, shaking off the weight of the conversation. "Come on people, enough brooding. These books aren't going to shelve themselves."

I surveyed the growing stacks, the titles blurring together into a mess of letters. "Can we shelve them by color?" I asked, half-joking, half-desperate.

"It's a library, Keith," Sunshine added, shaking her head. "Not an influencer's bookshelf."

Bobby said with a smirk, "Pretty sure that's not how libraries work."

"It would look cool," I argued, eyeing the stacks warily. The thought of sorting through all those jumbled titles made my head ache. "And alphabetizing will take me forever."

Barb pressed her lips together like the idea physically pained her. "They've already been sorted. Just put those books on the shelf."

Bobby opened a box and set the first book on the shelf in front of her. "I love it when my friends expect free manual labor. I should've brought my tip jar."

Oz rolled his eyes as he unfastened Liam's onesie and grabbed a fresh diaper. "You wouldn't know manual labor if it smacked you in the face." He lifted Liam's legs, sliding the new diaper underneath with practiced ease.

Bobby scoffed, crossing her arms. "Excuse me? I'm the one over here shelving books while you're playing with Liam."

A small smile tugged at my lips as Oz settled into a chair and offered Liam a bottle. The baby latched on immediately, his tiny hands gripping Oz's shirt.

"You're just jealous of my multitasking abilities," Oz said, shifting Liam slightly as he rocked him.

I'd never been much of a planner, but in this moment, thoughts of the future crept in. Would Rachel want to have kids with me? The image of a tiny hand and a cap of blonde hair in my arms. Would she have her sparkling blue eyes or my stubborn streak?

Raising Sunny hadn't been easy, but a child of my own? With Rachel? The thought warmed me like sunlight pouring through the window. I'd do that in a heartbeat.

Finally, I settled into the rhythm of shelving the books, the familiar motion calming my nerves. Barb directed where each genre should go, her voice steady and confident, while the rest of us handled the heavy lifting.

I let my thoughts drift in the steady hum of our teamwork. As the books found their place on the shelves, something inside me clicked. I had created a home for her inside my space.

Would Rachel see it? A place where we could belong together. An offer for the future. A chance to build something bigger than both of us.

The thought of her sitting up here filled the hole in my heart. Every book I placed felt like one more step toward showing her I was all in. I loved her, and I would fight for our future. Confidence settled in my chest as I grabbed another stack of paperbacks and placed them on the shelf.

"So, who's taking bets on how long it takes before Rachel reorganizes this entire place?" Evan asked.

Barb snorted. "Oh, it's inevitable."

Oz slid Liam into a pouch strapped to his chest. "I say she lasts a week."

Bobby shook her head. "Three days. Max."

I found myself smiling, the knot of worry in my chest loosening even more. I could picture Rachel standing in this very spot, her hands on her hips, muttering about the inefficiency of our system before diving in and fixing it. The thought warmed me.

When the last box lay empty, Oz dusted off his hands, baby Liam snoring away. "Not bad for a bunch of amateurs."

I stepped back, taking in the finished library, the weight of it settling around me like a vow. This wasn't just a room full of books. It was a promise. A promise that I was ready to build a future with her.

Chapter 28

Rachel

What would you do to win your lover's trust back?
a) Apologize sincerely, then slowly prove you're worth believing in again.
b) Shower them with honesty, leaving no room for doubt, hoping they see your vulnerability.
c) Earn their trust with small, thoughtful gestures—one moment at a time, making sure they feel safe.
d) Prove your devotion with an unforgettable gesture that shows you're committed to making things right... and to them.

Standing in front of the mirror, I admired my gold and copper dress as it shimmered under the soft light. The fabric hugged my curves just enough to make me feel confident without being uncomfortable. I'd styled my short hair, sweeping it back, and added a few touches of makeup.

A quiet strength I wouldn't have recognized a few weeks ago filled my heart. For once, I didn't feel like I had to pretend. I looked good, and I knew it. The reflection staring back at me wasn't just a woman in the mirror. It was someone who owned her place, ready to take on whatever came next.

Today was the staff day. The last day before winter break. A day to tie up loose ends, drink an excessive amount of coffee, and hear everyone's plans for the holidays. But Keith and I were also presenting to the staff today.

A few weeks ago, I wanted to crawl under a rock before standing up in front of the faculty. I'd have been the awkward, autistic girl, stammering and second-guessing myself, making a mess of the whole thing. I wasn't that person anymore.

The road here hadn't been easy. I'd put up walls and the doubts and the fears made them hard to tear down. But now I was relaxed and ready to stand in front of a room full of teachers and face my fears.

With Keith.

It was time to face him too. To show him that I'd changed. I'd found room for him in my heart, and I wanted forever with him.

As I got in my car, I thought about our latest awkward exchange. He'd sent me the slideshow, apologizing for any mistakes I might find. I'd thanked him, wishing we were face to face so I could say everything I wanted to.

Instead, I'd written them into the slides because the words were about more than co-teaching. They were about us. About me opening up, about the two of us changing to meet the other.

The slides showcased the effort we'd both had to put in, not just as colleagues, but as two people navigating the complicated space between us, trying to make it work.

Arriving at school, I found Keith outside the library, looking every bit the professional teacher. His dark button-up shirt brought out the warmth in his eyes and paired with chinos and polished shoes, he took my breath away.

When he saw me, his eyes widened. His smile was full of admiration and a hint of surprise. He stood a little straighter, a spark of heat lighting up in his gaze. "Wow," he said, his voice low and appreciative. "You look… amazing."

I returned his smile, feeling the warmth of it spread through me. "You, too."

He shifted his feet, looking down. "I'll speak for us if you want…"

The nerves in my belly twisted, threatening to rise, but I locked them down, refusing to let them win. "No. We'll do it together."

In the library, I felt a strange mix of emotions. The familiar scent of books settled my nerves, but a different kind of tension quickly took its place. This wasn't just a presentation. It was a leap of faith. A step into the unknown, where I trusted myself and Keith.

Mr. Kline nodded to us from where he stood at the front. "Welcome, everyone," he said, his voice warm and inviting. "I'd like to turn this meeting over to Rachel and Keith. They attended a conference at the beginning of the month and are going to share some information about co-teaching."

His eyes flicked toward us, and I took a deep breath as Keith clicked to the first slide. "Co-teaching isn't just about sharing a classroom," I began, my voice steady, confident. "It's about dividing responsibilities and tasks."

Val and Audrey sent me big grins and thumbs up from their seats near the front, each wearing colorful DIY Christmas sweaters that made them impossible to ignore.

Keith clicked to the next slide, his lips moving slightly as he read. Would he recognize the deeper meaning behind them? "Any partnership requires us to be vulnerable. We must let go of our preconceived notions, and be open to each other's strengths and weaknesses, so we can move forward as a team."

There was a murmur in the room, some quiet exchanges among the teachers. Keith smiled at me, and my chest swelled with warmth.

He spoke up then, his voice warm and calm. "Exactly. You can't co-teach without compromise. But it's also what makes it hard. Because trust has to be earned."

Clicking to the next slide, my gaze briefly met his. For a split second, everything else in the room faded, and I wondered—did he know how much his patience meant to me? It was more than just support; it was a lifeline.

I smiled at Keith, hoping he could see the love behind my words. "But that kind of teamwork takes time and commitment—not just from the teachers, but from the administration too. Principals have to understand how much effort it really takes. Partnerships like this don't just happen overnight. The teachers need to show up not just as coworkers, but as people who genuinely care—about the students, and about each other."

Keith nodded, his eyes never leaving mine. "Admin needs to remember that it's okay to not have it all figured out. What matters is that teachers keep trying. We keep pushing through the difficult moments. And keep moving forward together."

The truth of the words sent a shiver down my spine. Time slowed down as I looked into his eyes. He understood. He'd gotten my message and had responded in kind.

A soft snicker from Bobby broke the moment.

Evan leaned over to whisper something to her, his voice barely audible. "I swear, if the next slide is *How to Be a Better Man*, I'm walking out."

A few chuckles rippled through the room, and Keith's lips twitched into a grin. He raised an eyebrow at me, a playful glint in his eyes. "Guess I'll skip the next slide," he said, his voice lighter now. "But I do have a few tips on how to survive group projects."

Everyone laughed, and the warmth of shared understanding settled in. Whatever happened, we were all in this together.

Mr. Kline glanced around the room, his gaze sharp with disapproval. "Let's focus, everyone. Please continue."

"Conflict is inevitable," I continued. "But it's important not to close yourself off from finding a resolution. When someone's past actions leave you questioning their intentions, it's easy to let doubt creep in. But the only way forward is open communication and trust that things can change."

I looked up at Keith, my gaze steady. We'd both made mistakes and done things we regretted. But I'd chosen to move forward. It was time to be open to what Keith and I could build together.

"I'm sorry," I said softly, my voice carrying the quiet promise of something real, something that wasn't going anywhere.

Instantly a weight lifted from my shoulders, and I could breathe easier. My feet itched to move, to dance, to celebrate.

I turned back to the room, letting my gaze linger on my friends before landing on Keith one last time. "Co-teaching is a constant learning process," I summed up. "It's trial and error. Making mistakes and learning from them. But the rewards are immeasurable because we all bring something valuable to the table, and it's in the collaboration where the magic happens."

A new understanding blossomed between us. He wasn't just the guy with a reputation anymore; he was a man who had grown and changed. Just as I wasn't the awkward, uncertain woman I'd been. I'd found my strength and learned to embrace all of myself.

The room fell quiet for a beat, then Audrey and Val were out of their seats, giving us a standing ovation. Keith's grin was enough to make my heart skip a beat. We hadn't just shared a lesson on co-teaching, but also a piece of ourselves.

And in that moment, it felt like our hearts aligned.

Mr. Kline stepped forward again, looking slightly confused. "Well, I have to say, I learned a lot about co-teaching today," he said, rubbing his hands together, clearly excited. "Would anyone like to summarize what they've learned?"

Audrey, never one to shy away from adding fuel to the fire, leaned forward with a smirk. "Seems like Keith and Rachel have the perfect chemistry," she said, her voice low and suggestive, earning a few appreciative whistles from the crowd.

Val raised her hand, her tone teasing. "They've learned to mix business with pleasure," she said, her voice carrying just enough edge to make the room burst into laughter.

Even Mr. Kline couldn't hold back a smile. "Okay, okay," he said, raising his hands in mock surrender. "Let's keep it professional, folks."

But the room erupted into laughter anyway.

Finally, Mr. Kline clapped his hands together. "I think it's time we wrap up and start the holidays a little early! Enjoy your much-deserved time off. You've all worked hard this semester, and I think you've earned it. Happy holidays! Take care, rest up, and we'll see you all next year!"

The staff erupted in applause, some cheering, others eagerly packing up their things to head out before the principal changed his mind.

As the crowd began to thin, I took a deep breath, letting the relief settle into my bones. My eyes met Keith's across the room, and I smiled. A quiet understanding passed between us, tension replaced by something steadier. Trust. Love.

Chapter 29

Keith

What would you do if your lover rocked your world with their brilliance and made you so proud?
a) Shower them with compliments, then spend the rest of the night plotting ways to show just how much you admire them.
b) Give them a lingering kiss, whispering how incredible they are—and how you can't wait to celebrate.
c) Playfully tease them about being so perfect, then suggest a little "reward" for their brilliance later.
d) Take them by the hand, lead them somewhere private, and show them how proud you are in ways words can't express.

The meeting wrapped up, and the staff slowly filtered out of the library, talking about their holiday plans and the usual end-of-semester chaos.

We'd done it. Rachel and I had pulled off the presentation, and in the midst of it, Rachel had made a quiet but powerful declaration.

She'd forgiven me.

We were together.

But there was still more to do. I needed to show her the library. More than just romance books, it was proof that I loved her. Things had changed, for good.

Evan appeared beside me, giving me a nudge with his elbow. "Nice job, man," he said with a grin, his tone warm but knowing. "Loved the dig at admin."

I nodded. "Rachel put that in." My eyes lingered on her as she shut down the laptop, nodding as Val and Audrey spoke to her.

Evan didn't miss the direction of my gaze, and he raised an eyebrow. "Have you shown her the library yet?"

I gave him a pointed look. "I'm inviting her over after everyone leaves."

Evan chuckled, slapping me on the back. "The two of you are good together, Keith."

I smiled, nodding. "Yeah, yeah, yeah, I hear you. Don't screw it up."

Evan laughed. "Took the words right out of my mouth."

A few minutes later, we were alone. She picked up the laptop, her gold dress catching the light with every movement. I watched her, stunned for a moment—not just by how beautiful she looked, but by the way she carried herself. Quiet strength showed in her posture now, a confidence that hadn't been there before.

She cradled the laptop in her arms like it was no big deal, like she hadn't just stolen the air from the room.

"Hey," I said.

"Hey."

"I have a surprise for you at my house. Wanna come over and check it out?"

Her eyebrows furrowed slightly, and I could see the wheels turning, a flicker of curiosity dancing in her eyes.

"What is it?" she asked, her voice laced with caution but also intrigue.

I grinned, trying to keep the mystery alive. "I could tell you, but that would spoil the fun."

She hesitated for a moment, then smiled, a soft laugh escaping her lips. "You're really going to make me wait, huh?"

"Yep," I said, stepping closer, my gaze never leaving hers. "But I promise, you're going to love it."

Almost as much as I love you.

She nodded, her lips curling into a smile that made my chest tighten. "Okay, lead the way."

I couldn't suppress the grin that spread across my face as she placed her hand in mine. The anticipation felt electric. This was just the beginning of something that would change everything between us.

We walked out to the parking lot together, and I turned to her with a grin. "Drive with me," I said. "We'll come back for your car later."

She looked at me for a moment, clearly intrigued, but she didn't question me. I could feel the curiosity in her growing, but she didn't press for details. I liked that. I would never take her trust for granted again.

When we reached my house, I parked in the driveway and turned to her. "Before we go inside, I want to tell you I love you, and I'm asking you to trust me."

She looked at me, lifting her eyebrow. "Okay."

I nodded, reaching for the scarf I'd hidden in the passenger seat. "I want to blindfold you. Just for a minute. It's part of the surprise."

Rachel raised an eyebrow, her lips curling into a playful smirk. "Alright, but if this involves a creepy clown, I will kick you," she joked.

I smiled and moved to help her out of the car, slipping the blindfold over her eyes gently. "Deal."

With her eyes covered, I took her hand, her fingers warm in mine. She followed without hesitation, and that trust meant everything. My heart pounded, not just from the excitement of showing her the library, but from knowing what this moment meant. Her trust was a gift, one I'd never take for granted. Step by step, it felt like we were exactly where we were meant to be.

When we reached the top of the stairs, I paused for a moment to steady my nerves. This was it. Time to show her everything.

I gently removed the blindfold, taking a step back to give her space as she blinked, her eyes adjusting. The faint smell of books and wood filled the air. I took a deep breath, trying to steady the rapid beat of my heart.

"I built this for you, Rachel. A space where you'll always be understood, where your world, your books, can live alongside mine. I want you here. In my life, in my house with me."

I stepped closer, my heart pounding as I tried to find the right words, but they seemed to come naturally, my chest opening up with every breath.

"This library," I said, gesturing around the room, "it's more than a place for your books to find a home. It's a place where they can have their own happy-ever-after, where every story— yours, mine, ours—can be cherished."

I could feel my pulse in my throat, my palms sweating despite the calm tone in my voice. It was one thing to show her this room, but another thing entirely to show her the depth of what it meant. More than just a physical space, it was a home for her, for us, in my life. A place where she wouldn't just fit in, but where she would be cherished.

I looked around the room again, at the shelves stacked with her books, the soft lighting, the cozy chair I'd put near the window for reading. Everything had been chosen with her in mind. "I want you to be a part of my life in every way," I added quietly, my voice more serious now, more vulnerable. "Not just when it's easy, but when it's complicated and messy. Even when we're figuring things out. I want you here with me."

She turned toward me, the surprise still clear on her face. "You really built this... for me?" she asked, a mix of disbelief and something else that softened her features.

"Yeah." I smiled, trying to keep the emotions at bay, though it was hard. "I love you, Rachel. This library is my love story for you. I can't read it to you, so I built it."

Rachel slowly turned in a full circle, her gaze drifting over every detail in the room. Her fingers lightly brushed the books, as if was she trying to absorb everything in the room. The cozy armchair near the window, the plush throw pillows, the little reading nook I'd made specifically for her. I'd created this space, not just as a place for her books to call home, but as a reflection of how much she mattered to me.

She pulled a dog-eared romance book from the shelf, the cover featuring a brooding duke with a smoldering gaze and a windswept heroine clinging to his arm, her corset undone.

"Are these my books?" she asked, one eyebrow raised.

"They sure are, Princess," Keith said with a smirk. "Think *Ocean's Eleven*, but way more intense—Barb's the mastermind, and honestly, I was just the getaway driver."

Her breath caught, and I could see her eyes soften as she looked at the shelves again. I knew she was processing everything, each little detail, and I could feel her coming to terms with the enormity of it, taking in the warmth of the room, the thoughtfulness that went into each piece.

Finally, she turned to face me, her eyes searching mine, full of affection and something even deeper. "I never thought," she said quietly, "that anyone would do something like this for me.

Keith... I love you. I love you in ways I never thought possible. I'm sorry I didn't trust you."

The raw sincerity in her words and voice told me everything. I stepped closer, reaching out to gently take her hand in mine. "I love you too, Rachel."

Her lips curved in the smallest, softest smile that lit up her eyes. "And here I thought you were taking me to your bedroom," she teased.

I chuckled, stepping closer. "Oh, that's what the chaise longue is for." I gestured to the overstuffed chair that sat in the corner of the attic library, bathed in light from the skylight. It was a chair designed for indulgence—for losing oneself in a story, for quiet moments of reflection, or, if I had my way, for sharing stolen kisses with the woman standing in front of me.

Her smile softened, and she stepped into the circle of my arms.

"Okay, here first and then the bed," she whispered, her gaze locking with mine.

Chapter 30

Rachel

What would you do if your lover designed and made you a library?
a) Gush about how thoughtful they are... then start rearranging the books to make it *perfect*.
b) Pretend to be shocked, but secretly plan to spend every free moment in there, just you and them.
c) Playfully ask if there's a secret passageway hidden somewhere, hoping they'll lead you to something more... intimate.
d) Let them back you into one of the shelves, their hands roaming as they kiss you hungrily.

The attic library enveloped us like a secret world. Moving around the room, Keith lit the candles. They flickered along the shelves, their soft light making the space feel even more intimate. The scent of aged paper and fresh wax mingled with citrus and vanilla.

I barely had time to breathe it in before Keith's lips were on mine, kissing me like he never planned to stop. His tongue danced with mine to the quiet instrumental music he'd turned on, romantic and low.

My breath hitched as my fingers curled into his shoulders. A delicious shiver ran down my spine. The rasp of his beard against my skin sent sparks skittering through me, and when his teeth grazed my earlobe, a quiet gasp slipped out before I could stop it.

Keith chuckled, low and satisfied, his hands tightening on my waist. "You have no idea what you do to me," he murmured, his lips trailing down my neck, lingering in the hollow of my throat as he backed me toward the chaise.

Pulling back just enough to look at me, his dark eyes brimmed with emotion. Without a word, he lowered me onto the chair, knocking a pillow to the floor.

"Hot Girls Read Smut," I read the words on the pillow with a grin as I wound my arms around his neck. "I love that pillow."

He chuckled, his breath warm against my skin as his fingers traced the hem of my dress, slowly sliding it up. My breath caught when he reached the apex of my thighs.

I reached for him, my fingers threading into his hair, pulling him closer. "I love you," I whispered, the words tumbling out.

Keith stilled, his forehead pressing against mine as he exhaled shakily. "Rachel... I love you too." His hands tightened at my waist, grounding us both. "I've loved you for so long."

I cupped his face, tilting it just enough to meet his eyes, needing him to see everything I felt. "Show me," I murmured. "Show me how much."

His fingers moved higher, slipping beneath the fabric with deliberate slowness until they found my soft, bare folds. A low groan rumbled from his chest as he pressed closer, the heat between us crackling.

His eyebrow arched, that wicked smile spreading like sin across his face. "Princess," he murmured, voice thick with heat, "did you really go to school commando?"

I blinked. "Um, I couldn't wear my underwear with the dress; it showed under the fabric."

His hand cupped me, possessive and teasing, and I gasped as his thumb dragged a slow, aching circle.

"So, it wasn't to drive me crazy?" He pushed the hem higher, exposing my wet folds.

I smirked, my breath hitching as his fingers teased along the sensitive skin of my thigh. My nails grazed the back of his neck. "Driving you crazy is definitely a perk."

He let out a low chuckle, his grip tightening as he moved lower. "Is that so?" Keith's lips skimmed along my thigh, his voice rough with amusement. "Because if that was your plan, sweetheart, you should know—I've been gone for you since day one."

Sensation gathered deep within me as he trailed kisses up my inner thigh. His tongue claimed me, urging me toward climax, but I refused to give in.

"Day one? That's a bold claim," I teased though my breath came out in pants.

He hummed, the vibration zipping through me while his fingers traced slow, torturous patterns against my clit. "Mmm.

Maybe it was day two. Had to pretend I wasn't instantly wrecked by you."

"And now?" I could hardly think, hardly breathe as I squirmed beneath him, my breath catching as my hips moved to match the slow, sensual rhythm of his lips, heat curling low in my belly.

"Now, I don't have to pretend at all." His chuckle rolled over me like pure sin, his breath hot against my center. "Merry Christmas to me."

I could feel my body curling in on itself, tensing as his teeth nipped and soothed my clit, his soft beard intensifying the sensation against my skin. Gasps of pleasure mingled with my panting for air. I clawed at his hair, holding him to me and demanding more.

His name slipped from my lips, a breathless plea for him to stop teasing me. I arched into him, every nerve alight, every part of me alive under his touch. "Don't stop."

"Never." The word vibrated through my core, sending shivers pulsing through me. My back arched tight as waves of pleasure rocked through me.

"Never." The word vibrated through my core, sending shivers pulsing through me. My back arched tight as waves of pleasure rocked through me, each one more intense than the last.

I felt unmoored, undone—every nerve alight, every breath stolen by the way he touched me, the way his hooded gaze skimmed over me. My thoughts scattered, all logic replaced by the raw sensation.

"So beautiful," Keith murmured against my thigh, his voice rough. He eased the dress from my body, unhooked my bra with a slow, practiced flick, but left my boots on like he couldn't bear to take away the last bit of attitude. Then he kicked off his shoes, peeled away his shirt and pants, and lay down beside me, all muscle and quiet intensity. When he pulled me close, his skin against mine, it felt like gravity had shifted, and he was the center of my universe now.

He saw me.

Not just my body, but all the layers I tried to hide. The way I sometimes stumbled through conversations, missed cues, or clung to routines like lifelines. The softness I didn't always know how to show—emotions that felt too big or too quiet, all jumbled up inside. He saw that, saw me, and instead of flinching, he leaned in like it was the most natural thing in the world.

Before I could stop myself, I blurted, "I'm definitely taking notes on your technique so I can use it when I write a romance novel. I'll call it the *I'm Autistic, He's Hot, Let's Get Naked*."

Keith raised an eyebrow, then smirked, his voice dropping low with a teasing edge. "I'll be sure to sign the rights over to you, but only if you promise to write a sex scene in every other chapter."

He leaned in, his breath warm against my ear, sending a shiver down my spine. "And I'll make sure you have plenty of inspiration and material."

The words sent a shiver down my spine, heat pooling low in my belly. His hands skimmed over my breasts sending sparks zipping across my skin, each touch making my pulse race faster.

I tangled my fingers in his hair, pulling him closer, needing more. "Please," I whispered, my breath hitching as his lips found mine again, demanding, claiming. Each touch, each kiss was a silent promise.

My body responded, aching for more, for the next wave of pleasure that was just within reach. His fingers slipped lower, and the intensity of his touch made me tremble, my heart racing, desperate to feel him closer.

My head spun as I pushed him back against the chaise, kissing my way down his body. His hard cock fascinated me. The skin so soft, but with steel beneath. I ran my finger across the crease along the top, loving the hiss of his breath.

My hand fisted around his length, stroking him, pumping up and down. His eyes closed and he growled low in the back of his throat.

Pride and love swept through me. This man loved me. He'd opened his heart to me and was completely mine.

His breath hitched as I ran my tongue over him, exploring, learning every reaction, every shiver. My mouth closed over him, following his movements, leaning what he liked. I reveled in the way he surrendered to my mouth.

"Rach, please," he begged, his hips arching up. His voice was thick with need, and the raw edge to it sent heat through me. "I can't wait any longer."

In one movement, he reversed our positions, pressing me back against the chaise and bracing himself above me, his eyes dark with heat. "Rachel," he murmured, his lips trailing over my jaw, down my neck. "You're all mine."

And then he was inside of me, hard and fast, claiming my body. My hands roamed across his back and shoulders, my legs wrapped around his hips, claiming him back.

"Look at me," he coaxed, as I raced with him toward another climax, our bodies moving in sync, demanding release.

I tipped my head back to meet his hazel eyes. And saw the emotion in them, so sharp and sweet. It pierced my heart. Love overwhelmed me, send me flying into a world of sensation. One that swept us both up and over the edge.

We watched the sun move across the skylights, our bodies tangled in each other on the chaise lounge, basking in the afterglow. At some point, Keith had thrown a soft gold blanket over us. The lamps added to the candles warm glow in the room.

Keith's hand rested on my stomach, his thumb tracing lazy circles on my skin as he watched me with soft, contented smile.

"Penny for your thoughts?" he asked, his voice low and amused, the hint of a smile tugging at the corners of his mouth.

I shook my head, not able to keep my grin at bay. "How did you know I always wanted a library?"

Keith chuckled, his breath warm against my skin. "You were saving those boxes of books for something, right?" he said dramatically like he was some sort of detective.

I snorted. "I didn't know what to expect when you put that blindfold on me. The craziest ideas popped into my head like a room full of horrible antique clowns."

He cupped my cheek, whispering, "How would that have given you the perfect happy ending?"

He kissed me, his hands roaming down my side, and I swallowed hard. He knew exactly how to make me melt—understood how the slightest graze of his finger could make me feel so alive.

I let out a breathy laugh, turning to kiss his jaw. "But it's not an ending, right?" I asked as I pulled back.

Keith's eyes twinkled mischievously. "Nope, this is just the beginning."

My heart fluttered, a bubble of joy filling my chest. His presence, the warmth of his touch, made everything feel right, as if this was always meant to be. "I love you."

He placed a gentle kiss on the top of my head. "I love you, Rachel," he murmured, his voice low and sincere. "I'm never letting you slip through my fingers again."

His words were a promise for a future I never expected to have. "Promise?" I whispered, my voice almost trembling with the weight of everything that everything could be.

A slow grin spread across his face that made my stomach do a flip. He leaned in, his lips brushing mine with quiet intensity. "Promise," he said, and kissed me like we had all the time in the world.

I sighed into him, my fingers tangling in his hair, and for the first time in what felt like forever, I felt at peace. The truth in his kiss aligned my universe, and I was finally where I belonged.

No more hiding, no more pretending.

No more doubts.

Just love.

What Kind of Romance Are You In?

I hope you had fun with the Pop Quiz at the start of each chapter! Spoiler alert: there's no answer key, but your results should reveal your romance reader personality.

💔 **Mostly A's: The Slow Burn Masterpiece** – You love your tension thick, your stolen glances longing, and your emotions painfully unresolved. You resist, you overthink, and you pretend not to care. Until one touch, one look, one perfectly timed confession, and suddenly, you're all in. You believe love is worth the wait, and once you let someone in, you love them *hard*.

📚 **Read This:** *Love Hypothesis* by Ali Hazelwood & *Book Lovers* by Emily Henry

🔥 **Mostly B's: The Enemies-to-Lovers Showdown** – You thrive on banter, eye rolls, and unresolved frustration that leads to *very* resolved tension. You don't just fall in love—you battle for it first. You're the type to swear you *hate* someone while secretly obsessing over every little thing they do. Love for you is explosive, exhilarating, and impossible to ignore once the walls finally come down.

📚 **Read This:** *The Hating Game* by Sally Thorne & *How My Neighbor Stole Christmas* by Meghan Quinn

💜 **Mostly C's: The Second Chance Romance** – You believe in fate, personal growth, and the fact that sometimes, timing *is* everything. You might run, hesitate, and fight it, but love always returns to you. Whether it's an ex you can't forget, a childhood sweetheart who still knows how you take your coffee, or the one who got away, your heart believes in do-overs. And this time, you're going to get it right.

📖 **Read this:** *Dr. Strangebeard* by Penny Reid & *Reckless* by Elsie Silver

☕ **Mostly D's: The Spicy Rom-Com** – You dive in headfirst, embrace the chaos, and live for the swoon. Whether it's a steamy fling, a flirty friendship, or a whirlwind romance, you're here for the *fun*. You love grand gestures, ridiculous misunderstandings, and moments that make you laugh *and* blush. If there's a love confession, it better be dramatic. If there's tension, it better be *scorching*.

📖 **Read This:** *It Happened One Summer* by Tessa Bailey & *Sex Ed* by Kristen Bailey

About the Author

M. Jayne LaDow combines her love of storytelling with her background as a longtime educator. When she's not creating fictional worlds where coffee is plentiful, snowstorms are romantic, and teachers always have a happy ending, you can find her at the beach, spending time with her family, or being distracted by her cats. She lives in Virginia Beach with her husband, kids, and a bunch of furry and reptilian friends.

Acknowledgements

First and foremost, thank you to my amazing readers—without you, this journey wouldn't be nearly as much fun. You all bring the magic to my words, and I'm so grateful for each of you.

To my incredible family: Jim, you've been my rock, my sounding board, and the one who gets why I'm always talking to myself (I promise, it's all for the plot!). A special shout-out to Miles and Megan, who cheer me on even when I'm glued to my computer, typing away about fictional characters while completely ignoring the laundry.

To Liz: Thank you for reading late into the night, for your endless support, and for always being my favorite sister. I'm lucky to have you by my side.

To Lauren: Marchfield wouldn't exist without you. You're my brainstorming partner, my researcher, and the best cheerleader I could ask for. Thank you for answering my endless questions and always pushing me to be better.

To Suzanne: My accountability partner in writing and crime— you keep me on track, even when the words aren't flowing.

M. Jayne LaDow

Thank you for always being there with a kind word, a pep talk, and a good laugh.

To Dave: Thanks for allowing me to write in my fictional world while you take care of things up north. I appreciate you more than you know.

To Nancy: Thank you for asking me how it's going at least once a week and listening to me vent with such patience and kindness.

To my wonderful editor, Erin: You took my wild, messy manuscript and worked your magic to make it shine. Your patience, expertise, and incredible eye for detail have made this book something I'm truly proud of.

And finally, to all the teachers and educators out there who inspire everything I write. Your passion, humor, and heart make a difference every day, and I can only hope my characters reflect even a fraction of the amazing work you do.

Thank you, thank you, thank you!

Stay Tuned for:

Tardy Pass, No Questions Asked

A new Marchfield Middle Novella
featuring Bobby and Mel.

Bobby Nooney has survived war zones, but nothing prepared her for middle school science class. Trading combat boots for lab coats in the quirky town of Marchfield, she's not looking for love... until she accidentally scares the daylights out of a guidance counselor in a dimly lit records room. Sparks fly, and suddenly, lesson plans aren't the only thing on her mind.

Mel Brannaghan thought she'd flunked love. When her cheating husband died in his lover's arms, she left her hometown for a fresh start. Dating wasn't part of Mel's plan, but Bobby's presence makes it hard for her to deny their growing attraction.

Spicy, swoon-worthy, and laugh-out-loud funny, *Tardy Pass, No Questions Asked* is the queer love story that started it all at Marchfield Middle. With heart, heat, and just the right amount of school mayhem, this prequel proves that love shows up— whether you're ready or not.

Coming in June 2025

Books by M. Jayne LaDow

One Night Stands and Lesson Plans
Learning Goals and Dancing Poles
Pop Quizzes and Stolen Kisses
Tardy Pass, No Questions Asked (Coming June 2025)